KAREN KINCY

STORMS OF

LAZARUS

CURIOSITY
QUILLS PRESS

A Division of **Whampa, LLC**
P.O. Box 2160
Reston, VA 20195
Tel/Fax: 800-998-2509
http://curiosityquills.com

© 2014 **Karen Kincy**
http://www.karenkincy.com

ISBN 978-1-62007-916-4 (ebook)
ISBN 978-1-62007-917-1 (paperback)
ISBN 978-1-62007-918-8 (hardcover)

To everyone who loved the first book and wanted more.

1913

ONE

I n the dead of night, the necromancer started singing. **Ardis** braced herself at the edge of the ridge, kicking her boots deeper into the snow, and glanced backward. Wendel wasn't more than a few paces behind her. He trudged with his head bowed, his ragged black hair shadowing his face, his breath milky in the moonlight.

"*Stille Nacht*," Wendel sang, "*heilige Nacht, alles schläft; einsam wacht.*"

His honey-gravel voice lent itself well to the melody, even if he wasn't entirely on key.

"Silent Night?" Ardis said, also in German. "Really?"

Wendel raised his head, his pale green eyes glittering with amusement.

"Of course," he said. "It's Christmas Eve."

Was it? Ardis had lost track of time, somewhere between fleeing Constantinople and hiding from an ancient society of assassins.

"You have a lovely singing voice," Ardis said, "but—"

"Why, thank you."

"But be quiet. We're escaping."

"Escaping." Wendel grinned like he couldn't help himself. "Exactly."

Her sigh fogged the air, and she rubbed her mouth to hide her smile.

"How close are we to the border of Bulgaria?" Ardis said.

Wendel shrugged. "Who knows? We don't have a map, remember?"

She narrowed her eyes and resisted the urge to snap at him. "I hope we aren't lost."

Wendel climbed the last few feet between them. He hooked his arm around her shoulders and tugged her against him. "Look." He pointed at distant lights glittering beyond the forest. "We aren't lost. We can spend Christmas in that village."

Ardis wanted to believe him, but was afraid they had come all this way for nothing. Because she hadn't seen him this happy before, not in the time she had known him, and the necromancer seemed cursed by sadness.

She couldn't tell him that, of course. She had to be strong for them both.

"I don't suppose you have any of your inheritance left?" Ardis said.

Wendel snorted. "I'm dead broke." He paused. "Though at least I'm not dead."

She elbowed him. "I told you not to keep joking about that. It's morbid. You of all people should know that."

He rubbed his ribs and backed away from her. "Thanks for the mortal wound."

"Oh, you're fine."

Ardis rolled her eyes and kept walking. Truthfully, the necromancer *was* fine. Even though she had watched him die.

She blinked away those memories and concentrated on her footsteps. "Since we have no money, we should look for a nice barn to sleep in."

"Or a stable. That's the Christmas spirit."

Ardis glanced sideways at Wendel. He was trying not to grin, and failing.

"I hardly think I'm the Virgin Mary," she said dryly.

"Not a fan of immaculate conception?"

A blush blazed across her cheeks. "Not a fan of babies."

"Even the Baby Jesus?" He laughed. "Heretic!"

Down below the ridge, flashlights swept the forest. Ardis skidded to a halt and grabbed a tree branch to steady herself, whispering, "Quiet."

Wendel crouched beside her and touched her elbow. "What is it?"

She pointed. "There."

A flashlight beam swung across the trees and illuminated the bushes behind them. Ardis scooted deeper into the underbrush and flattened herself against the trunk of a pine. Wendel tensed but stayed where he was.

"Come closer," Ardis hissed. "They'll see you."

Wendel shrugged, his eyes narrowed, and reached inside his coat. He stopped himself halfway. Ardis knew he was looking for Amarant, but of course he had lost the black dagger to the man who had killed him.

"There are only six of them," Wendel muttered.

Ardis stared down the ridge. He was right. Half a dozen men bundled in wool and furs approached, carrying flashlights.

"The Order?" Ardis said.

Wendel shook his head. "I don't think so. They still think I'm dead."

"Bulgarians, then?"

"Possibly."

Wendel lingered against the snow, his black clothes and black hair a stark contrast. Such an obvious target. Gritting her teeth, Ardis lunged to her feet, grabbed his arm, and dragged him down to hide beneath the pine.

"Why would the Bulgarians be looking for us?" Ardis said.

Wendel paused. "We are both fugitives."

The six strangers climbed the ridge, their flashlights growing brighter.

"But we never did anything illegal in Bulgaria," Ardis said.

"Well…"

She shot a glance at Wendel. "Really?"

"It wasn't my idea."

Which meant the Order of the Asphodel had commanded him to kill.

Wendel raised his finger to his lips and flattened himself to the ground. He grabbed Ardis's shoulder and pushed her down. She huddled against him, her heartbeat thudding, and held her breath so it wouldn't cloud the air.

Boots crunched the snow. A man halted inches from Ardis's hand.

All they had to do was look down. All they had to do was see the footprints in the snow.

The man shone his flashlight up the ridge. He swept the beam over the snow, casting nightmare shadows, then waved his comrades onward. He stood close enough that Ardis could have touched him. Her lungs burned as she forced herself not to exhale. Finally, the man clomped away, kicking flecks of snow into her face.

Ardis let her breath escape in a puff of white.

Wendel stiffened, his shoulder pressing hard against hers. She glanced at him as he flared his nostrils, but didn't see why.

"*Grok!*"

The hoarse croak startled Ardis. Her head snapped toward the noise. A bough in the pine tree bounced, shedding a flurry of snow.

"*Grok!*"

A black bird landed with a thump on a fallen tree. It was too big to be a crow, with a wicked beak and glittering eyes. The raven cocked its head and stared at Wendel. Expectantly. Ardis knew what it wanted.

"Wendel," she whispered. "Hide your necromancy."

"What?" he whispered. "I am!"

Ardis jerked her head toward the raven, as if Wendel wasn't already staring at it. His eyebrows angled into a frown, and he glared like he wanted to incinerate the bird with his mind. The raven ruffled its feathers and hopped nearer.

This was bad. If the Bulgarians noticed—

A flashlight swung in their direction and spotlighted the raven. Glossy black feathers gleamed as the bird pumped its wings. It swooped low over the snow and landed on the lowest bough of the pine tree.

Right over the necromancer.

"*Grok!*"

The Bulgarians stared at the bird. One of the strangers pointed his flashlight into Ardis's eyes. Blinded, she crawled backwards.

"Halt!" said the stranger.

In German or English?

Ardis froze with her hands flat on the snow. She could feel it melting beneath her palms.

"On your feet," said the stranger.

That was definitely English.

Ardis climbed to her feet, squinting at the flashlight, and held her hands above her head. The stranger was still a silhouette. Slowly, Wendel also stood, though he spread his hands at his sides in an appeasing gesture.

"*Entschuldigen sie,*" Wendel said, "*suchen Sie für uns?*"

The stranger shone his flashlight in Wendel's face. "No German."

Wendel sighed, as if he had a right to be peeved, and repeated himself in English.

"Are you looking for us?"

Make that flawless English. Ardis narrowed her eyes at him for neglecting to mention his fluency earlier. He spoke with a subtle crispness that had to be the accent of a Prussian prince. Which, of course, he was.

"Perhaps," said the stranger.

"Who are you?" Ardis said.

"Officer Zlatkov of the Bulgarian border patrol."

Wendel snapped his fingers. "I owe you, Ardis. This *is* Bulgaria."

Ardis glared sideways at him.

Zlatkov lowered his flashlight; Ardis glimpsed the nervous twitch of his mustache. He rattled off something in Bulgarian to his comrades. The smallest man among them stepped forward, a hooded cloak obscuring his face.

Wendel's arrogant confidence faltered. Ardis didn't know why.

Nobody moved for a moment. Somebody shoved the smallest man, stumbling, and his hood fell back. He wasn't a man at all, but a woman. She had porcelain skin and cornsilk blonde hair, cobwebbed with white, though her face looked young and beautiful.

Wendel stared at the woman. He closed his mouth, then opened it again. "You can't be."

The woman edged closer to him. When the light caught her eyes, they flashed like those of a wolf. Wendel's lips parted with what could be fascination or repulsion. The woman stopped inches from the necromancer. He tilted his head and narrowed his eyes, and lifted his hand as if to stroke her cheek.

"Yes," the woman said, the word a little sigh.

She closed her eyes, her face tight with longing, and leaned closer to Wendel.

It looked like they might kiss.

Two men jumped forward and grabbed the woman's arms. They dragged her backward, yelling in Bulgarian, though she didn't resist.

Officer Zlatkov drew a pistol from his jacket and aimed between Wendel's eyes. "Don't move."

Out here on the border, they couldn't count on the Hex to negate gunpowder.

Ardis did as he said, her hand halfway to her sword, and glanced at Wendel. The necromancer seemed too shaken to react with his familiar bravado. He raised his hands and looked down the barrel of the pistol.

"You found me." Wendel licked his lips. "Where did you find *her?*"

The woman stared at Wendel through the hair tumbling over her face. She looked as though she wanted to tell him, but didn't dare.

Officer Zlatkov shook his head with a grim smile. "You are under arrest."

At least the Bulgarians didn't want to kill them on the spot.

Ardis attempted to sound innocent. "Why?"

"You know why."

Zlatkov's men patted down Wendel, who clenched his jaw but let them do it. They handcuffed him without further ceremony, then turned to Ardis. Her hand jerked involuntarily toward her sword. Zlatkov trained the pistol on her head. Swallowing hard, she forced herself not to fight. Another man unbuckled her scabbard from her belt and confiscated her weapon, then cuffed her arms behind her back. He reached under her jacket and ran his hands along her waist, lingering longer than necessary.

Ardis's face burned. She distracted herself by imagining revenge.

"Come with us," Zlatkov said.

"I would rather decline your invitation," Wendel muttered.

He was rewarded for his sarcasm with a rough shove between the shoulders.

They hiked down the ridge toward the village. The raven flew from tree to tree overhead, never letting the necromancer out of its sight. Wendel kept glancing at the raven, a crease between his eyebrows, but Ardis was more worried by the woman with the wolfish eyes, who listed toward Wendel like she was lovesick.

Who or what was she, and why did the necromancer want to touch her?

Candlelight flickered behind frosted windows in the village. It would have been quaint if Ardis and Wendel weren't being marched through its streets. They crossed a cobblestoned town square and entered a brick building under construction. The foyer was dark and dank, with a hallway that branched both left and right.

"Ardis," Wendel said.

The border patrol steered him to the right and shoved her down the opposite hallway.

"Wendel!" Ardis said. "Don't—"

A man shoved a hood of rough burlap over Ardis's head. She had never been arrested before, and panic clawed inside her ribs like a rat trapped in a cage. She tried to force down the feeling, tried to count their steps.

A turn to the left. A turn to the right. A rusty screech of a door opening.

Someone shoved her into a chair. Cold steel bit into her wrists as they chained her down. She held perfectly still, her breathing muffled, the moldy stink of the burlap in her mouth.

The door groaned shut. Footsteps retreated down the hallway.

Ardis was alone.

Her heartbeat pounded in her ears. As she sat in the darkness, it slowed to the drumming of dread.

The handcuffs were just a little looser than they should be. One size fits all, no doubt, and they likely hadn't been designed with the smaller bones of a woman in mind. Ardis flexed her fingers, then folded them together tight and yanked.

"Come on," Ardis said through clenched teeth.

Damn it, this would be easier if she could see. Maybe she could—

The door screeched open. Footsteps clicked across the floor and stopped in front of her. She tensed, her shoulders rigid. The burlap sack was yanked from her head.

Officer Zlatkov stood holding a lantern that cast ghoulish light on his face. He set the lantern on a table before dragging another chair closer and sitting. He crossed his legs, flicked a match on the table, and lit a cigarette.

Zlatkov blew smoke toward the ceiling. "Ardis."

She swallowed and tried not to cough.

"What do you know about Yu Lan?" Zlatkov said.

Ardis's heartbeat stumbled and came back galloping. Her name— her old name—sounded odd in his voice. In this dark room.

"Yu Lan killed a man in America," Zlatkov said. "Didn't she?"

Ardis said nothing. She didn't see how speaking would help her.

Zlatkov dragged on his cigarette. The end glowed red. Ardis stared at it, thinking of how her sword smoldered with magic.

Where had they taken Chun Yi? She needed to find it.

"Answer the question," Zlatkov said.

She bit the inside of her cheek. "Yu Lan killed a man in self-defense."

"Self-defense?" Zlatkov had a gravelly laugh. "If she was innocent, why did she flee? Why did she hide as a fugitive here?"

Ardis stared at the space between his eyes. "She knew they wouldn't believe her."

Zlatkov scooted his chair closer and leaned into her face. He tapped the ash from the end of his cigarette. It drifted into her lap.

He almost smiled. "Is that the truth?"

"Yes," she said, looking anywhere but him.

"Then tell me the truth about the Russians," Zlatkov said.

Ardis frowned. "The Russians?"

Zlatkov slapped her across the face, hard enough to knock a gasp out of her. The stinging faded to heat in the shape of his hand.

"Isn't Yu Lan innocent?" he said mockingly. "Isn't Yu Lan honest?"

Ardis bared her teeth. "Yu Lan is dead."

"Not yet," Zlatkov said.

"I'm Ardis now."

Zlatkov sucked on his cigarette and blew the smoke into her mouth. She coughed and squinted, unwilling to break eye contact.

"I know," Zlatkov said. "I know Yu Lan was a little whore, just like her mother."

Ardis laughed bitterly. "You don't know the half of it."

Zlatkov shook his head and smiled. He waved his cigarette in her face as he talked, the smoke curling through the air. "This little whore killed a man when she should have just done her job. Then she ran off and played at being a mercenary. But she did a piss poor job of that, too, didn't she? She whored herself out again to the

Russians when they paid more money than the archmages. Greedy little bitch."

Blood rushed through Ardis's ears so loud she could hardly think. "I didn't betray the archmages."

Zlatkov slapped her again. Her eyes watered at the pain.

"What happened in Constantinople?" he said.

Ardis doubted he would believe the truth, but she had nothing else. "The Grandmaster. He betrayed the archmages. He sold their secrets to the Russians. We tried to stop him."

Zlatkov stared at her like he couldn't believe what a pathetic liar she was. He leaned close enough that his smoker's breath soured her nostrils. He grabbed her chin, his fingers bruising, and stared into her eyes "Liar."

Ardis sneered at him. "As if you could tell."

Zlatkov didn't slap her again. He bent her over, roughly, and unchained her from the chair so he could drag her upright. He groped her breast, his fingers gripping hard enough to bruise, before fumbling to unbuckle his belt. Acid rose in Ardis's throat. She pretended to fall to her knees, forcing him to stumble away.

Zlatkov panted. "Bitch."

Ardis felt the weight of the handcuffs at her wrists. She narrowed her eyes.

"I've heard it all before," she said. "Can't think of anything creative?"

Ardis wrenched against the handcuffs and twisted her left hand loose. She surged to her feet and punched Zlatkov in the jaw. His head snapped back. She kneed him in the groin and kicked him in the stomach before he hit the floor. He curled like a worm. Breathing hard, Ardis glanced at the door.

She could run away, or she could incapacitate him.

Obviously, the second option was the superior one.

Ardis waited for Zlatkov to uncurl, and kicked him in the face. Her boot connected with his nose. His eyes rolled back. Blood trickled across his cheek. She stared at him until she was sure he was out cold, then crouched and searched his pockets for the key to her handcuffs. She freed herself and grabbed his pistol.

Only then did she realize she was shaking all over. From adrenaline. From memories.

She leaned against the wall and forced herself to inhale. She had escaped what had happened in America, but didn't think she could ever escape the fear. A sour taste lingered on her tongue; for a second, she thought she might vomit. She coughed and pressed her hand to her mouth.

She had to get out of here. She had to find Wendel.

TWO

rdis didn't look at Zlatkov as she left the room. She unlatched the door and nudged it open with her toe, then peeked around the corner. No sign of anyone in the hallway. She retraced her steps to the foyer, then headed down the hallway where she had last seen Wendel. She followed several disorienting twists and turns, hoping she wouldn't lose her way. Her breathing sounded too loud in the silence.

A door stood slightly ajar. Muffled voices leaked through the crack. She couldn't identify the words, but could identify Wendel's voice anywhere. She sucked in a breath, cocked her pistol, and kicked the door open.

A man with his back to the door whirled around and reached into his jacket.

Ardis shot him in the shoulder; the bullet staggered him, but he cocked his gun. Without thinking, she aimed for his head and shot him between the eyes.

Shaking, Ardis lowered her gun. She glanced at the man as he lay dying at her feet.

"Ardis," Wendel said.

He sat chained to a chair, bruises on his cheekbones, bleeding from his lip. Otherwise, he didn't look worse for the wear.

Wendel smiled, then winced and licked his split lip. "My savior."

Ardis shook her head and crouched over the man she had shot. His limp hand lay near his jacket. She searched his pockets until she found a hunter's knife. She still had Zlatkov's handcuff key, and used it to free Wendel.

"Take this." Ardis held out the knife. "But remember, they have guns in Bulgaria."

"I noticed."

Wendel climbed to his feet and took the knife from her. He glanced at her face, then touched her on the shoulder. "Are you all right?"

"I'm okay." Ardis shrugged off his hand. "You?"

He nodded. "Let's end this chat before our friends join the conversation."

Ardis left the room first, since she was the one with the gun. The hallway was still empty, though she knew they had only eliminated two of the six men who had brought them here. And certainly not the entire border patrol.

"This way," Ardis said, trying to sound confident.

Wendel held the knife ready as they skulked down the hallway. Ardis peeked around the corner.

"Ardis," Wendel hissed. "Stop."

She glanced back at him. "The coast is clear."

He shook his head, his face pale beneath the blood and the bruises. She didn't like the look in his eyes. That gleam awfully like fear.

"What is it?" she said.

Wendel gripped her arm and dragged her into a run. They swung around the corner and rushed down the hallway. She didn't know why he was running, but the sooner they got out of this godforsaken place, the better.

Wendel skidded to a stop. "Ah, damn."

A pair of gaunt figures lingered at the end of the hallway. They shuffled nearer, as if hesitant, their faces shadowed. One was the woman with wolfish eyes. The other was a man with the same strange eyes and deathly skin.

Ardis stared down her pistol's sights. "Don't move."

When they ignored her, she shot the man square in the kneecap. He barely stumbled, but the bullet got his attention. He whirled on her and bared his teeth.

No, make that fangs.

Ardis swore under her breath. "Vampires? Really?"

Wendel made a face. "Not my fault!"

"But you knew—"

Ardis never finished her sentence.

The vampire she had kneecapped sprinted at her with a snarl. She had never fought vampires before, had never even seen one, though she knew most had been hunted down and beheaded over the past century.

Beheading sounded good. Ardis reached for her sword that wasn't there. "Christ."

Ardis decided to improvise. When the vampire closed in, she pistol whipped him, hopefully hard enough to knock out some of his teeth. The vampire's head jerked sideways as he hit the wall. He staggered away, bleeding from the mouth.

Wendel treated the vampires with considerable wariness. He circled the woman, his eyes glittering with intensity, nearly within her reach. When she tried to touch him, he lunged and grabbed her by the throat. Her fingers flew to meet his. She let out a strangled gasp, but didn't fight him.

"Stop," Wendel murmured.

Ardis stared at him. "Are you actually trying to—?"

Movement in her peripheral vision. The male vampire charged, flinging her hard into the wall. She raised the pistol against his ribs and fired point blank, but a bullet did nothing against a heart that had already stopped.

His hand closed around her shoulder, fingers knotting in her hair.

Adrenaline pulsed in Ardis's blood. She pushed against the wall, fighting for leverage against her opponent, but couldn't match his supernatural strength. He pressed against her with a growling sigh and yanked back her head to bare her neck.

She sucked in air to scream, but the vampire clamped his hand over her mouth.

Ardis bit him first. Her teeth sank into his fingers. He grunted but didn't let go; she wondered if he even felt pain.

The vampire closed his eyes and bent over her neck.

His teeth pierced her skin with blinding pain. The agony increased until it shattered into pleasure. It shocked her how sweet it felt. Shivering, she clung to him as the strength melted from her muscles. Pinpricks danced over her skin, and her heartbeat whooshed gently in her ears like the sea.

The bite ended, but the sensation lingered.

He released her and let her slump against the wall. She slid down to the floor, her eyesight blurry, and struggled to focus. Voices murmured nearby, sounding underwater. A blond man lifted his hands, flames crackling at his fingertips, before hurling fire at the vampire

Ardis squeezed her eyes shut. The burning hurt to look at.

Distantly, she was aware of the cold concrete beneath her cheek. She ran the palm of her hand flat against the floor. She felt something warm, and looked at her fingers. Red. Blood. Frowning, she touched her neck.

Why did nothing hurt?

"Ardis. Damn it, Ardis, look at me!"

She blinked, her vision a blur, until she focused on Wendel. He was kneeling over her, shaking her by the shoulder. He didn't have to be so rough. The shaking jarred her out of the sweet euphoria of the vampire's bite.

"Wendel," Ardis muttered. "Quit that."

The blond man bent over Ardis, squinting, his eyes as blue as the sky. Frozen breath frosted the scarf over his mouth. He unwound the wool clumsily, his hands armored in intricate mage's gauntlets, the steel clicking like insects.

"Konstantin." Ardis smiled. "What a surprise."

Konstantin's eyebrows angled in a frown. "Help her stand."

"What's wrong with her?" Wendel said.

"It's just the vampire's venom," Konstantin said.

"Just? *Just?*"

"She needs to walk it off."

Wendel spoke through clenched teeth. "If you turn out to be wrong about this, so help me God, I will kill you myself."

Konstantin blanched and raised his hands. "The venom has a half-life of only two hours."

"This isn't one of your textbooks," Wendel said icily.

Wendel hooked his hand behind Ardis's neck and looked into her eyes. His were so serious. "I need you to hold on, Ardis. I will try not to hurt you."

"It doesn't hurt," she said.

That didn't seem to reassure Wendel.

Ardis laced her fingers behind Wendel's neck, and he lifted her into his arms. She rested her head against his chest. His heartbeat thumped in her ear. Blood stained his shirt, and she realized her neck was still bleeding.

"I'm sorry," she said.

"Why?" Wendel said.

Ardis laughed softly. "I'm bleeding on your shirt."

"Wendel." Konstantin cleared his throat. "You should put her down."

Wendel muttered some profanity, but lowered Ardis to her feet. Her legs wobbled. She held onto him so she wouldn't fall. Konstantin caught her other elbow. The metal of his gauntlets felt hot against her skin.

"Try to walk," Konstantin said. "Physical activity should help counteract the venom."

Ardis nodded. The movement made her head spin. She managed a step forward, but her next step turned into a stumble. Wendel caught her before she could fall. He lifted her back into his arms and started walking.

"I have a better plan," Wendel said.

Konstantin followed alongside. "Which is?"

"We're getting the hell out of here."

Ardis winced as the bite on her neck throbbed.

Wendel glanced at her face. "Why is she still bleeding?"

Konstantin raised his finger as he walked. "Vampire venom acts as an anticoagulant. That, and a rather powerful anesthetic."

"And?" Wendel said. "How do we fix it?"

"I could cauterize the wound."

Wendel grimaced. "Ardis?"

She squinted at him. Everything still looked blurry, though less of a pleasant blur. "That sounds smart."

They navigated the maze of corridors and stepped into the night. Cold rushed over them, and Ardis's teeth started to chatter.

Konstantin held out his hand, flames rippling at his fingertips, his gauntlets glowing yellow with magic. "Try not to move."

Ardis stiffened in Wendel's arms. Konstantin pressed his fingertips to her neck. Magic seared her skin and burned the bite. She gasped at the pain and forced herself to hold still as he stopped the bleeding with fire.

Konstantin lifted his fingers. "Done."

Shivering, Ardis felt a lot more awake. She gripped Wendel's shoulder. "It hurts now."

"Good," Konstantin said.

Wendel glared at the archmage.

"I think the venom is starting to wear off." Ardis blew out her breath. "Damn."

Ardis lifted her head to look around. Her neck throbbed with sickening pain. Konstantin hovered nearby and glanced between her and his gauntlets. Behind him, the windows of the brick building stared at them like the empty eyes of skulls.

Wendel nodded at Konstantin. "Archmage."

He said it the same way he did every time, his flippant disdain at odds with the begrudging respect in his eyes.

"You're welcome?" Konstantin said.

"Now is when we say goodbye," Wendel said.

Without waiting for a reply, Wendel strode across the cobblestones. Ardis held on and tried to breathe evenly.

"I was looking for you," Konstantin said.

Wendel stopped with his back to the archmage. He waited for a moment.

"Why?" he said.

"They said you were dead, but they never found a body."

Slowly, Wendel turned around. He kept his tone perfectly bland when he spoke. "You contacted the Order of the Asphodel?"

"I had to." Konstantin dragged his fingers through his windblown tangle of blond hair. "I need you."

"For nostalgia's sake?" Wendel bared his teeth. "You had us arrested, archmage."

Konstantin bit his lip and averted his gaze. "I'm afraid things went terribly wrong. I'm lucky I came when I did."

"Very lucky," Wendel said sardonically. "We almost escaped without you."

"How did you find us?" Ardis said.

A little smile curled Konstantin's mouth. "Vampires. The best bloodhounds to hunt down a necromancer. They crave the taste of a man who can control the dead."

Wendel stiffened. Ardis flinched at his fingernails digging into her back.

"Put me down," she said.

Wendel let her slide to her feet. Her knees wobbled, but she managed to hide it.

She hugged herself and rubbed her arms. "What do you want from us?"

Konstantin's jaw hardened. "You owe a debt to the archmages."

They did—Ardis couldn't deny it. Not only had Wendel sabotaged Konstantin's *Eisenkrieger* project, but Konstantin had let Ardis run away to Constantinople to save the necromancer. She knew they should repay him.

And in all fairness, Wendel deserved some sort of punishment.

"Follow me," Konstantin said, "and I will answer all of your questions on the way."

Wendel stared at him. No doubt calculating the odds of the situation.

"This is our best option," Ardis said, mostly because they didn't have another one. "Let's go."

Ardis took a step toward Konstantin, which was a mistake. The world tipped around her like a chessboard losing all its pieces. She stumbled onto one knee and caught herself with her hand splayed on the cobblestones.

Wendel clutched her shoulder. "You shouldn't be walking."

"Can I lie down?" Ardis said.

He squinted. "Of course not."

Ardis staggered to her feet and sucked in a long breath. Stars danced in the corners of her eyes. Her neck ached almost as sharply as the instant the vampire's fangs had pierced her skin. Wind chilled her sweaty face.

"Wendel," Konstantin said. "For once, don't be an idiot. You can't keep running, carrying Ardis through the snow, praying the assassins don't realize you're alive. Come with me and you can have a real shot at survival."

Dizziness rippled over Ardis, and she blinked fast.

"Very well," Wendel said. "You win."

Judging by the ice in his voice, he hated saying every word.

"This way," Konstantin said.

Wendel helped her stagger across the town square. They reached a sleigh hitched to a matched pair of black draft horses. The great beasts snorted and pawed at the snow, heat from their nostrils fogging the air. Konstantin hopped in and held out his hand. Ardis shied away from the steel of his gauntlets, the fire at his fingertips still bright in her memory.

"Let me help you," Wendel said.

With his hands at her waist, Wendel boosted Ardis into the sleigh. She clambered in gracelessly and slumped in the corner. Wendel settled next to her with a thud. He leaned back and stretched out his legs.

Ardis touched her fingers to her forehead. "Where are we going?"

"Not to our deaths, apparently," Wendel said.

Konstantin shook his head. "Logic escapes you, doesn't it?"

"I don't trust you," Wendel said, with more than a little insolence. "Do I need to explain the concept of revenge to you, archmage?"

Konstantin leaned across the gap between them. His eyes looked frosty. "You are more useful to me alive. Necromancer."

Wendel looked smug, as if he had known he was invaluable all along.

At Konstantin's command, the driver urged the horses into a trot. The sleigh lurched into motion and scraped over the snowy road. Blearily, Ardis gazed at the sky. Snow like powdered sugar drifted onto her face.

"Where are we going?" she said again.

"Phillipopolis," Konstantin said.

That sounded vaguely familiar to Ardis, so she nodded.

Darkness swallowed the village. Only the lanterns hanging from the sleigh lit their way. The horses plodded through a forest of pines, their harnesses creaking. The slicing of runners across snow underscored the silence.

Ardis tilted back her head and watched the boughs of trees pass overhead.

"*Grok!*"

"Oh, damn," Wendel said.

Wingbeats whooshed between the trees. The raven fanned its tail and banked over the sleigh, before settling on a low-hanging branch. Wendel pantomimed throwing something at the bird to scare it away. The raven chattered in a bratty way, glided down to the sleigh, and landed behind the oblivious driver's back.

Konstantin stiffened. "Get rid of your minion."

"My what?" Wendel retorted.

"That crow."

"The *raven* isn't undead, archmage. I can't control him."

Konstantin arched his eyebrows. "Then why—?"

"He's clever, that's why." Wendel smiled. "In his greedy little head, a necromancer is nothing more than a glorified sous chef for scavengers. If he follows me long enough, he might find his dinner. Something nice and dead."

Konstantin eyed the raven with considerable disgust and a hint of fascination. "Don't tell me you have undead nearby."

"All right," Wendel said flippantly, "I won't."

Konstantin spoke in a dangerous murmur. "I am absolutely serious."

The raven clambered nearer to Wendel, its claws clicking on the lacquered wood of the sleigh. Wendel gazed at it rather fondly. Ardis suspected he liked the bird only because the archmage didn't.

She smiled. The lingering venom in her blood weighed down her eyelids. They had barely slept a night since Constantinople. A hard bench in a sleigh was a luxury after huddling together in a cave in the wilderness.

Ardis rested her head against Wendel's shoulder.

If she closed her eyes, she could almost imagine they were alone. They were safe. She let this delusion lull her to sleep.

San Francisco never slept through the night. Red lanterns hung like garlands of glowing fruit over the streets of Chinatown. Ardis ran over the cobblestones, dodging the crowds, ducking into alleys wherever she could. She loved the feeling of cutting her own way through the city, of finding things she had never seen.

Outside an herbalist's shop, a man sat on the sidewalk and played a haunting melody on a two-stringed *erhu* from China. The song reminded her of romantic maidens in flowing robes. She lingered until the man pointed with his bow at the box of coins by his feet. Then she shook her head and kept running.

She passed a restaurant, which smelled of sizzling and simmering, and an opium den, which smelled of burnt poppies. The odd, sweet aroma always provoked a shiver down her spine, though she had never been tempted.

Ardis ducked her head and ran faster. She would be late. Again.

Her mother's brothel looked almost respectable from the outside, with bright red paint and a bit of gilding around the doorways. Inside, the smoke of incense perfumed the air and twisted serpentine between lamplight. A courtesan lounged on a divan, chatting with a man who wrung his hat in his hands. A new customer, clearly, one who hadn't been seduced yet. Ardis raised her eyebrows, and the courtesan smiled.

Her mother's office was at the back of the brothel, down a long hallway.

"Yu Lan," her mother called. "Hurry."

Ardis brushed aside a velvet curtain and crossed the threshold.

"Yu Lan!"

"I'm coming," Ardis said.

When she stepped into the office, there were only shadows.

THREE

When Ardis woke, clouds blotted out the stars and the moon. Wendel brushed a snowflake from her face with his thumb. She had fallen asleep with her head in his lap. In other circumstances, without Konstantin watching, this might not have been such a bad arrangement. Blushing, she sat upright and straightened her clothes.

The sleigh still glided through a dark forest. Pines swayed in a gust of wind.

"Ardis," Wendel said. "How do you feel?"

She blinked a few times. "Better."

"You slept for over an hour. Is the half-life finished, archmage?"

Konstantin sighed. "That isn't how half-lives work."

"Don't tell me." Wendel held up a hand. "I don't care to know."

Ardis yawned. The venom must have faded from her blood, but she still felt exhausted. Like she hadn't slept a minute. Gingerly, she touched her neck. Her skin ached from where Konstantin had cauterized the wound. The memory of the bite flashed through her mind. The pain. The pleasure.

Shame scorched her face. She closed her eyes for a moment.

"I shouldn't have let him get so close," Ardis said. "That was stupid of me."

"Don't blame yourself." Wendel's words roughened. "We all made mistakes."

She shivered. "What happened to the vampires?"

"I underestimated them." He twisted his mouth. "The dead don't usually fight back."

"Are they immune to your necromancy?"

"When I touched the vampire, she resisted my command. She felt dead, but there was a pricking energy beneath her skin. By the time I forced her to obey, I saw the other one biting you. I should have seen him sooner."

Konstantin fidgeted with his gauntlets. "I eliminated that threat."

"That's a polite way of putting it." Wendel flicked his eyebrows upward. "I had no idea vampires were so flammable."

Konstantin coughed. "I apologize for the way things went."

Wendel inspected his nails. "Thank you so much for conveniently swooping in and rescuing us, archmage."

A hint of pink touched Konstantin's cheeks. He narrowed his eyes. "Next time, maybe you should pay less attention to finding a shiny new minion and more to staying in one piece."

Wendel snorted. "My shiny new minion distracted the border patrol."

Ardis imagined the vampire sinking her teeth into Officer Zlatkov's lifeless body, which gave her a perverse satisfaction.

"Oh, right," Wendel said. "You could have called off the border patrol yourself."

Konstantin's gauntlets clinked as they clenched into fists. "I would have."

Wendel curled his lip. "Before or after the Bulgarians interrogated us?"

"They interrogated you?"

Wendel laughed scornfully. "God, what did you think would happen?"

"They acted against my orders. I didn't ask them to treat you like criminals."

They could be considered criminals, though Ardis neglected to mention that.

"What did you tell them?" Wendel said. "They knew an awful lot about my past and present. They promised a rather unpleasant future."

Konstantin spoke crisply. "The Archmages of Vienna research each of their employees."

"Employees?" Wendel said the word with spectacular derision. "I'm not your employee."

"You will be once we work on the Eisenkriegers."

"Am I getting one of those little flower pins, like Ardis?"

Konstantin scoffed. "No."

Wendel started to speak, but Ardis interrupted him.

"Stop," she said. "Both of you. Just stop."

They stared at her, nonplussed.

"All I want for Christmas is one day without fighting," she said.

Konstantin furrowed his brow and looked almost wistful.

"Fine." Wendel looked considerably less wistful. "But you may be disappointed."

Before Ardis could ask what he meant, the sleigh driver reined in his horses. They had arrived on the outskirts of a city.

"Phillipopolis," Konstantin said. "We have to walk from here."

Snow hushed the city and lay unbroken on many roads. Streetlights gleamed like fireflies, scattered here and there, and suffused the fog with gold. Ardis jumped from the sleigh, pinpricks dancing through her numb legs.

"I feel undead," she muttered.

Wendel arched an eyebrow. "Believe me. You aren't."

She stared at him for a moment. "I'm afraid to ask."

Konstantin climbed from the sleigh and fished out a pocketwatch from his coat. The dial glowed with technomancy. "It's two o'clock. Technically, it's Christmas."

Wendel leapt to the ground with surprising grace; Ardis had guessed his muscles were as stiff as hers.

"Technically, it's my first Christmas as a free man," Wendel said.

Konstantin looked sideways at him. "How sad."

Wendel hated pity in all its varieties, but this time he faked a flattering smile. "Can you make it all better, archmage? Can you give me the Christmas gift I have been dreaming of?"

Konstantin pursed his lips. "And what would that be?"

"Don't take the bait, Konstantin," Ardis said.

Wendel grinned. "Too late."

Konstantin shook his head and started walking, but Wendel followed at his heels.

"I want asylum," Wendel said.

"Asylum?"

"I'm tired of everyone trying to kill me."

"You belong *in* an asylum," Konstantin muttered.

Wendel forced his laugh into a frown, as if he hadn't meant to humor the archmage. "Is that a no?"

"Talk to me after you fix my Eisenkriegers."

"You drive a hard bargain, archmage."

Konstantin snorted. "Yes, because not killing you is a bargain."

"As if you would."

"God." Ardis sighed. "I'm so tired of you two bickering."

Shivering, she plodded through Phillipopolis.

In a frosty field near the center of the city, a sleek zeppelin with a sky blue gondola hovered at a mooring mast. Ardis recognized the golden flower on the airship's fins as an edelweiss, the symbol of the archmages.

"We're traveling by airship?" Wendel said.

"Obviously." Konstantin broke into a boyish smile. "I love zeppelins. I can't be bothered with those buzzing little airplanes."

Wendel's shoulders stiffened. He slowed and craned his neck to inspect the zeppelin. Ardis wondered if he didn't like flying, but had seen him on an airship twice before, and he hadn't been this suspicious.

"Excuse me," Ardis said. "Konstantin, where are we flying?"

The archmage's smile faltered. "My apologies. You fell asleep before I could explain things a bit more clearly to you."

"Our destination?"

"Prussia."

"Prussia?"

Ardis glanced at Wendel, but he had the face of a statue. He tilted his head as he gazed along the zeppelin. She had no way of knowing how he felt about returning home. If he even thought of Prussia as his home anymore.

"Why?" Ardis said.

Konstantin touched his knuckles to his mouth. He sucked in a breath, then sighed. "We are at war."

Ardis stared dumbfounded at him for a minute, though she had known there would be a war. They all had. "With who?"

"Blame Russia," Konstantin said. "They declared war on us."

"On Austria-Hungary?"

"And Germany. By necessity."

Kaiser Wilhelm II of Germany and Tsar Nicholas II of Russia may have been cousins, but that didn't mean they had aced diplomacy. A tangle of alliances meant yet more countries would be dragged into the fight—starting with Germany and Austria-Hungary on one side, Russia and Serbia on the other.

"Did Russia say why?" Ardis said.

"To retaliate against Project Lazarus." Konstantin met her gaze. "They won't tolerate an army of Eisenkriegers. When the Order replied to my telegram, they accused Wendel of selling our military secrets to the Russians."

Zlatkov's words echoed in her ears.

She whored herself out again to the Russians when they paid more money than the archmages. Because she was a greedy little bitch.

Ardis's pulse beat in her throat. "You can't think it was us, or I wouldn't be talking to you now."

"Wendel said it was Thorsten Magnusson," Konstantin said.

"Thorsten betrayed the archmages. He told the Russians about Project Lazarus."

Konstantin shook his head. "Ardis, I—"

"We tried to stop him. Thorsten didn't care what the consequences would be. He even said that war was good for business."

"Ardis." He met her gaze. "I believe you."

Her breath escaped in a sigh. "I should have done more."

"The archmages tried to stop this war. But the Hex wasn't enough."

Konstantin touched her back and nudged her toward the zeppelin. "The Russians are invading East Prussia. It's not too late to stop them."

Ardis glanced at Wendel. "Is that how you convinced him?"

Konstantin's smile looked distant. "It seems he still has some loyalty to his family, as much as he would like to deny it."

Certainty settled over Ardis with the weight and comfort of armor.

This would be her future.

She strode to Wendel and waited by his side. When he looked at her, she recognized the tension of worry in his face. "Wendel, are you ready?"

Wendel sighed but said nothing.

They walked beneath the zeppelin's underbelly, and climbed the stairs corkscrewing inside the mooring mast. Konstantin bounded up the tower, his boots clanging on steel; Ardis followed at his heels. The railing felt slick with ice under her hand. She reached the nose of the zeppelin, where a swaying gangway led inside.

A man in a smart blue uniform saluted her. "Welcome to the *Wanderfalke*."

Peregrine falcon. Ardis hoped this airship was as fast as its namesake.

"Thank you," she said.

Konstantin waved at her. "Captain Himmel, meet Ardis. She's one of our mercenaries."

Himmel glanced at Ardis with honey-colored eyes. A smile curved under his waxed mustache. She arched her eyebrows, and he broke into a grin. If Himmel was flirting, Ardis doubted Wendel would appreciate that.

Shockingly, she didn't hear a single sarcastic comment.

Ardis frowned and glanced back over the gangway. Empty. She squeezed past Konstantin and ran back to the mooring mast.

Wind whistled in her ears and tugged her toward the edge. Wendel stopped halfway with his hair in his eyes, clutching the railings on either side.

"Wendel!" she said.

He lifted his head and spoke through clenched teeth. "Yes?"

"What are you doing?"

A muscle in his jaw twitched. "Catching my breath."

Ardis narrowed her eyes. She didn't believe Wendel for half a second, but knew he wouldn't tell her the truth with Konstantin and the airship captain watching.

She waved him onward. "We don't have time for this."

Wendel's grip on the railings tightened, and he yanked himself up a few stairs. He ran the rest of the way, stopping where she blocked him.

Panting, Wendel stared at her. "Excuse me."

She lowered her voice. "What's wrong?"

Wendel shook his head, still breathing too hard.

"Tell me later." She stepped aside to let him pass, and watched him cross the gangway with his head high and his shoulders rigid.

At last, they all boarded the *Wanderfalke.*

Konstantin thinned his lips. "Wendel, how good of you to join us."

Wendel didn't even retort, though he eyed Himmel.

"Captain Himmel, this is Prince Wendel of Prussia." Konstantin coughed. "Formerly, anyway."

"There's no need for obsolete titles," Wendel muttered.

"Sir." Himmel stood at attention. "This is the necromancer?"

Konstantin gave him a meaningful glance. "I'll take them from here. Prepare to cast off, and plot the fastest course to Prussia."

Himmel saluted the archmage again. "Yes, sir."

Konstantin led them deeper into the zeppelin. The gangway had no walls, like it might on a passenger airship, and the duralumin skeleton of the zeppelin gleamed in the dim light. The floor leveled out as they reached the lower deck. Konstantin held the door and waved them through into a corridor. They passed doors marked as the kitchen and the wireless telegraphy room.

"Your cabins are on the upper deck," Konstantin said.

Ardis raised her eyebrows. This must be a flagship zeppelin.

They followed Konstantin upstairs to a deserted lounge and dining room. On both the port and starboard sides, promenade decks slanted to overlook the ground. Ardis wandered to the windows and stared at the snowy roofs of Phillipopolis. With a jolt, the zeppelin cast away from the mooring mast and floated into the sky.

"How long is the trip to Prussia?" Ardis said.

Konstantin joined her on the promenade and stood with his hands clasped behind his back. He frowned, his face thoughtful. "Fifteen hours in good weather, though airship travel has been restricted ever since the declaration of war."

"Are there enemy airships?" Ardis said. "I didn't think Russia had any."

"They don't." Konstantin smiled grimly. "But Britain does, and there's talk of them allying with Russia against us."

"Wonderful," Wendel said.

Ardis glanced over her shoulder. Wendel lingered in the shadows, not looking at the windows, his arms crossed. Her chest tightened as she realized why he had been acting so wary. He was afraid of heights.

Or perhaps Wendel was afraid of falling.

Ardis would never forget the look on Wendel's face as he plummeted to his death, but had assumed he had forgotten it all. Did he remember her standing on the Serpent's Tower as he dropped through the darkness?

Did he remember dying?

Ardis shivered and hugged herself. Konstantin was staring at her now.

"Sorry," she said. "It's a little cold."

Konstantin dipped his head. "The *Wanderfalke* is outfitted with shielding technomancy, though temperature regulation isn't a primary concern. We care more about hydrogen containment." He cleared his throat as if realizing he had gone off on a tangent. "May I suggest your cabins? They tend to be warmer."

Wendel waved at nothing in particular. "Lead the way."

They left the dining room and walked down a corridor lined with doors.

Konstantin pointed out the first and second doors on the left. "These will be your cabins. Let me know if you need anything."

"Thank you," Wendel said. "You make a decent airship steward, archmage."

Konstantin coughed. "Good night."

Ardis opened the door to her cabin and discovered a small bare room with a single berth. Light glowed from a wall lamp shaped like a porthole. She glanced back at Konstantin, who hesitated in the doorway.

"Merry Christmas," Konstantin said. It almost sounded absurd.

Ardis nodded. "Merry Christmas."

Wendel lingered behind the archmage. Ardis caught his eye, but Konstantin let the door swing shut between them.

Ardis tried not to worry about Wendel. Frowning, she kicked off her boots and killed the light. She crawled into the berth, still fully clothed, and yanked the blankets over herself. The moment her head hit the pillow, exhaustion anchored her there and dragged her down. She drifted underwater in an ocean of sleep.

Outside the window, a maidenhair tree danced in the wind and scattered its golden leaves over the streets of San Francisco.

Ardis sat at the dinner table. The naked blade of a *jian* rested on the old wood. When she touched the Chinese sword, it ignited under her fingertips. Enchanted flames crawled over the steel and whispered against her skin.

"Chun Yi," she whispered.

Her sword smoldered with its own fire, brighter than the autumn leaves.

"Yu Lan!"

Her mother, Jin Hua, swatted away her hand. Jin Hua looked distracted, her long dark hair twisted back in a careless bun. "Put down that sword."

Ardis did as she was told. Jin Hua delivered plate after plate of delicious food until the table groaned under its burden. A whole pot of wonton soup, an embarrassment of dumplings, roast duck swimming in sauce, pork cooked with mustard greens, and Ardis's favorite, sesame chicken with handmade noodles.

Her mother pressed a pair of chopsticks into her hand.

"You need to eat," Jin Hua said. "For the baby."

"What baby?" Ardis said.

Jin Hua poured her a cup of fragrant jasmine tea. "Don't be silly, Yu Lan."

When Ardis looked down, the world went askew. She was pregnant? She rubbed her round belly. Very pregnant.

"Mama?" Ardis said, her words unsteady. "I'm having a baby?"

Jin Hua smiled. "Sooner than you think."

FOUR

rdis jerked awake and clutched fistfuls of sheets in her hands. Her pulse hammered in her ears. She pressed herself to the mattress, trying to piece together the fragments of the dream, but it still didn't make much sense.

Unless…

Ardis slipped her hand under her shirt and touched her belly. It felt as flat as it ever did. But that didn't stop the panicky little jitter to her heartbeat. She had been careful; she had taken precautions. She couldn't be pregnant.

Though, with enough bad luck, she knew she could be.

God, what would Wendel say about her dream?

Talking to him about babies didn't seem like a conversation they could have right now. Or ever. She had never been remotely intrigued by the realm of tiny helpless wailing things that demanded tributes of milk.

Ardis propped her elbows against the berth and pushed herself upright.

"It was just a dream," she muttered. "A nightmare."

Because of course an accidental baby would be a nightmare. She was a mercenary, for heaven's sake. She pressed her lips together and decided to stop thinking about it. The part with the sword was the most interesting, anyway.

Barefoot, Ardis tiptoed to the next cabin and slipped inside.

Wendel lay with his arm curled around a pillow. He lifted his head.

"Ardis?" he whispered.

Her stomach tightened. "I couldn't sleep."

"Ah."

Wendel swung his legs over the edge of his berth and patted the spot next to him. "Join me in the insomniacs club. Very exclusive. Only the best clientele."

She sat close to him. Her dream darted through her mind again. She inhaled and held the words in her mouth.

Wendel's smile faded. "What is it?"

Ardis touched her belly. There was no baby. Maybe there never would be. "Nothing."

"Don't lie to a liar," Wendel said gently.

"You first." Ardis raised her eyebrows. "Tell me why you couldn't sleep."

He laughed and rubbed his thumb over his lip. She studied his face, though she couldn't read him well in the shadows.

"I couldn't stop thinking about the vampires."

That wasn't what Ardis had expected. "Are you angry Konstantin saved me?"

"No."

Wendel stared at the floor. His eyes narrowed slightly. "What did it feel like?"

Her stomach clenched. She knew what he was asking, but didn't know how he would look at her if she told him the truth.

"Like bliss," she whispered.

Wendel looked at her with a strange curiosity in his eyes, then looked away.

"Fifteen hours is a long flight for a zeppelin," he said. "They will have to stop to refuel. We can still escape to Switzerland."

"You don't want to go home?" she said.

Wendel was silent for a moment. "Prussia isn't home."

"But you have family there."

"Correct." Wendel clucked his tongue. "I doubt they will abandon Königsberg."

"Königsberg?"

"The capital of East Prussia, and the name of our ancestral castle there."

Ardis gawked at him. "Castle?"

Wendel grimaced. "Tragically, Königsberg isn't much of one. Back when the Teutonic Knights built it, the castle was a crusader fortress, but over the centuries it has been dandified, for lack of a better word."

"I'm still amazed you have an ancestral castle."

"We won't for long when the Russians invade," Wendel said. "Juliana and Wolfram may have the sense to flee, but my father isn't the kind of man who surrenders. And I know my mother would stay by his side."

Ardis touched his arm. "Are you worried about them?"

Wendel laced his fingers together and inspected his hands. "Yes."

"Then you should help them."

"You don't have to tell me that," he said dryly. "I'm not heartless."

She poked him in the ribs. "Tempted by the thought of being a hero?"

"Hardly."

She smiled at him. "I can't imagine you riding into battle on a white stallion. You're too devious for that. I expect you to skulk into the castle under cover of darkness and let an army of undead do all your dirty work."

He laughed. "I have a reputation to maintain."

Ardis started to stand, but Wendel caught her wrist and tugged her down. She fell sideways against him, halfway in his lap, and he held her with an arm behind her back. He smiled, dipped her lower, and stole a kiss. His lips felt divine against hers. She melted against him, craving the heat of his skin.

His stubble grazed her cheek as he moved to whisper in her ear.

"I'm still tempted to escape," he said, "so we can spend more time alone."

She licked her lips. They hadn't been alone like that in days. She ran her hand over his cheekbone and combed her fingers through his ragged hair, remembering how long and beautiful it had been when she first met him.

"I should trim your hair," she said.

"Not handsome enough for you?"

"You look rough around the edges."

He lowered his voice. "Rough isn't always bad."

Blushing, she pushed him away. "Calm down."

"I'm calm."

When he adjusted himself beneath her, Ardis knew he wasn't exactly telling the truth. He attempted to look innocent.

"Your turn," Wendel said. "You never told me why you crept into my cabin."

"To seduce you, clearly." Ardis hoped her smile looked real.

"I'm all for seduction," he said, with a raised eyebrow, "but this isn't fair. I want to know what keeps you awake at night."

Anxiety prickled along Ardis's skin. She tried to sound flippant. "San Francisco."

Wendel hesitated. "The man who wouldn't take no for an answer?"

Ardis pressed her hands between her knees. "Not him." She wasn't brave enough for the rest.

"It was just a dream," she said again, as if repetition would make her words real.

Wendel held her hand. "Stay with me. I can't sleep without you."

She met Wendel's eyes, and he looked back at her with a vulnerability he didn't often reveal. She slipped her hand behind his neck and captured him in a kiss. They dropped onto the berth. After an awkward moment of elbows and knees, they fit together.

He lay on his back and Ardis lay with her head resting on his chest. His heart thumped under her ear.

Ardis unbuttoned his shirt and stroked her hand over his warm skin. He flinched when she found a few of his scars, but he had so many that she couldn't touch him without reminding him of his memories. She wanted to touch him until he forgot the pain and felt only pleasure.

"Before I met you," Wendel said, "it was easier to fight."

She frowned. "Are you saying I'm a liability?".

"You misunderstand me." Wendel paused, his face only inches from her own. "In some ways, it is easier to face death alone."

An ache both sick and sweet panged in Ardis's chest. "You aren't alone."

"Exactly," he said. "I don't want to see you hurt."

She smiled, her eyes stinging. "That sounds awfully heroic of you. I think I might be ruining your reputation, Wendel."

He laughed. "To hell with my reputation." He kissed her.

Ardis deepened the kiss. Wendel's hand slid under her shirt, and she arched against him. His thumb rubbed circles over her nipples, first one, then the other, until the tight pleasure made her moan softly into his mouth.

"I love you," Wendel whispered in her ear.

Ardis swallowed hard. Was this the part where she said the same?

She had told him she loved him the night he died, the night she brought him back with borrowed magic. But of course he hadn't heard her then. Somehow, parroting the words back to him now felt like it cheapened them. Her hesitation fed the guilt in her gut. And so she hid her emotions behind a smile.

"You should love me," Ardis teased. "I saved your life."

"Oh?"

She couldn't see Wendel's face, though she was sure from the sound of his voice he was raising one of his eyebrows.

"Are we keeping count?" he said. "Last time I checked, I rescued you."

"But I was smart," she said. "I never swore fealty to you."

"How evil of you," Wendel said, with suppressed laughter in his voice. "I suppose this means I'm still yours to command."

Ardis smiled in the dark. "I command you to lie back and close your eyes."

"Yes, mistress."

She laughed and swatted him. "Don't call me that."

"Technically, it's true. We aren't married."

Ardis shook her head and climbed onto Wendel. She straddled him on her knees. He untied her braid, then combed his fingers through her loose hair. He had such a gentle touch for a man who fought with his hands.

"For me to be your mistress," Ardis said, "I would have to be a kept woman."

"I see," Wendel said.

He didn't sound like he was paying much attention. He seemed to be more fascinated by running his hands along the curves of her hips.

"Considering how you have no money," Ardis said, "you can't afford a courtesan."

Wendel lifted his head and dragged the pillow closer, as if to give himself a better view.

"I know little about courtesans," he said. "Please, by all means, educate me."

She scoffed at him. "I could be insulted."

"Are you?"

"No."

Ardis bent down to kiss him. His hands cradled her face tenderly; his fingers tangled with her hair, and he kissed her more fiercely. He caught her lower lip in his teeth and bit her just hard enough to make her gasp. Panting, her face flushed, she broke away. Desire burned in his eyes. The look was more lust than love, but she would take it. She wasn't sure what love looked like, anyway.

Wendel distracted Ardis from her thoughts by thrusting against her. She rubbed him and savored how hard he had become. She leaned back and stripped off her shirt. Before she could unbuckle her belt, Wendel hooked a hand over her shoulder and flipped her onto her back.

"Allow me." The rasp in his voice made her shiver.

Ardis loved seeing him like this. He unbuckled her belt and lingered to kiss the inside of her thigh. She helped him by wriggling out of her trousers. She laughed when the cloth bunched at her ankle and he struggled to tug it over her foot.

"That was a mistake," Wendel said. "Imagine something much more seductive."

She smirked. "Oh, I'm imagining all sorts of things."

He knelt over her. "I'm listening."

"I'm imagining you naked, first of all."

"Done."

Wendel slid off the berth and stripped in remarkable time. When he walked toward her, she couldn't stop staring at his silhouette. She reached out and wrapped her fingers around him. He sucked in a breath and staggered nearer, his knees bumping against the berth.

"That feels good," Wendel said, his voice gravelly.

Ardis stroked him. He groaned and closed his eyes. With her other hand, she gripped his buttocks, his muscles clenching under her fingernails. She stroked him faster, then stopped and climbed onto her knees. He was inches from her mouth.

"Ardis?" Wendel said.

She was surprised how coherent he was. Still.

"I'm imagining something," Ardis whispered.

When her breath breezed over him, he swayed, his hands clenching.

"God," Wendel said, "don't make me guess."

Ardis smiled wickedly. "Is this torture?"

"If this is torture, I would sign up willingly."

They had been through hell together, including actual torture, and Ardis didn't want him thinking about that right now.

She didn't want him thinking about anything right now.

Licking her lips, she bent forward and looked up at him through her eyelashes.

"Do you want me?" Ardis said.

Wendel growled the words. "I want you more than anything."

She laughed, and took him in her mouth. He gasped. She ran her tongue around the tip of him before sliding down a little deeper. His fingertips brushed the back of her head. She sucked on him, and his fingers tightened in her hair.

"Ardis," Wendel said.

She drew back and looked at him. "Yes?"

His face tensed. It took him a moment to articulate his thoughts.

"Tell me what you want. I want to know exactly how you imagine this ending." Wendel exhaled shakily. "Please."

Ardis smiled at his attempt to be polite. "I want you to moan."

He shuddered, involuntarily, and she licked the length of him. When she lifted her head, he was clenching his jaw tight.

"To tell you the truth," Ardis said, "I've never done this before."

Wendel sucked in a shaky breath. "Never?"

She laughed. "Don't sound so surprised. I was a good girl in San Francisco."

"I'm honored to be your first," he said.

"How gentlemanly of you." She felt a nervous flutter in her stomach. "Any requests?"

"Whatever you are comfortable with."

She smiled. "That's a dangerous thing to say. I never said I was that innocent."

"I'm quaking in my boots."

"You aren't wearing any."

"A minor point."

Ardis arched her eyebrows. "You are altogether too witty."

"I don't—"

Ardis licked Wendel again, and his words became a gasp. She stroked him in her hand, caressing him with her fingers and her tongue. He uttered something unintelligible. She smiled, and he flinched at the light touch of her teeth. She kissed him as an apology, but he backed away from her.

"I won't last like this," Wendel said.

Ardis couldn't stop smiling. "I'm good?"

He raised his eyebrows, as if this question were far too obvious for a reply.

"Or," she said huskily, "very, very bad?"

Wendel let out a growling sigh. Ardis slid her lips around him and enjoyed every gasp and shiver she elicited. He groaned and closed his eyes, his head tilted back. She stopped only when her jaw started to ache.

"Ardis?" he said.

She rubbed her cheek. "My jaw hurts. I blame you."

"What? Why?"

"Try to be less well-endowed next time."

He laughed. "Apologies." He didn't sound sorry at all.

Wendel stepped away, every muscle in his body taut, and bent to grab his coat from the floor. He rummaged in a pocket until he found what he was looking for.

He held the preventive high. "Yes?"

Ardis plucked the preventive from his hand and tossed it away. "No. I want to finish what I started."

She grabbed him by the hips and dragged him closer, and bent over him again. His breath became ragged.

"Ardis," he said. "I'm close."

She paused. "Good."

She bent down again. She loved to explore him with her mouth, to find the places that pleased him the most. He held his breath and tensed. It didn't take long to find his breaking point. He groaned as he let go.

She held still as he shuddered. The taste of him surprised her, and she swallowed.

Wendel staggered back. He looked weak at the knees. He dropped onto the berth, wrapped his arm around her waist, and dragged her down to him. She lay against his chest, his heartbeat hammering against her cheek.

Ardis touched her fingers to her mouth, and Wendel kissed the top of her head.

"Mmm," he said.

She smiled. "Is that all you have to say?"

He tweaked her ear. "There's still the preventive."

"Ambitious?"

"Very."

"I'll take the moment to catch my breath."

Wendel's laugh vibrated through her chest. His arm tightened around her in lopsided hug. She kissed the hollow of his neck, then curled against him to steal the heat of his skin. His hand smoothed the tangles from her hair.

She couldn't remember why she had looked for him. There was no past, and no future, only this time in his arms.

Ardis sighed and shut her eyes. She drifted through the darkness.

"Don't fall asleep," Wendel said.

"I'm not."

He slipped out from underneath her and kissed her softly. He wasn't soft elsewhere, though. She wanted to tease him about his impatience, but he kept kissing her until the feeling seared away her thoughts. He left her breathless while he found the preventive, until he held himself over her.

"Wendel," she said.

"Yes?"

She smiled. "I felt like saying your name."

He smiled in return, though his was far more wicked. "I want you to moan."

"Thief," she said. "That was my line."

"I'm not giving it back. I will, however, give you something else."

As he slid into her, she savored every inch of him. She tilted her hips and pressed tight against him, until they were as close as they could possibly be. He drew back, and she whimpered an involuntary protest. When he thrust again, she urged him on with her fingernails biting into his buttocks. They found a rhythm together, hard and fast and unrelenting, her heart pounding a staccato beat.

He never stopped, never faltered, and her anticipation built until she could barely breathe.

Ardis gasped. "Wendel."

"Moan," he said. "I love it when you moan."

After an instant of self-consciousness, she moaned. The sound encouraged him to thrust even harder. She clung to him as she teetered on the edge, then fell over the brink and tumbled into ecstasy. He thrust one last time, shuddering, and held her tight. Wordless with the echoes of pleasure, she kissed him.

Wendel tucked Ardis into the crook of his arm.

With a sigh of sheer contentment, she closed her eyes. Now she could sleep.

FIVE

On Christmas morning, Ardis woke in Wendel's arms, and the luxury of peace felt like the best gift in the world. She had spent far too many Christmases alone.

When Ardis stirred, Wendel's arms tightened around her.

"Are you awake?" he whispered.

"Yes," she said. "How long have you been awake?"

He laughed quietly. "I can never sleep on Christmas morning."

Ardis imagined Wendel as a little boy, too excited to stay in bed, and found the thought both sweet and sad. Wendel had been only eleven when his family discovered his necromancy and disinherited him. She doubted he had much of a childhood in Constantinople, during his time with the Order of the Asphodel.

"Can't wait to see what Santa Claus brought you?" Ardis said.

Wendel paused. "In Germany, children find their gifts under the tree on Christmas Eve. So today would be too late."

"I didn't know that," she said.

"Why? Haven't you been working for the archmages for several years?"

Ardis blushed. "Yes, but I spent the holidays alone. One Christmas, I did buy a new tassel for my sword, after the old one fell off."

Wendel lifted himself on his elbow and looked into her face. "Are you joking?"

"No," she said, still blushing.

Wendel laughed, hard enough that he doubled over and pressed his face to the pillow. Ardis swatted at him to make him stop, but it only made him laugh more. She started laughing with him, until her eyes watered and her ribs hurt. When at last their laughter faded, they both lay silently.

Wendel cleared his throat. "I didn't mean to laugh, but then I imagined how pitiful that tassel must have been."

Ardis sighed and dabbed her eyes. "I haven't laughed that hard in months."

Wendel sat upright and flicked on the light. The porthole lamp glowed softly. "Ardis, I promise you we will have a proper Christmas."

"It's not too late for gifts?" she said.

"We can cheat."

She grinned. "Can I have you for Christmas? Wearing nothing but a bow?"

"If you have a bow."

Wendel kissed her on the cheek, then leaned back and frowned. "Though I'm afraid that was the last preventive."

Ardis crawled off the berth. She searched her clothes, turning out every pocket, but returned to him empty-handed. "Sadly, you're right."

Her dream from last night crept back into her head. Her stomach squirmed. She didn't want to take any chances.

What if it was already too late? A baby wasn't the Christmas gift she wanted.

Blinking away those thoughts, Ardis grabbed her shirt. Wendel stretched out on the berth and watched her dress. His hand strayed lower, and she glared at him. He didn't even bother to look innocent.

"Am I not allowed to touch myself?" Wendel said.

"No." Ardis smirked. "Save your strength."

She sat on the berth to tug on her boots. He knelt behind her and kissed the back of her neck. She shivered, but tried not to let him notice.

"I'm hungry," she said. "I want breakfast."

His sigh stirred her hair. "I suppose I can put on clothes."

She snorted. "It's a crime, I know."

Wendel didn't stop smirking the whole time he got dressed.

They found Konstantin in the zeppelin's dining room, at a table laden with food, though he didn't seem to be eating. He hunched over a newspaper, a pat of butter precariously balanced on the knife in his hand.

"Good morning," Ardis said.

Konstantin startled, barely avoiding dropping the butter. "I'm sorry; I didn't see you there. Please, help yourself to breakfast."

Ardis tugged out a wicker chair. It felt surprisingly lightweight, as did most zeppelin furniture, with a cushion filled by air. Wendel sat to her right, opposite Konstantin, and reached for a platter with slices of meat and cheese.

"Did you sleep well?" Konstantin said.

Ardis nodded and hoped he couldn't see her blush. She doubted Konstantin knew she had spent the night in Wendel's cabin, though hopefully no crewmembers had rapped on her door in the morning before she woke.

Wendel sucked in his breath. "Is that really...?"

Ardis glanced at him. "Really what?"

"*Lebkuchen.*"

Wendel rubbed his hands together and dragged a plate of cookies closer. They looked rather like gingerbread. He handed one to Ardis. The cookie was shaped like a heart, frosted with a shiny white glaze that cracked under her teeth. Lebkuchen tasted sweetly spicy, like almonds, ginger, cinnamon, and orange.

"Delicious," Ardis said.

Wendel looked wistfully at the cookie in his hand. "They remind me of Prussia."

Konstantin folded his newspaper. "They aren't Prussian. They are Austrian, from Vienna."

"Ah," Wendel said.

Ardis cocked her head. "You come from Austria, don't you, Konstantin?"

"Yes," the archmage said. "Salzburg."

Frowning, Konstantin sipped his coffee. Wendel bit a lebkuchen heart in half. Both of them looked secretly homesick.

"I have you both beat," Ardis said.

Konstantin peered over his cup of coffee. "What do you mean?"

"I'm the farthest from home this Christmas," she said. "San Francisco must be over five thousand miles from here."

"You win." Wendel twisted his mouth. "Congratulations."

"Did you eat Chinese cookies at home, Ardis?" Konstantin said.

She knew he was trying to be polite, but his curiosity made her blush.

"Fortune cookies," she said.

Konstantin nodded, squinting. "A cookie for luck, then?"

"Not quite. When you break open the cookie, you find a little piece of paper with your future written on it." Ardis didn't believe in fortunetelling, so she shrugged. "They aren't actually Chinese. Someone invented them in San Francisco."

"But they remind you of home," Konstantin said.

"Yes."

Ardis helped herself to a slice of pumpernickel and slathered it with plum jam. She bit the bread and chewed for a moment. "Not that I'm dying to go home."

"Agreed," Wendel said.

"Speak for yourselves," Konstantin said. "Salzburg is a lovely place."

Wendel arched an eyebrow. "Why not take a slight detour, archmage? Salzburg must be better than flying to the front lines."

Konstantin glanced heavenward as if both tempted and exasperated. "I would love to go home, but I'm too busy saving yours."

Wendel shrugged. "Prussia has an army."

Konstantin glared at him. "And so does Russia. Theirs is bigger."

"Ours is better."

"So I should ignore the wireless telegram that came this morning?"

Wendel waited for the archmage to tell him what the telegram said, but Konstantin sipped his coffee and looked at him coolly.

Ardis broke the silence. "What did it say?"

"The Russians are marching on Königsberg," Konstantin said.

"Königsberg?" Wendel straightened, his fork in his fist. "No one loots that castle except me. It's my birthright, damn it."

Ardis sighed. She didn't know why Wendel insisted on acting like such a bastard around the archmage, when she knew he cared about saving his home and his family. Would it kill him to admit he had a heart?

"Your uncle isn't too happy about that, either," Konstantin said.

"Uncle?" Ardis said.

"Wilhelm." Konstantin paused. "King of Prussia, Emperor of Germany."

Ardis's jaw dropped. "How far from the throne were you, Wendel?"

Wendel waved away her comment. "Never close enough to count." He looked Konstantin in the eye. "Archmage, I hope you have an excellent plan for our arrival in Prussia. One that involves undead Russians."

Konstantin's smile looked secretive. "Perhaps I will tell you more about my plans."

A *rap-rap-rap* came from the window of the starboard promenade deck. Konstantin frowned, puzzled, and Wendel looked at him as if the noise were his fault. Ardis, however, pushed her chair from the table and stood. She walked to the promenade deck, leaned over, and peered out the window.

A raven perched outside on the railing. It pecked on the window.

"Wendel?" Ardis said. "You won't believe this."

The raven shuffled along the railing, its claws knocking down small puffs of snow.

Wendel looked out the window. "My God." He laughed. "He's a persistent little devil."

He fiddled with a latch and slid the window open. The raven eyed his hand as if he might be hiding food. Wendel tried to pet the raven, but it hopped away and croaked at him, rustling the glossy feathers at its throat.

"For heaven's sake," Konstantin said. "Close the window!"

"Can I keep him?" Wendel said, smirking.

"No." Konstantin tossed aside his napkin. "Just, no."

Wendel ignored him and offered a crumb of lebkuchen to the raven. The bird flew into the zeppelin and landed on the back of a wicker chair. Wendel tossed the bird the crumb, and it caught it, blinking as it swallowed.

Konstantin stood. "Get that bird out of here!"

"I'm naming him Krampus," Wendel said.

"Him?" Ardis said. "How do you even know it's a him?"

Wendel shrugged. "You know, it's been far too long since I've had a pet. Krampus will have to be my Christmas present."

With another crumb, Wendel coaxed the raven to hop onto his wrist.

"Krampus likes me," Wendel said. "See? He knows I'm a good necromancer."

"That's a little creepy," Ardis muttered.

Konstantin let out a sighing growl. He slid the window shut himself, then raked his fingers through his already wild curls.

"If that bird dirties this zeppelin," Konstantin said, "I will hold *you* responsible."

Wendel flashed a smile. "I don't think he's housebroken."

Konstantin sucked in his breath, but was interrupted by the arrival of Himmel. The captain held a bottle of crystal clear liquor in his hand. He saluted Konstantin, then glanced at the raven and raised his eyebrows.

"Who brought the raven?" Himmel said.

"No one," Konstantin said. "It must have followed us here."

"Doubtful, sir." Himmel shrugged. "At this altitude, the *Wanderfalke* flies about twice as fast as a raven. So it must be a stowaway."

Konstantin rubbed his beard. "I hadn't taken the raven's speed into account."

Perched on Wendel's wrist, Krampus croaked and cocked his head. Wendel stroked the raven's scaly foot until he bit him. Wendel flinched and inspected his thumb, though it looked like nothing more than a playful nip.

"Never mind the bird." Himmel lifted the bottle. "I wanted to invite you for a drink."

"Oh?" Konstantin said, clearly still distracted by the raven.

"Apricot schnapps. I saved a bottle for Christmas."

Ardis eyed the bottle. She liked the sound of schnapps in the morning. But Konstantin kept frowning at Krampus.

"If the invitation isn't exclusive," Ardis said, "I would love a shot or two."

Himmel dipped his head. "Please, join us."

"And I can take the archmage's drink," Wendel said.

Konstantin blinked. "No, you won't. Himmel, I hope you have enough for four."

Himmel had a husky laugh. "Don't worry, this schnapps will knock you on your ass. Pardon my language. I'm off duty."

"Don't mind me," Ardis said.

Himmel smiled. "My quarters?"

Konstantin nodded. His cheeks looked pink, and Ardis wondered why he was blushing.

Wendel glanced around the room. "What's that noise?"

A wasp buzzed overhead. It landed on the table, its antennae twitching, and scuttled over to Ardis's abandoned plate where it chewed on a crumb.

"You let a wasp in through the window," Ardis said.

The wasp buzzed to her and landed on her arm. She held her breath. Ordinarily, wasps wouldn't attack unless provoked.

But this was no ordinary wasp.

She hadn't noticed at a distance, but the wasp's legs clicked with tiny mechanical joints. It reshuffled its wings, fashioned of silk and wire, over its enameled exoskeleton.

Mesmerized, Ardis lifted her arm to her face. "It's a clockwork wasp!"

With a flickering of its antennae, the mechanical insect dipped its abdomen and plunged its stinger into her skin. She swore at the piercing pain and swatted at the wasp, but it zoomed away before she could smash it.

"Allow me to kill it," Wendel said.

"Don't kill it!" Konstantin said. "Catch it."

Wendel curled his lip. "Why?"

"So I can inspect it."

"Oh, obviously."

The wasp circled them in drunken figure eights, then landed on the table again. Wendel snatched an empty glass and clanked it over the insect. Unbalanced, Krampus leapt from Wendel's wrist and flew to a chair with a croak. The wasp scuttled against the glass, the clink of its tiny feet audible.

"Are you all right, Ardis?" Wendel said.

She winced and rubbed her arm. Pain burned from the sting. "One little wasp sting won't kill me."

Wendel's eyebrows angled into a frown. "Unless, of course, the poison is fatal."

"Are you that paranoid?"

"Not for an assassin. If I were the Russians, my clockwork wasps would be deadly."

Himmel stroked his mustache. "We do have a doctor on board."

"I'm fine." Ardis sighed. "If I feel worse, I'll go."

Wendel glowered at her. "It could be a slow-acting poison. It—"

She silenced him with a look.

Konstantin knelt by the table and peered at the wasp. He tapped the glass, and the wasp buzzed its wings furiously. "What a marvelous piece of clockwork!"

"Archmage," Wendel said. "Watch out."

"I'm not letting it out," Konstantin said. "I'm perfectly safe."

"No, watch out!"

Another clockwork wasp swooped from the ceiling and landed on Konstantin's back. Himmel smacked it onto the table, then crushed it beneath the bottle of schnapps. The crunch of gears reminded Ardis of tiny bones breaking.

"Save the schnapps!" Wendel said.

Himmel snorted. "Alcohol makes a decent blunt weapon."

He peeked beneath the bottle. One of the wasp's crooked legs twitched, and he smashed it until he pulverized it into pieces of metal.

"Still think it's marvelous, archmage?" Wendel said.

Konstantin pursed his lips. "The clockwork is incredibly intricate. Archaic, but intricate." He peered at the trapped wasp. "With that level of sophistication, this wasp could only have come from the House of Fabergé."

Wendel cocked his head. "Why does Fabergé sound familiar?"

"The House of Fabergé is famous for jewelry and decorative technomancy. Tsar Nicholas himself has commissioned pieces."

"The Russians," Himmel said grimly.

"Consider me unimpressed," Wendel said. "Wasps?"

Himmel looked at the necromancer as if unimpressed by his arrogance.

"These wasps found us at an altitude of two hundred meters," the captain said.

Ardis agreed with Himmel. Clockwork wasps from Russia couldn't be a good omen. "Scouts?"

"Likely," Himmel said.

Wendel stepped toward the table. "Allow me to kill the second one."

Konstantin gripped the glass over the trapped wasp. "No. Bring me a container so I can save it for future study. I would like to take it to my laboratory in Prussia."

Himmel sighed. "Yes, sir."

The captain left the dining room.

Ardis stared at her arm. The wasp's sting had swollen into a red bump as big as a penny, but the pain had faded to itching. "Sorry, Konstantin, but I'm smashing anything else I see."

"I only want this one specimen," Konstantin said.

Himmel returned with a jar that still had a sauerkraut label on it. He handed it to Konstantin, who slid the glass to the edge of the table and knocked the wasp into the jar. Konstantin clapped the lid on and screwed it shut as tight as it would go. The wasp buzzed and pinged off the glass.

"Satisfied?" Himmel said.

Konstantin completely missed the sarcastic quirk of Himmel's eyebrows. "Yes. For now."

Himmel lifted the bottle of schnapps. "I really could use that drink."

"Me, too," Ardis said.

Konstantin cradled the jar with the wasp. Awfully close for comfort, in Ardis's opinion, but then again, the archmage did love technomancy.

"Falkenrath?" Himmel said. "Will you be joining us for schnapps?"

Konstantin nodded. "If the invitation still stands."

Himmel smiled. "It does."

"Sans wasp," Wendel muttered.

Krampus hopped onto the table, stared at the smashed wasp, and pecked at the pieces until Wendel shooed him away.

"No," Wendel said sternly. "Don't choke on clockwork and die."

Krampus looked at him with one eye and blinked.

Nobody but Konstantin wanted the wasp, so they detoured to his cabin, where he stashed the sauerkraut jar. They descended the staircase to the lower deck and followed Himmel to his quarters. The captain's cabin was more spacious than the cabins on the upper deck, with enough room for a couch and chairs in the corner.

"Please, have a seat," Himmel said.

Konstantin settled on a chair and crossed his legs. Ardis leaned back on the couch, and Wendel sat next to her. She rubbed the bump on her arm, which was still a bit itchy, and resisted the temptation to use her fingernails.

"Krampus," Wendel said. "Krampus, stop."

The raven perched on his shoulder, nibbling his hair.

Ardis smiled. "He's preening you."

"Do you think he's an orphan raven?" Wendel said.

"Probably."

Krampus hopped onto the arm of the couch, where he started smoothing his wing feathers with his beak. Wendel smoothed his hair, which the raven had disheveled, and Ardis hid her smile behind her hand.

"Here you go," Himmel said.

The zeppelin captain slid four glasses across the table and expertly poured them each a shot of apricot schnapps.

Konstantin took his glass first. "A toast?"

"Do you have one in mind?" Himmel said, sitting by the archmage.

Konstantin's ears reddened. "No."

"I have one." Himmel lifted his glass. "To a Christmas with clear skies."

"Without wasps," Ardis added.

"Hear, hear."

They all clinked glasses. Ardis knocked back her shot. The alcohol scorched her throat the whole way down, and the sweet taste of apricot lingered on her tongue.

She made a satisfied murmur, then lifted her glass again. "To good schnapps."

Himmel laughed and poured her another shot. Konstantin still had half of his. He drank it fast, coughed, and put down his glass. Wendel smiled wickedly and scooted Konstantin's glass closer to the bottle.

"Another for the archmage," Wendel said.

"I'm fine," Konstantin said.

But Himmel poured him another shot. Konstantin took his glass from him. Wincing, he sipped the apricot schnapps.

"You don't drink very often," Ardis said, "do you?"

Konstantin's eyes widened. "Alcohol and technomancy aren't compatible."

Himmel laughed. "An experiment gone wrong?"

A spectacular blush reddened Konstantin's face. He tried to look serious, but he fidgeted too much for it to be convincing. "I would never experiment with alcohol while in the laboratory."

His eyes twinkling, Himmel nudged Konstantin with his elbow. "I believe you. Archmages are straightlaced men."

Konstantin swigged the rest of his schnapps and grimaced at the ceiling. Then he glanced sideways at Himmel and raised his finger. "Relatively. After all, zeppelin captains are reckless men."

Ardis laughed at the surprise on Himmel's face.

"How reckless are we feeling today?" she said, and everyone looked at her with curiosity. "Reckless enough for a game of poker?"

"Gambling isn't allowed on this airship." Himmel winked. "Technically."

"Quite right," Konstantin said, missing the wink.

"We don't have to play for money," Ardis said. "We could play for peanuts."

"We don't have any peanuts," Wendel said.

Inspiration struck Ardis, and she couldn't stop grinning. The heat of the schnapps glowed from her belly and warmed her skin.

"When we Americans invented poker," she said, "we also invented a few spicier versions. Ever heard of strip poker?"

SIX

Wendel, who was drinking his second shot, spluttered and wiped his mouth with a napkin.

"Yes!" Wendel said. "Yes, we should definitely play strip poker."

Ardis rolled her eyes. "I'll beat you, Wendel."

"I love a challenge."

She didn't mention strip poker was a popular game at her mother's brothel in San Francisco, but Wendel should know better.

"What are the rules of strip poker?" Konstantin said.

"You play for clothes," Wendel said.

Konstantin squinted. "I don't need any more clothes."

Everyone but Konstantin laughed, and the archmage looked so red in the face that Ardis touched the back of his hand.

"Every time you lose," Ardis said, "you lose some of your clothes."

Konstantin tugged on the wool scarf at his neck. "Well. I see. Though I do appear to be wearing quite a few articles of clothing." He articulated his words so carefully that he must have started feeling the alcohol.

"I'm game," Wendel said. "Are you, archmage? Feel like losing today?"

Konstantin narrowed his eyes, then smiled thinly. "Oh, I won't be the first one out."

Ardis laughed. "Himmel, are you in?"

The captain shoved his chair from the table. He rummaged in a shelf and returned with a deck of playing cards. Himmel tossed the cards to Ardis. She caught them and started shuffling them on the table. Wendel watched her with a vague smile, and Konstantin toyed with his shot glass. Krampus continued preening.

"Is anyone a poker virgin?" Ardis said. "Speak now or forever hold your peace."

Himmel and Wendel shook their heads.

"I'm familiar with the general theory," Konstantin said.

"Five-card draw," Ardis said. "The ante will be one piece. If you fold, you strip. If you bet more and lose, you strip more."

Himmel nodded. "Sounds fair."

"I'll deal." Ardis tapped the cards on the table. "Cut the deck, Archmage Konstantin."

Squinting, Konstantin split the shuffled deck in half. Ardis took the deck back and dealt everyone five cards facedown.

"First round of betting," she said.

Konstantin let out a puff of air. "I may be a virgin, but I know how to play."

Wendel laughed, his eyes sparkling, and Himmel struggled to keep a straight face. Konstantin sighed and reached for the bottle of schnapps, but Himmel slid it out of his reach. The captain caught the archmage's eye.

"Slow down there," Himmel said.

"It's only two shots," Konstantin said.

"Of schnapps."

Konstantin snorted. "I'm not inebriated."

"Yet." Himmel curled his mustache. "Feeling reckless?"

Konstantin met his stare. "Possibly."

Wendel stole the bottle and helped himself to a third shot,

which he knocked back.

"Are we playing or not?" he said.

"Once we all look at our cards," Ardis said.

They each picked up their hands. Ardis had one pair—an eight of hearts and an eight of spades. Wendel smirked for an instant, Konstantin licked his lips, and Himmel leaned back in his chair. Ardis kept her face blank.

"Now we bet?" Konstantin said.

"Yes," Ardis said. "Clothing instead of chips."

"I bet one," Wendel said.

"I call," Himmel said.

Konstantin chewed on his lip. "Wendel, I'll see your one and raise you two."

Wendel whistled low under his breath.

"I fold," Ardis said, and tossed her cards onto the table.

"I'll call your bet, archmage," Wendel said.

Himmel relinquished his cards. "I'm out."

"Since I folded…" Ardis took off one of her boots. "There."

Himmel kicked off both of his boots and wiggled his toes.

"Not too bad," the captain said.

"Now we draw?" Konstantin said.

Ardis nodded. "You and Wendel are at three, counting the ante."

Konstantin shook his head and didn't draw. Wendel discarded a card and took another from the deck. He looked rather smug.

"I check," Konstantin said.

"Check," Wendel said. "Show me your cards, archmage."

Konstantin had a serene smile. "My pleasure."

Wendel slapped his cards on the table. Konstantin bared his with a flourish. Wendel had two pair, but Konstantin had a straight.

"Damn it," Wendel growled.

Konstantin grinned and tossed his scarf over his shoulder. "You thought I was bluffing?"

Wendel sighed and kicked off both his boots, followed by his coat, which he draped over the back of the couch. "I need another drink."

They passed around the schnapps.

When Ardis drank her third shot, she barely noticed the burn. "Ready for another round?" Everyone nodded, and she passed the deck to Wendel. "Your turn to deal."

Wendel shuffled with skill, glaring at Konstantin the whole time, then dealt their hands. Ardis had two pair—a pair of aces and a pair of eights. Giddiness bubbled in her chest, though that may have been the schnapps. She forced a poker face and glanced between the others. Wendel still glared at Konstantin, who seemed pleased by his hand. Himmel ran his tongue over his teeth and narrowed his eyes at his cards.

"Bet or check?" Wendel said.

"I'll bet my hat," Himmel said.

"I call," Konstantin said. "Though I don't have a hat."

Himmel tipped his hat to Konstantin, who smiled shyly.

"Okay," Ardis said, "I'll call."

She knew she had a good hand, but didn't want to look too cocky.

"Call," Wendel said. "Time to draw."

Himmel discarded and drew two cards, pokerfaced, though he did tweak his mustache. Konstantin replaced only one and puffed his cheeks in a sigh. Ardis kept her two pair and discarded a card, then drew a third ace.

Full house. Ardis curled her toes and resisted the urge to grin.

When Wendel tossed three of his cards onto the table, they skidded off the edge and fell. He ducked under the table and grabbed them, then flounced back in his seat. Ardis giggled, a bit giddy. Wendel pretended to glare at her, then meticulously discarded his cards and drew three. He flicked his eyebrows upward.

"Check," Himmel said.

"Very well," Konstantin said. "I'll check."

Ardis paused. "I'll bet three."

Everyone glanced at her, and she chewed on the inside of her cheek.

Wendel tilted his head. "You must be bluffing."

Ardis smirked at him. "Do you call?"

"Why the hell not?" Wendel said, with tipsy bravado.

Konstantin swallowed. "I fold."

Himmel eyed Ardis for a long moment, then met Konstantin's gaze.

"I call," Himmel said. "Showdown."

Ardis watched them reveal their hands. Wendel had one pair, and Himmel had two pair.

She spread her cards on the table. "Full house."

"I can see that," Himmel said dryly.

Wendel swore at great length in more than two languages. "Is this the part where I get naked?"

Ardis grinned. "You knew the stakes."

He sighed. "Your wish is my command."

Wendel climbed to his feet and dipped into an exaggerated bow. He unbuttoned his shirt and flung it away, then balanced on one foot to peel off his sock. He hopped onto his other foot, wobbled, and almost toppled before he defeated his second sock. Barefoot, Wendel unbuckled his belt and kicked off his trousers.

"Voila," Wendel deadpanned.

"No undershirt?" Himmel remarked. "Your loss."

Ardis grinned at Wendel as he stood there in his drawers. He caught her gaze and arched his eyebrows. She rather appreciated the loss of his clothes, which no longer hid his pale skin or the lean angles of his body.

"Do the belt and trousers count as two?" Wendel said. "Or do the drawers go?"

"Let's stop at that," Ardis said.

Konstantin's face reddened to the roots of his hair, and he looked everywhere but Wendel. Ardis couldn't blame him, considering their history. Wendel had kissed him, picked his pockets, and destroyed their work together on Project Lazarus. Flying to Prussia was Wendel's last shot to redeem himself.

Himmel looked Wendel over from head to toe, then shoved his chair from the table.

"Strip," Wendel said, slurring just a little. "Nudity loves company."

Himmel did. Jacket, overshirt, undershirt, and a single sock. Ardis caught herself staring at Himmel's surprisingly muscled chest. Finally, Himmel took his captain's hat and dropped it on Konstantin's head.

"You folded, Falkenrath," Himmel said.

"What? Pardon?" Konstantin stammered. "Oh, yes, I suppose I did."

Konstantin fumbled with his boots. The captain's hat almost teetered from his head, but Himmel straightened it for him.

"Hand me the schnapps," Wendel said.

"How many shots have you had?" Ardis said. "Four?"

"Yes. This will be my fifth."

"Impressive."

"Trust me," Himmel said, "don't underestimate schnapps."

"I can hold my liquor," Wendel scoffed.

Himmel shrugged. "You might win the vomiting match later."

Konstantin laughed and clapped his hands. He seemed to have a perpetual blush at this point. Wendel poured himself a fifth shot and sprawled back on the couch with a sloppy grin. Ardis leaned across the table and tugged the bottle of schnapps from Wendel's hands. He frowned and tilted his head.

"Do you always drink this much?" Ardis said.

"Don't you drink to get drunk?" Wendel laughed. "Heaven forbid I go to Prussia sober."

With that, he downed the schnapps.

Himmel started shuffling the cards. "Another round?"

"I'm in," Konstantin said. "I feel lucky."

Himmel winked at Konstantin, whose blush went from red to volcanic. Ardis squinted at the two of them. Perhaps Himmel knew

Konstantin preferred gentlemen. Was the archmage too oblivious to notice any flirtation?

"To tell you the truth," Wendel said, "I hate Prussia."

"Oh?" Himmel said, who seemed the most sober.

Wendel leaned forward with his hands on his knees. "I would have been a prince, and I never even liked Prussia. We lived too far north. Too damn cold." He snorted. "Who knows? Maybe the wind and the snow won't bother me now. I don't feel cold much anymore, after the whole returning from the dead thing."

Himmel stared at him. "Excuse me?"

"You know, when Thorsten stabbed me in the heart and threw me from a tower." Wendel pantomimed something tiny falling from the table to the floor. "Plenty of sharp rocks below, too. Must have been quite a crunch."

Ardis's stomach writhed with anxiety, and the alcohol wasn't helping.

"Christ." Himmel let out a bark of a laugh. "You have a sick sense of humor."

Wendel pretended to gasp. "What? Didn't the archmage tell you?" He pointed at Konstantin. "Shame on you, keeping this handsome captain in the dark. You should have told him he has a dead man on his zeppelin."

All the blood drained from Konstantin's face. "Wendel... I didn't know—"

"Nobody told you?" Wendel sneered. "How tragic. You so touchingly hunted me down, but you never heard the truth."

Ardis felt like she might be sick. Acid climbed in her throat. "Excuse me."

Ardis stumbled out of the captain's cabin and strode down the hallway. She spotted a bathroom and shoved her way inside. The moment after she clicked the lock shut, she dropped to her knees and bent over the toilet.

Saliva rushed into her mouth. She gagged, but nothing came up.

Plenty of sharp rocks below, too. Must have been quite a crunch.

How much did Wendel remember? Because she remembered it all. Every damn thing.

Her name, halfway spoken, in his last few heartbeats. His cold lips under her own. Her kiss that brought him back.

His borrowed necromancy shivering like lightning over her skin.

Ardis uncurled her hands and stared at them. Healing scars crisscrossed her palms. She had grabbed the broken glass of the window without even thinking, when she leaned out to see Wendel falling from the tower.

He hadn't even noticed she had been hurt that night. That she was still hurting.

Ardis bent over the toilet and vomited. She lost three shots of schnapps, and breakfast besides, and retched until she could breathe again. Shaking, she flushed the toilet and washed herself in the tiny sink. She stared at her reflection in the dim little mirror. She looked awful, her face splotchy, her eyes bloodshot.

There was a hesitant rap on the door.

"Just a minute," she said.

"Ardis? Are you all right?"

It was Konstantin. It wasn't as if Wendel was sober enough to care.

"No," Ardis said.

A pause. "Are you ill?"

Ill. Such a polite way to put it.

"I blame the schnapps," she said.

She unlocked the door. Konstantin lingered outside with worried eyebrows. He still wore the captain's hat.

"Come on," Ardis said. "I don't want to spend Christmas in a bathroom."

She tried to smile, tried to keep walking, but Konstantin caught her arm.

"Wendel can't be dead," he whispered.

Bitterness lingered on her tongue. "I watched him die."

"But how did—?"

"Necromancy."

Konstantin narrowed his eyes. "He resurrected himself?"

"No, I did."

"How?"

"Listen, why don't you ask Wendel? I'm not the expert here."

Konstantin bit his lip. He fidgeted as though he desperately wanted to ask questions and take notes, maybe even write a scientific paper. She looked the archmage in the eye and waited for him to stop looking so impatient.

"When do we get to Prussia?" Ardis said.

"Soon." Konstantin blinked a few times. "Himmel would know."

Ardis returned to the captain's cabin. Wendel and Himmel stood by the couch. Wendel was halfway dressed, barefoot with an unbuttoned shirt. Himmel looked flustered, a few strands of his slicked hair falling over his face.

Konstantin cleared his throat. "Are we interrupting anything?"

"Not at all," Himmel said. "Just a little chat with the necromancer."

Wendel met Ardis's gaze. His eyes glittered with an emotion she couldn't put a name to. "Ardis?"

"I'm fine."

Wendel furrowed his brow, like he knew she was lying. He stepped closer, but Himmel grabbed him by the shoulder.

Wendel curled his lip. "Unhand me."

"Sit down," Himmel commanded.

Wendel obeyed, helped by a shove toward the couch.

"Be a gentleman," Himmel said. "Apologize."

"Yes, sir," Wendel said, his words still a drunken drawl. "Please accept my most sincere apologies for drinking too much of your schnapps. And for telling the truth about my untimely demise at such an inappropriate time."

Himmel glared at him. "You should be apologizing to Ardis."

"Forgive me." Wendel met her gaze. "Did I upset you?"

"Yes," Ardis said.

"I'm terrible with this whole honesty thing. You know I make a much better liar."

She snorted. "Not judging by your skill at poker."

Konstantin laughed, but disguised it by clearing his throat.

"Do I need to drop to my knees and grovel?" Wendel said. "Because I can."

Ardis sighed. "Don't."

A knock on the door interrupted them. Himmel shrugged on his jacket and stole his hat back from Konstantin. When Himmel opened the door, Ardis glimpsed an officer with an impressive handlebar mustache.

"Captain," the officer said. "You might want to come see this."

Himmel frowned. "Explain."

"We spotted an airship off our starboard bow. It appears to be American."

Ardis felt a jolt of surprise. "American?"

"Have they hailed us?" Himmel said.

"No, sir," the officer said. "Though I would suggest hurrying to the Control Room. The airship should still be within sight."

Himmel glanced over his shoulder. "Stay here."

Konstantin stepped forward, his eyes bright, but the captain frowned.

"You, too," Himmel said. "Until you aren't so tipsy."

Himmel exited the cabin and shut the door behind him. Konstantin stared at the door, his hands curling into fists at his hips.

"I want to see this airship for myself," Konstantin said.

"Same here," Ardis said.

Konstantin waved her onward. "Shall we?"

"Shall we what?"

"Head to the balcony at the nose of the zeppelin?"

Ardis grinned. "After you."

"Wait for me." Wendel yanked on his boots. "I'm almost decent."

He didn't seem too drunk to walk, though he staggered when wind jostled the airship. Ardis caught his elbow and straightened him.

"If anyone should stay," she said, "it should be you."

Wendel tossed his hand. "I'll live."

Konstantin peeked out of the cabin, then cracked open the door and slipped through. Ardis crept after him, Wendel following last. They ran to the bow of the zeppelin. Konstantin stopped outside a door labeled Navigation and Meteorological. He rubbed his beard as he searched the area, then pointed when he spotted a ladder.

"This way," Konstantin said in a stage whisper.

Wendel snickered. "You aren't even slightly stealthy, archmage."

Konstantin shushed Wendel and climbed. Ardis clambered after him. Schnapps still blurred her eyesight, so she paid careful attention to the placement of her feet. Konstantin bumped his head, rubbed the bruise, and flung open a hatch. Glacial wind gusted into the airship. The archmage scrambled up and out.

Ardis clasped Konstantin's hand. He helped her to her feet.

"It should be off our starboard bow," Konstantin said.

Clouds like mountains of cream drifted through the cold morning. No airship in sight.

"Christ almighty," Wendel said.

Ardis discovered Wendel sitting with his hands on the deck. He had crawled through the hatch, but hadn't gotten to his feet yet. He scooted away from the railing. She wondered if he was having another spell of vertigo.

"There!" Konstantin said.

Ardis looked back to the sky in time to see an airship of titanic proportions plow through the clouds. It looked twice the size of their zeppelin, with a rigid skeleton and a triple-decker gondola armored in metal.

Ardis felt considerably more sober.

"Good God," Konstantin breathed. "She should be on the other side of the Atlantic."

"You recognize the ship?" Ardis said.

"The USS *Jupiter.*" Konstantin said the name with hushed reverence.

As the *Jupiter* sailed nearer, its shadow reached out and dwarfed the *Wanderfalke.* Awestruck, Ardis stared at the airship. An American flag had been painted on each of its immense tail fins. A gleaming steel spike at its nose pierced the air.

"Oh my God," Konstantin stammered. "Tesla."

"Who?" Ardis said.

"Nikola Tesla."

"I don't know who that is."

Konstantin gawked at her with eyes like saucers.

"How can you not know of Nikola Tesla?" he said. "He has been living in New York City for years. His work on steampowered mechanical oscillators should have made the newspapers, at the very least, and then there are his experiments with atmospheric electricity and the wireless transmission of energy."

"What are you babbling about?" Wendel said.

"Tesla!" Konstantin said. "The man is an absolute genius."

Still sitting on the deck, Wendel leaned back on his elbows and laughed.

"Ah," he said, "one of your idols."

Dreamily, Konstantin drifted to the edge of the balcony. He leaned over the railing to wave at the airship. His boot lifted from the deck. He teetered on the brink until Ardis grabbed him by his scarf and reeled him in.

"Himmel was right about you being tipsy," Ardis said.

Konstantin straightened his scarf. "Ardis, we have to tell Himmel. Rumors have been flying for years, but I'm not sure how much he knows."

"Tell him what?" Wendel said. "That you adore Tesla?"

Konstantin ignored him. "We may be witness to one of Tesla's greatest works to date." He looked skyward. "The USS *Jupiter.*"

SEVEN

To the Control Room!" Konstantin said.

The archmage jumped down the hatch and descended the ladder. Ardis followed after him, her heartbeat hammering in her throat. On the upper deck, they walked to the nose of the *Wanderfalke* and entered the Control Room. Ardis scarcely had time to stare at the intricate instruments before Himmel halted them.

Himmel saluted. "Archmage Konstantin."

"Captain," Konstantin said, a bit breathlessly. "I know that airship."

"Who are they?"

"The USS *Jupiter*."

Himmel furrowed his brow. "I haven't heard of them."

"Have they hailed us?" Konstantin said.

"Not yet."

Konstantin paced by the windows. "Send them a wireless telegram."

Himmel hesitated as if unsure the archmage was sober enough to dictate.

"What should we say, sir?" Himmel said.

"Identify ourselves as a zeppelin under the command of the Archmages of Vienna, and request information on their current course." Konstantin squared his shoulders. "Remind them they are flying over Austria-Hungary."

Himmel nodded. "Right away, sir."

The telegraph operator began to tap out the message in Morse code.

Ardis stood by the windows and pressed her hands to the cold glass. She peered at the immensity of the USS *Jupiter*. "What's America's stance on the war?"

"Neutral, ma'am," Himmel said. "Though I question why they would send such an enormous airship across the Atlantic."

"Why would they build the USS *Jupiter*?" Ardis said.

Konstantin raised his hand like a schoolboy. "Nikola Tesla."

"Pardon?" Himmel said.

"Hasn't anybody heard of Tesla?"

Himmel shook his head. "Enlighten me."

Konstantin shifted his weight from foot to foot. "There has been speculation for as long as I can remember. Tesla was commissioned by the Americans to build a magnificent electric airship. A marvel of technomancy."

"Electric how?" Ardis said.

"I haven't the slightest clue," Konstantin said, "which is why this is all so thrilling."

"Captain," said the telegraph operator. "The USS *Jupiter* informs us that they are on an observation mission, and that they are aware of their current coordinates over Austria-Hungary. They request our destination."

"Archmage Konstantin," Himmel said. "Your orders?"

"Tell them Vienna," Konstantin said. "We will stop there to refuel."

The telegraph operator sent the message, then received the reply.

"They report that Vienna is also their destination," said the telegraph operator. "They have offered to rendezvous with us there."

"Excellent!" Konstantin said.

Himmel clasped his hands behind his back. "Full ahead! Match their airspeed."

"Sir," said the navigator, "they appear to be travelling about ten knots faster."

"Then they will have time for tea in Vienna."

Wendel walked into the room with his head tilted back, pinching his nose between his fingers. Blood leaked from his nose and trickled over his mouth.

"Excuse me," Wendel said stuffily, "but does my nose look broken?"

"Wendel!" Ardis gawked at him. "What happened to you?"

"The wall."

Himmel's eyes flashed. "Get him out of here. See that he doesn't bleed everywhere."

A burly officer grabbed Wendel by the elbow. Wendel tried to shrug him off, but couldn't manage it while holding his nose. The officer escorted him from the Control Room. Ardis backed away from the window as the USS *Jupiter* powered above the clouds, then ran after Wendel.

"You have been an idiot this time," Ardis said.

"Agreed," Wendel said.

The officer hauled him to the dining room and dumped him in a chair. Wendel leaned back and squeezed his eyes shut.

"Do you need medical assistance, sir?" the officer said gruffly.

When Wendel nodded, blood gushed from his nose. He cursed and grabbed a napkin. "Please."

He sounded so miserable Ardis couldn't be angry at him. She nudged a chair closer and sat. The officer left without ceremony.

"How did you walk into a wall?" Ardis said.

"I didn't," Wendel said. "I jumped off the ladder and the wall was there."

She sighed. "Stay away from schnapps."

"I'm not that drunk."

"Nice try."

They sat in silence for a while.

Ardis inspected the blood staining his knuckles. "Wendel?"

"Yes?"

"Are you afraid of heights?"

"Yes." Wendel didn't even scoff.

Ardis considered the truth-telling properties of alcohol. "Have you been sleeping?"

He paused. "No."

"At all?"

Wendel met her gaze. Pain glittered in his eyes, perhaps from his wound, perhaps from something that cut much deeper. "I can't sleep. I can't stop dreaming of it, Ardis."

"Of what?"

"Of falling."

She knew he meant dying. Hurt burned in her throat like an ember.

"What do you remember?" she whispered.

Wendel laughed, and blood trickled to his lip. He dabbed himself with the napkin. "Sorry. I'm making this conversation gratuitously gory. Though I suppose a little blood doesn't bother you."

Ardis inhaled. "Blood isn't what scares me."

"I'm an idiot." Wendel met her gaze. "I never meant to hurt you."

She stared at the scars on her palms and tried to remember the pain of the broken glass. She barely could. The pain of Wendel's death eclipsed everything else.

He reached across and touched her wrist with his fingertips. "Ardis. I'm alive. I'm here."

She blinked away the threat of tears. "Please don't joke about dying."

"I won't."

The door to the dining room swung open. A woman swept inside hauling a black bag, wearing an immaculate white apron over a gingham dress.

She scrutinized Wendel through silver-rimmed spectacles. "What happened?"

"Wendel walked into a wall," Ardis said. "Drunkenly."

The woman sniffed. "I smell the alcohol."

Wendel straightened in his seat and bunched his eyebrows in a pitiful expression. He lowered the napkin. "Please tell me my nose isn't broken."

The woman arched an eyebrow. "It could be."

Wendel groaned. "Not my face. I have scars on almost every square centimeter of my body, but not my beautiful face."

Ardis slapped her hand to her forehead. "God, Wendel."

"Nurse," Wendel said. "Can you save my nose?"

The woman dropped her bag on the table and unlocked the clasp. "I'm a doctor, not a nurse. And you should be glad for your good fortune that I was travelling aboard this airship."

Wendel's eyebrows shot skyward. "A doctor!"

"Dr. Ursula Lowe. And don't move."

The doctor lowered Wendel's hand. She examined his nose, prodding it with her fingers; he flinched.

"Your nose isn't broken," Ursula said.

"Oh, thank God," Wendel said.

"Bend over."

"And bleed on the floor?"

"You don't want blood to travel down the nose to the stomach. It can cause gastrointestinal upset and vomiting."

Wendel bent over. He held the napkin under his nose. "Now I feel sick."

"Likely the alcohol," Ursula said. "Avoid drinking for several days."

Wendel groaned. Blood pattered onto the napkin. "Isn't this punishment enough?"

Ardis squeezed Wendel's shoulder. Her stomach hurt just looking at him. "Can't you give him something for the pain?"

"Laudanum," Ursula said.

Wendel brightened. "Yes, please."

Ursula rummaged in her doctor's bag and withdrew a tiny green bottle marked with the words *LAUDANUM* and *POISON*. "Bring me a glass of water."

Ardis fetched a glass and a pitcher from a nearby table. Ursula poured water to the halfway mark, then unscrewed the laudanum and squeezed drops into the glass. The dark syrup swirled and dissolved in the water.

"Take this," Ursula said.

Wendel knocked back the dose of laudanum. He clanked the glass on the table and twisted his face in a grimace.

"Laudanum and blood taste quite repulsive together," Wendel said hoarsely.

"The nosebleed should resolve soon," Ursula said. "You should sleep."

Wendel's shoulders stiffened as he stared into the empty glass.

Ardis swallowed. "He hasn't been sleeping."

When Ursula looked to Ardis, her spectacles flashed in the sunlight.

"Insomnia?" Ursula said. "For how long?"

"I don't know," Ardis said.

Wendel folded the bloodstained napkin neatly on his knee. "Days."

"Why?" said the doctor.

Wendel narrowed his eyes and said nothing. Ardis didn't know how to help him if he wouldn't help himself.

"Nightmares," Ardis said.

Ursula stared at Wendel for a long moment.

"Laudanum will help," she said. "Return to me if he worsens."

The doctor sterilized her hands with alcohol, returned the laudanum to its place, and locked the clasp on her doctor's bag.

"Thank you," Ardis said.

"Don't thank me," Ursula said. "It's my duty."

Ardis thought she saw a flicker of a smile before the doctor left the room.

"Impressive bedside manner," Wendel said.

He stood, still clutching the napkin to his nose, though the bleeding had slowed. He looked pale, and Ardis hoped the laudanum would start working soon.

She wrapped her fingers around his wrist. "Let's wash that blood off you."

He smirked. "Before I'm accused of murder."

Ardis walked with him to the bathroom, where she cleaned his face with a wet washcloth. He winced as she touched his nose, but made no complaint. He looked everywhere but her eyes.

"It stopped bleeding," Ardis said.

"Finally."

"Come along." She washed and dried her hands. "Bed."

He couldn't help smiling. "I love it when you say that."

He was flirtatious even while drunk, wounded, and dosed with laudanum.

She sighed. "You aren't in any shape for that."

Wendel allowed her to escort him from the bathroom to the cabin. He sprawled on the berth and closed his eyes.

"Feeling a bit better," he murmured. "I love laudanum."

This hardly surprised Ardis. Wendel had scars from so many wounds.

"Try to sleep."

"I will," he said.

She kissed him on his forehead. "I'm worried about you."

He made a quiet murmur in his throat, but nothing articulate. When she drew back, his fingers closed around her hand.

"Ardis," Wendel said. "I remember…"

She waited for him to speak. His hand slipped from hers.

"I remember everything," he whispered.

She stared at him, her heart pounding. His breathing slowed to the gentle rhythm of sleep, and she didn't want to wake him.

Not even to hear the truth.

As Ardis walked down the corridor by the cabins, a sharp ache panged where she had been stung. She clutched her arm. The jagged pain throbbed in time with her heartbeat. Anxiety crawled like ants in her stomach.

Was Wendel right? Was this the poison?

Damn it; the doctor had left only minutes before.

Ardis broke into a run and rounded the corner. She almost collided with a crewman, who apologized and backed away.

"Excuse me," Ardis said. "I need the doctor."

"Right this way."

The crewman backtracked and brought her to a cabin. Still clutching her arm, Ardis rapped on the door. Ursula answered it right away. The doctor adjusted her spectacles, her lips pursed, and stared at her.

"Dr. Lowe," Ardis said. "Can you take a look at this?"

Her arm panged with an even sharper stab of pain, and she gritted her teeth.

"What happened to your arm?" Ursula said.

"A clockwork wasp stung me."

Ursula backed away. "Come in and sit down."

Ardis hesitated, since she didn't want to intrude, but the steely look in Ursula's eyes hardly invited argument. She ducked into the cabin and dropped onto the berth, tightening her fingers around the sting. "It didn't hurt like this until a minute or two ago."

"Let me look," Ursula said.

Ardis lifted her fingers. Ursula rubbed her thumb over the tender skin, then pressed hard against the bump. A brilliant shard of pain sliced through Ardis. She gasped, her eyes watering, and yanked her arm away.

"This may hurt," Ursula said. "Hold still."

It already hurt, but Ardis nodded and braced herself.

Ursula unlocked her bag and reached inside. Steel flashed in her hand. A scalpel. Ardis sucked her breath through her teeth. Ursula poured alcohol onto a cloth and dabbed the sting, then reached for the scalpel.

"What is that for?"

"There's something under your skin," Ursula said, "that doesn't belong there."

"God, are you serious?"

"Yes." Ursula angled the scalpel over Ardis's arm. "Ready?"

Ardis swallowed hard. Blood rarely turned her stomach, but she preferred the steel of a sword to the steel of a scalpel.

"Do it," Ardis said.

Ursula lowered the blade, her eyes sharp with concentration. She sliced into the inflamed skin and cut a tiny incision less than an inch long. Ursula turned away, bent over her bag, and returned with forceps.

"I almost have it."

Queasy, Ardis wasn't sure she wanted to know what "it" was.

Ursula reached into the incision and picked out a miniscule metal worm. It wriggled against the forceps, gears whirring inside its segments. The doctor dropped the worm into a glass vial and sealed it with a stopper.

"God." Ardis pressed her hand to her mouth. "What is that?"

Ursula held an eye loupe to her glasses and inspected the worm. She tilted the vial, and the creature rolled with a rattle. "It appears to be a clockwork larva."

Ardis shuddered. "That's repulsive."

"I see writing carved into the steel. Possibly Russian."

"I don't suppose you can read Russian?"

Ursula lowered the loupe. Unmistakable curiosity glinted in her gray eyes. "No, but I believe the archmage may know more. You should bring it to him for further examination."

Ursula bandaged Ardis's arm with gauze. The pain from the sting had faded.

"Thank you, doctor." Ardis hopped off the berth. "I feel better without that worm."

Ursula met her gaze. "Don't speak too soon. I would rather know the purpose of the larva before making a prognosis."

That was less than reassuring.

"Take it to the archmage and report back."

Ardis pocketed the vial. With a nod goodbye, she went off in search of Konstantin. She found the archmage walking downstairs near the gangway, and she hurried to match his long stride.

"Konstantin," she said.

"Care to join me for lunch, Ardis?" He smiled absently. "I'm venturing to the mess hall."

Ardis wasn't sure the crew would be comfortable eating with the archmage. But Konstantin leapt off the stairs and turned the corner. She sighed and followed him. When they stepped into the mess hall, they interrupted a conversation between crewmates.

Himmel shoved his chair from the table and saluted. "Archmage Konstantin."

The rest of the crewmates realized who stood in the doorway, and all of them leapt to their feet with a scraping of chairs.

Konstantin's cheeks reddened. "Please, sit down. This is terribly embarrassing."

A few of the youngest crewmen shared glances. Perhaps they expected the archmage to be strict with formalities.

Himmel furrowed his brow. "Did you have something to say, sir?"

Konstantin pinched the bridge of his nose. His ears looked scarlet.

"I thought we might join you for lunch," he said. "Considering how empty the dining room would be above deck."

"Very well, sir," Himmel said. "You can be my right-hand man."

Himmel dragged two more chairs to the table. Konstantin perched on the chair to the captain's right. Ardis took the last seat and stared at her napkin. After the captain sat again, his crew dropped back into their chairs.

"Eat," Himmel said. "That's an order."

He winked, which didn't help Konstantin's blush in the slightest.

Ardis fingered the vial in her pocket. Lunch didn't seem like the best time to whip out a clockwork larva, but she had lost her appetite. The others ate rye bread, cheese, cold meats, and apples from the last autumn. She had dined alone for years, always the stranger in the corner, and didn't know how to join the chatter of conversation. Konstantin seemed just as tongue-tied while Himmel talked about the weather.

"On a winter day like this," Himmel said, "the sun can be an advantage."

Konstantin ruffled his curls. "How so?"

"When things heat up, our lifting power increases."

"Ah! I know exactly what you mean. Elementary physics."

Ardis reached halfway to a slice of cheese, then stopped, her stomach still unsettled. She nudged Konstantin's elbow.

"Yes?" he said.

"Look at this," she whispered.

Ardis hid the vial in a napkin and slid it to Konstantin. He unwrapped it and squinted. Then his eyes widened.

"Where did this come from?" he said softly.

"The clockwork wasp," she said, keeping her voice down. "The doctor cut it out of me."

Konstantin blanched. "Cut it out…?"

"From my arm. And look, there are letters carved on it."

Konstantin pinched the vial between his fingers and lifted it to his eye. The larva curled on the bottom. The archmage looked torn between fascination and revulsion. A few of the crew glanced sideways at him.

"Can you read Russian?" Ardis said.

"Not a word." Konstantin squeezed his eyes shut. "But I'm sure I have seen a clockwork creature such as this before." His eyes sprang open. "Yes! I remember reading a textbook, rather obscure, that dealt with espionage."

Ardis felt her stomach plummet. "Such as?"

"Clockwork creatures with technomancy for tracking and spying."

"Konstantin? Smash the worm."

"Oh, God." He stared at the larva. "The Russians."

The zeppelin shuddered. Ardis caught her fork before it fell off the table.

Konstantin laughed nervously. "I don't suppose that's turbulence?"

Himmel threw down his napkin and shoved his chair from the table. He peered through the portholes along the wall.

"Doubtful," the captain said. "We—"

The zeppelin lurched sideways. Its nose careened downward at a steep slant. Everything on the table jolted off and clattered on the floor. The crew scrambled to their feet, stumbling over chairs, as Himmel shouted orders.

"All hands on deck! Officers report to the Control Room!"

Outside the zeppelin, Ardis glimpsed a flicker of red.

Fire? Magic?

Ardis jumped over a fallen chair and dodged people running to their posts. A glass shattered under her boot.

A blur of crimson whipped past the portholes. It vanished an instant later.

"Ardis!" Konstantin called.

She looked back at the archmage. He braced himself against the doorframe. The two of them were the last ones left.

"Ardis," he said, "we can't stay. We—"

The zeppelin plunged earthward and flung them both off their feet.

EIGHT

Ardis slammed against the wall. Konstantin clung to the doorframe until he fell and hit the floor beside her. She crawled to her feet, her ribs bruised, and helped him stagger upright. They leaned against the slanted wall.

"Abandon ship," Konstantin said. "We have to abandon ship."

"Already?" Ardis said.

Konstantin's eyes looked glassy with panic.

"Hydrogen," he said. "Highly flammable. Technomancy can't shield us forever."

"Go to Himmel. Stay with him."

Konstantin scrambled out the door and ran at a stumbling lope down the crooked corridor. Ardis followed him, watching his back, and detoured to the dining room. She leaned against the windows of the promenade deck.

"Impossible," Ardis whispered.

A clockwork dragon soared through the air on wings of duralumin. Thousands of scales, each enameled in crimson, glittered along its length. Silvered cloth clung to its scything claws—a tatter torn from the zeppelin's skin.

The dragon glided away from the *Wanderfalke* and circled for another attack.

Ardis didn't wait to see if it breathed fire.

She sprinted from the promenade deck and ran to Wendel's cabin. Krampus hopped and scrabbled against the door. Ardis shooed him away and flung it open. Wendel curled around a lump of blanket with his back to her. Krampus flew over her shoulder and landed on his pillow.

"Wendel!"

Ardis shook his shoulder. He rolled over and squinted at her.

"What?" Wendel said. Sleep and laudanum thickened his voice.

"Get up," she said. "Now."

Wendel staggered to his feet. He looked only mildly alarmed.

"What is that terrible noise?" he said.

"The zeppelin. Crashing."

Ardis grabbed Wendel's wrist and hauled him out of the cabin. He stumbled behind her, still clumsy, but she didn't let go.

They ran to the Control Room.

Himmel called out orders to his crew, who scrambled to save the crippled zeppelin even as it plunged from the sky. Konstantin stood by the windows, his palms flat against the glass, frozen in a sea of pandemonium.

Ardis halted on the threshold. Powerless to help.

"Drop the emergency ballast," Himmel said. "Full astern!"

"Sir!" a man said. "No response from the starboard aft mechanic."

The navigator glanced from his instruments. "Captain, we can't do without that engine. We're losing altitude too fast."

Himmel's hands curled into fists. "Stop the engines."

"Sir?"

"We're going down, but we won't go down in flames."

The engines sputtered and silenced. In the eerie calm, the telegraph operator tapped out a message even Ardis understood.

S-O-S.

Konstantin twisted back to look over his shoulder.

"Himmel!" he said. "I see a lake."

The captain stared out the window for an instant, and turned on his heel.

"Sixty degrees starboard," Himmel said. "All ruddermen stay at their stations. Everyone brace for an emergency landing!"

Ardis locked gazes with Wendel. He grabbed her hand. She wasn't sure if he meant to steady himself or protect her from harm. He looked more lucid than before, though that might have been the gleam of fear in his eyes.

Bristling pines loomed beneath them. Rushing closer.

"Increase altitude!" Himmel said. "We won't make—"

The zeppelin snagged on a treetop and lurched sideways. The impact knocked Ardis against Wendel. His grip on her fingers was almost crushing. He hooked his arm around her shoulders and held her close.

Ardis clung to him. Praying they would land alive. Every heartbeat an eternity.

After a moment of silence, they hit earth. The zeppelin scraped the ground with a screech of metal on stone. It skidded along the rocks and plowed into the lake. Water absorbed their speed and dragged them down.

"Abandon ship!" Himmel shouted, his command all but lost in the chaos.

Ardis and Wendel fled the Control Room. She bolted for the stairs, but he pulled her to the promenade deck. Waves lapped at the windows. She realized his plan and hauled open a large window. Water poured inside, sloshing around her boots.

"After you," Wendel said.

"Can you swim?" Ardis said.

"Yes."

"Well?"

"Enough."

She climbed through and leapt into the lake.

Icy cold hit her like a sledgehammer. Ardis sank underwater, stunned, then kicked to the surface and sucked in air that scraped her throat raw. Now wasn't the time to tread water. Not when the cold could kill you. She swam toward shore, her lungs on fire, but could already feel her muscles stiffening and slowing.

Drowning. Hypothermia. Neither sounded like a good way to die.

Ardis clawed her way to the beach and staggered onto the rocks. Her teeth chattering, she searched the lake for survivors.

"Wendel!" she shouted. "Wendel!"

"Ardis."

She found Wendel farther down the shore, wading through the shallows with his hand clamped around Konstantin's arm. The necromancer towed the archmage out of the lake. Ardis ran to meet them.

"We have to go back," Konstantin said.

"We can't," Wendel said.

"But Himmel. He's still in the zeppelin."

"Along with the rest of his crew."

Konstantin stared at Wendel, his face white, his eyes feverish.

"We can't stand here and let them die," Konstantin said.

"If we go back," Wendel said, "both of us will die."

Ardis stepped between them. "Wendel is right. We—"

A shadow darkened them. She looked up as the clockwork dragon soared overhead. It swooped over the lake like an eagle hunting a wounded bird. The dragon missed the *Wanderfalke*, but circled over the trees.

"Himmel!" Konstantin said.

Ardis reached for him, afraid he would fling himself back into the water. But he pointed to a man clinging on the zeppelin's gondola. Even from here, they could see his captain's hat. Himmel's hands slipped on the steel as he struggled to hold on. But it was only a matter of time before his fingers became too numb.

The clockwork dragon swooped for another attack.

Oil slicked the water. When the dragon shredded the zeppelin's balloon, it tore deeper and clawed into the airship's duralumin ribs. The bent metal's screech was lost in the whoosh of hydrogen igniting.

In an instant, the *Wanderfalke* was ablaze.

Ardis glimpsed Himmel slip beneath the waves seconds before the oil caught fire. Reflected flames danced in the lake. Gorgeous, in a macabre way. The burning zeppelin began to sink into the water. Its silvery skin curled into ashes and bared its duralumin skeleton.

Ardis and Wendel shared a glance. His eyes hardened.

"I'm going back," he said.

"Wendel!"

Had he lost his sanity to laudanum?

"I don't feel cold much anymore," he said. "Remember?"

Wendel kicked off his boots and strode out into the lake. Ardis clenched her hands into fists and followed him. She would be damned if she let him go in there alone. She wasn't sure he was very good as a hero, anyway.

Ardis swam out to the zeppelin. A rush of intense heat buffeted her. As the zeppelin sank deeper into the lake, water conquered fire in a hiss of steam. She saw no sign of Himmel, but found a crewman fighting to stay above the surface, his skin ghostly, his eyes glassy. Ardis seized him by the arm and helped him swim to shore.

By the time they made it, both of them were shivering uncontrollably.

"Stay out of the wind," Ardis told the crewman. "Try to keep warm."

The crewman nodded and stumbled to the shelter of the trees. Konstantin huddled on the beach, shivering, hugging himself tight.

"I don't see him," Konstantin said. "I don't see anyone."

Two men walked from the water, dragging a third man by his arms. When Ardis ran to them, she realized three things.

The walking men were dead, they had been revived by Wendel, and they had rescued Himmel.

But was the captain still alive?

The dead men dropped Himmel on the rocks and walked away stiffly, returning to the lake to fish out more survivors. Ardis knelt next to him and pressed against his neck, searching for a pulse, but her fingers felt like icicles.

Faintly, she detected a heartbeat.

"He's alive," Ardis said. "Help me move him."

Konstantin's face looked blank with shock, but he did as she said. They carried Himmel to the trees and lowered him onto the pine needles. Himmel's right arm was wounded. Blood trickled from a ragged gash that cut to the bone. Worse, Himmel wasn't breathing.

"Did the doctor make it?" Ardis said.

"The doctor?" Konstantin stammered. "Yes. I saw her."

"Go get her."

Himmel wasn't losing much blood, which was one advantage of the cold. But Ardis didn't know how to save him. Konstantin returned with Ursula.

The doctor took one look at Himmel and grabbed his good arm. "Help me roll him over."

Konstantin obeyed. Ursula angled Himmel's head sideways. Water trickled from his open mouth. Himmel choked and coughed water from his lungs. Konstantin held his head until he could breathe.

"Thank God," Konstantin said. "You almost went down with your ship."

Himmel sucked in a rattling breath and tried to speak, but coughed again.

"Where is Wendel?" Ardis said.

Konstantin shook his head. "He must have come back by now."

Ardis stood, still soaking wet, and trudged through the trees to where the scattered crew huddled. She scanned the lake. The ribs of the zeppelin, warped by intense heat and cold, sank beneath the black waves. No sign of Wendel.

Fear clamped around her heart like a hand of ice.

"No," Ardis said. "Not again."

She ran to where the waves crashed into mist. A few survivors dragged themselves ashore, and she directed them to the doctor.

"*Grok!*"

The raven's cry floated on the wind. Ardis walked down the beach to a jumble of boulders. Wendel crouched behind them, his clothes heavy with water, and tried to coax a bedraggled Krampus into his hands.

"Wendel!" Ardis said.

"It's a miracle," he deadpanned, not looking up. "I found Krampus."

The raven croaked and puffed his feathers until he looked like a bristling black fruit. Wendel lunged and caught him, keeping the bird's wings tucked beneath his hands. Krampus curled his feet and blinked.

"You little wretch," Wendel said. "You look miserable."

Frost whitened Wendel's hair—and his stubble, which was beginning to resemble a beard. Ardis touched his cheekbone.

"God, you feel so cold!" she said.

Wendel winced. "I will admit to noticing the temperature at this point."

Ardis realized he was in fact shivering, so she grabbed his sleeve and tugged him toward the forest and the survivors. Under the shadow of trees, crimson flashed beyond the canopy.

"The clockwork dragon," Ardis said.

"It can't attack us in the forest," Wendel said.

"But the beach."

Ardis pointed to the survivors straggling toward the trees. Still out in the open. She ran back to them.

"Everybody take cover!" Ardis shouted. "Watch your backs!"

The survivors glanced at the sky, and fled as fast as they could to the safety of the trees. The clockwork dragon glided low over the lake, its metallic belly glinting in the firelight.

If the Russians wanted to attack Project Lazarus, they would kill the archmage.

Ardis returned to Konstantin, who sat by Himmel. Ursula bandaged the captain's wounded arm with a strip of cloth.

"We have to move," Ardis said. "It isn't safe here."

Konstantin met her gaze. "But this is Hungary. This is our territory."

"This is war."

Himmel grunted with pain as Ursula tightened the bandage.

"Captain," Ardis said. "Can you walk?"

Himmel shook his head. His eyes looked hollow. "I'm not a captain. Not without my ship. Not without my crew."

Ardis stared fiercely at him. "Your crew isn't lost. We have survivors, and we need to lead them to safety. Can you walk?"

"I can try."

Ursula finished bandaging him. Himmel staggered upright, and Konstantin steadied him with a hand on his elbow.

"Careful," Konstantin said. "You nearly drowned."

Himmel shrugged off the archmage's hand and walked stiffly on his own.

"Where are we?" Ardis said.

"Farmland," Himmel said. "Fifteen miles southwest of Budapest."

Fifteen miles. Too far for the wounded to walk.

"We should find shelter," Ardis said.

"There should be a village nearby. I'm not sure which direction." Himmel's jaw hardened. "The navigator is dead."

Ardis almost said she was sorry, but apologies wouldn't help them survive.

"Look!" Konstantin said.

Ardis braced herself for the clockwork dragon, the muscles between her shoulder blades stiffening in expectation of claws.

"The USS *Jupiter*." Konstantin squinted at the sky. "They must have heard our distress call."

"Too little, too late," Himmel said.

Engines droning, the *Jupiter* floated over the forest. As the airship advanced, the clockwork dragon pumped its wings and gained altitude. It circled higher in the sky, wheeling over the *Jupiter*, then flattened its wings and stooped into a dive. It flared its wings to slow its descent, then swung its claws forward like an attacking falcon.

The USS *Jupiter* hovered with idle engines. Not even trying to outmaneuver the dragon.

Ardis sucked in her breath. The dragon's outstretched talons gleamed over the airship, ready to shred its silver skin. A deep humming trembled the air. With a blinding burst, lightning arced from the spiked nose and struck the dragon.

Electricity shivered over the clockwork beast. Black smoke curled from its jaws. It froze in midair, tumbling from the sky. Seconds later, it jerked back to life. Its wings snapped open, straining against its plummet, and its belly skimmed the treetops. The dragon pumped its wings as it powered skyward, swerving behind a ridge and out of sight.

"Magnificent," Konstantin breathed. "It simply must be Tesla."

The *Jupiter* gave a wide berth to the *Wanderfalke*, even as the wreckage sank beneath the waves and the last of the fire sputtered out.

Konstantin stepped from the trees and waved his arms over his head. Wendel joined them, though he didn't look quite so enthusiastic. The necromancer had tucked Krampus inside his coat, and the raven blinked by his lapel.

"Are the Americans here to save us?" Wendel said.

"You sound so skeptical," Ardis said.

Wendel shrugged, which caused Krampus to fidget.

The *Jupiter* slowed over the beach. The airship vented hydrogen, descended to the water, and dropped anchor, hovering above the surf. At the bottom of the gondola, doors swung open like the wings of a beetle. Winches lowered lifeboats through the hatch and into the lake. The crew set the oars in the water and rowed.

Within minutes, the first lifeboat scraped the rocky beach.

The Americans scrambled ashore and approached the crew of the *Wanderfalke*. Himmel closed the gap. Ardis and Konstantin escorted the captain, while Wendel lurked behind them and looked sidelong at their rescuers.

An American woman took the lead. Fiery red hair escaped from under her hat, though her navy uniform looked immaculately ironed. She glanced between them, pursed her lips, and clasped her hands behind her back.

"Hello," the woman said, in broken German. "You need our help?"

"Yes," Ardis said, in English. "We have many wounded men and women."

The woman's eyebrows shot skyward. "Are you American?"

Ardis shook her head. "Just me."

Himmel squared his shoulders and spoke in German. "We were attacked by Russians. We lost our ship and lot of good people."

The American stared, uncomprehending, until Ardis translated.

"I'm Yeoman Breony Kay," the American said. "You must be Captain Himmel?"

"Correct." His right hand out of commission, Himmel offered his left. Kay shook it briskly.

"Our captain has invited you and your crew aboard," Kay said. "We can offer medical attention and passage to Vienna."

Ardis hadn't even finished translating before Himmel stepped back.

"I will take the last boat," he said, "after I direct my crew to safety."

"Captain!" Konstantin lowered his voice. "If anyone needs medical attention, it's you. Take the first boat."

Himmel stared him down. "Is that an order, archmage?"

Konstantin didn't blink. "It is."

"Very well, sir."

Konstantin walked Himmel to a lifeboat and waved him ahead. The captain didn't look pleased by this preferential treatment, but rather than argue with the archmage, he sat and cradled his wounded arm. After Konstantin, Ardis, and Wendel climbed into the lifeboat, the Americans rowed them to where the USS *Jupiter* floated inches above the water. Waves lapped at the underside.

"After you," Kay said.

One by one they disembarked the lifeboat and climbed aboard. As Ardis hopped aboard, she found herself staring into a man's piercing gray eyes. When she straightened, her head barely reached the shoulder of his suit. His dark hair and mustache looked immaculate.

Konstantin sucked in his breath with a strangled noise. "Forgive me, but are you Nikola Tesla?"

NINE

ave we met?" said the gray-eyed man. He spoke German with a soft accent.

Konstantin wrung his hands. "No, Mr. Tesla. You are Mr. Tesla, aren't you?"

A small smile curved under the man's mustache. "Yes, I am Nikola Tesla."

Konstantin's hand shot out. "Konstantin Falkenrath. I'm one of the Archmages of Vienna. This is an absolute honor."

Tesla stared at his hand, but didn't shake it. "We meet under rather unfortunate circumstances."

Konstantin withdrew his hand and rubbed it on his sleeve as if afraid he was dirty.

"Unfortunate is an understatement," Himmel said.

The captain's arms trembled as he shivered, but he tried to keep his back straight.

"Please," Tesla said, "don't risk hypothermia for conversation."

"Agreed," Wendel said.

Frost melted from Wendel's hair and dripped on the floor. Ardis picked at her shirt, which clung to her like a second skin.

Yeoman Kay beckoned them. "Right this way."

Ardis didn't need to be told twice. She glanced at Wendel, who had a wary slant to his eyebrows, and grabbed his hand.

"You feel like an ice sculpture," Ardis said.

"How poetic." Wendel grimaced. "I'm flattered."

Krampus peeked out from his coat and nibbled at a button. With utmost stealth, Wendel stroked the raven on the head.

"Perhaps we can talk later?" Konstantin said.

Ardis looked back. Konstantin still lingered hopefully by Tesla.

"Yes," Tesla said. "Later."

Himmel harrumphed. "Archmage."

Konstantin snuck a sideways look at Himmel before ducking his head and following Yeoman Kay.

"So this is the famous USS *Jupiter*," Wendel said.

As they travelled toward the tail of the airship, the gangway seemed to go on forever. No windows interrupted the duralumin walls, but electric lamps shone overhead like tiny suns. Ardis hugged herself, the stink of smoke lingering in her nose. A hum rumbled in her ribs—the airship's immensely powerful engines.

"Damn," Ardis said, for lack of a better word.

Yeoman Kay escorted them to a mess hall big enough to seat fifty. It looked utilitarian, lacking the flourishes of the *Wanderfalke*. Fog clouded the windows along the far wall and obscured the view of the lake.

A silver-haired man in a doctor's coat braced himself on the back of his chair and climbed stiffly to his feet. He stroked his walrus mustache. "Are these the first of them?"

Yeoman Kay nodded. "There should be at least a dozen more."

On cue, another lifeboat's load of survivors shuffled into the mess hall. All four men shivered, soaked to the bone, their clothes dripping on the carpet. One of them had singed hair and a burn seared across his cheek.

The doctor looked over his patients and zeroed in on Himmel.

"My name is Dr. Frost." He said this in English, slowly, as if talking to a small child. "Let me look at your arm."

Himmel stared at him. Did he not understand?

"Captain," Wendel said in German, "the doctor wants to see your arm."

Grimacing, Himmel held out his arm. Dr. Frost peeled the bandage aside and peeked at the wound, then clucked his tongue.

"That will need stitches," Dr. Frost said. "Can you wait?"

Wendel took the liberty of translating, which earned him a glare from Himmel.

"I understood that much." Himmel switched to English. "I can wait."

With an irritated look, Wendel peeled off his sopping coat and freed Krampus. The raven hopped to the back of a chair.

"That bird is unsanitary," Dr. Frost said.

"And?" Wendel said.

"Get it out of here."

Wendel tried halfheartedly to catch Krampus, who flew out of reach.

Yet more survivors arrived, two carrying an unconscious third with a blood-darkened shirt. Dr. Frost knelt by the man and questioned his crewmates, Ardis acting as translator. Konstantin fetched blankets and wrapped them around the survivors. Wendel stood empty-handed until the doctor noticed.

"You." Dr. Frost snapped his fingers. "Help me."

"What do I do?" Wendel said.

"I need a nurse."

Wendel twisted his face into a look of complete incredulity. "I'm not qualified for that."

"He really isn't," Ardis said. "I'll do it."

Dr. Frost furrowed his brow. "Miss, I need you to translate."

"Excuse me," Wendel said. "I speak German and English."

"I need you"—Dr. Frost pointed at Wendel—"to put pressure on this wound."

"Where?"

Dr. Frost showed him a gash on the unconscious man's chest. Blood trickled from the cut, though it looked as though no major vein or artery had been hit. Wendel knelt by the doctor, who pressed a wad of gauze to the wound.

"Hold this," Dr. Frost said. "Don't let go."

The doctor moved on to the next survivor. Ardis followed. Together, they questioned a man who didn't seem entirely lucid. Ardis waited as Dr. Frost checked his reflexes. She glanced over at Wendel, who held the gauze with a look of fierce concentration.

Konstantin hovered by Himmel. "How is your arm?"

Himmel shrugged lopsidedly. "The same."

"Is there anything I can get for you?"

"No, thank you."

"If only I could heal you with temporal magic. It's a shame I lost my technomancy gauntlets in the shipwreck."

Himmel looked him in the eye. "It's a shame we lost the ship."

Konstantin rubbed the back of his neck and looked like he wanted to help the captain, but hadn't the slightest idea how.

"Doctor," Wendel said.

"Yes?" Dr. Frost said.

"This man. He's badly hurt."

Dr. Frost looked anything but amused. "I'm aware of that."

"No." Wendel lifted his head. "He's dying."

Dr. Frost straightened. "What? How would you know?" He returned to the unconscious man, feeling for a pulse. Alarm flashed over his face. "There must be internal bleeding; his heart is failing."

"What do we do?" Wendel said.

"There's nothing we can do."

The doctor returned to his other patients, but Wendel still didn't step away from the man. The necromancer pressed his hand to the man's chest with a kind of blank determination. He closed his eyes for a second.

Wendel's jaw tightened. "He's dead." At last he let go. He might have been angry with himself, or with the man for dying, but when he stood, his face smoothed into a look that said he didn't give a damn. "Who's next?"

With the living saved and the dead buried, the USS *Jupiter* flew into the sky. Ardis stood by a window in the mess hall. Oil lingered on the water, the blood of a zeppelin now long gone. If she stared beneath the waves, she could barely make out the bones of the *Wanderfalke* at the bottom of the lake.

Hungary rolled beneath them as they set course for Vienna.

The ship's cook announced dinner and doled out chicken soup. Men who could walk brought soup to those who couldn't. After the crew of the *Wanderfalke* had been served, the crew of the *Jupiter* filed in and joined them. Americans sat shoulder to shoulder with Austrians or leaned against the wall together. Some ate in silence, while others chatted with the handful of words they had in common.

Ardis found Wendel sitting at a table opposite Himmel and Konstantin.

"Please, join us," Himmel said.

"Thank you," Ardis said.

Shadows darkened under Himmel's eyes, but at least Dr. Frost had stitched up his arm and bandaged it again. Konstantin kept blinking owlishly and shoving back his hair, which resembled the aftermath of a hurricane. Ardis sipped her soup. Heat trickled down her throat and pooled in her stomach.

"Ah," she said. "I finally feel thawed out."

"That water was damn cold," Himmel said.

The captain looked as if he wanted to say more, but stared into his soup. Konstantin nudged Himmel's spoon closer to him.

"Eat," Konstantin murmured.

Himmel clutched his spoon in his left hand. Clumsily, he dipped it into his soup, scooped up a carrot, and lifted it to his lips.

"Yes, sir," Himmel said. "And please tell me you won't pull rank all dinner."

Konstantin squinted. "Well, I don't see why I would."

Himmel's mouth twitched with a smile.

Wendel fidgeted with his sleeves. "I assume Prussia isn't on today's agenda?"

"Of course not," Himmel said. "Unless this USS *Jupiter* flies at a miraculous speed, plan on spending the night in Vienna."

"It might fly at a miraculous speed," Konstantin said, somewhat dreamily.

Himmel glanced out a window with a professional eye. "Not in this headwind."

Konstantin poked his spoon skyward. "It will be beneficial to rest a night in Vienna."

"I could rest a week," Ardis said.

"The war won't wait a week." The look in Konstantin's eyes darkened. "The Russians didn't even wait until after Christmas."

"We should send them a belated Christmas gift," Wendel said.

"Pardon?" Konstantin said.

"Something explosive." Wendel smirked. "I'm sure you can manage, archmage."

Himmel barked out a laugh. "I'll do the wrapping paper."

Wendel drained the broth from his bowl and leaned back in his chair for a second before hopping to his feet and disappearing in the crowd.

"Where did he go?" Himmel said.

Konstantin dabbed his mouth with a napkin. "Maybe it's that abominable raven of his."

"Krampus?" Ardis said. "He's oddly obedient for a raven, don't you think?"

When Wendel returned, it wasn't with Krampus. He carried a plate heaped with food that made her mouth water. Roast turkey, gravy, cranberry sauce, string beans, and steaming hot biscuits with a melting pat of butter.

"Christmas dinner," Wendel said. "The soup was just a first course."

Ardis stared openmouthed at the food. "I must be dreaming. It's so… American."

"Here," Wendel said. "Have my plate."

She pretended to dab her eye with a napkin. "I think I might cry."

Everyone laughed. Ardis smiled, even though her throat ached as she ate a bite of turkey, and her eyes stung as she swallowed. Because she was closer to tears than she would admit. Today had been, without question, one of the worst days of her life. And yet they willingly flew toward days even more dangerous.

Ardis stared at her plate. Melancholy dragged her down like an anchor.

Her thoughts were rather rudely interrupted. Out of nowhere, Krampus hopped onto the table and strutted toward her uneaten food. Wendel whipped a napkin at him, and the raven flew to the floor with an indignant croak.

"Off, you brat," Wendel said.

Krampus tilted his head and blinked. He looked dubiously innocent.

Secretly, Ardis tossed the raven a string bean. Krampus caught it and shook it like a worm that needed killing, then swallowed it in several gulps. Ardis hid her smile behind her hand and reached for another bean.

"Don't be nice to him," Wendel said. "He's already evil."

Ardis laughed. "Hypocrite."

The others fetched their plates, and they ate dinner together. Sunlight faded into the darkness of evening. The ship's cook delivered dessert with a flourish—plenty of plum pudding drenched with brandy sauce.

A bittersweet end for a Christmas in the sky.

⊰─────────────────────────⊱

After dinner, Ardis wandered down the gangway to the nose.

She discovered an observation deck and stopped there, her hands clasped behind her back, her heartbeat paradoxically calm.

She watched darkness fall on Vienna as they flew closer to the city, a headwind buffeting the airship. At this altitude, even the cathedral looked small, its tallest spire like a needle pricking the sky.

"Ardis?"

She turned her head and found Wendel there. He looked bedraggled and tired, though he managed to quirk his eyebrow.

"I wondered where you went," Wendel said.

Ardis looked back out over the city. "I wanted to see Vienna."

Wendel waited by her side, without touching her, and gazed out the window. The lights of the city glittered in his eyes.

Ardis rubbed his scratchy cheek. "When did you last shave?"

He squinted. "Constantinople."

"Eleven days ago? Impressive."

He arched an eyebrow. "Thank you."

"You're welcome, though you might want to shave in Vienna."

Wendel tilted his head as if considering this for a moment; he slipped his hand behind her neck and tugged her into a kiss. His lips felt soft on hers, but when he dipped his mouth to her neck, his stubble rasped against her skin.

Ardis sucked in her breath at the surprising pleasure.

"We have the night in Vienna," Wendel said.

She stepped back and lifted his chin with her finger. "You can't possibly be suggesting anything but sleep."

A devilish smile spread on his face.

Ardis laughed. "I'm sorry, Wendel, but I have ulterior motives."

"You do?" he said.

"A hot bath and a warm bed."

He touched his hand to his heart. "Am I invited?"

"Always."

Wendel stood behind Ardis and slipped his arms around her. She leaned against his chest.

The USS *Jupiter* moored at Aspern Airfield on the outskirts of

Vienna. As they disembarked from the airship, Ardis remembered catching an Orient Express Airways zeppelin from here to Constantinople.

How little time it had taken them to return, and yet how much had changed.

Ardis and Wendel crossed the gangway from the zeppelin to the mooring mast. Wind whistled around the tower and tugged at their clothes. When Wendel glanced at the ground, the color drained from his face.

"Afraid of heights?" Himmel said.

The captain and Konstantin waited on the gangway.

Wendel tore his gaze away from the ground long enough to glare at them. "Only with you lurking behind me like that."

Ardis prodded him in the back. "Keep walking."

When they stepped on solid ground, Wendel exhaled and stared heavenward. A tattered scrap of black flew from the airship and circled above them—Krampus. The raven disappeared over the rooftops.

Ardis smiled. "I'll bet you ten koronas Krampus will find his way back."

"I'm not taking that bet," Wendel said. "I'm penniless."

Konstantin stepped forward and raised a finger. "Meet tomorrow at the Hall of the Archmages. Seven o'clock sharp."

"We'll be there," Ardis said.

Konstantin ducked his head, then reached into the pocket of his jacket. He took out a golden pin in the shape of an edelweiss flower. Seeing it brought a lump to Ardis's throat. It was a badge of the archmages. *Her* badge.

"This belongs to you," Konstantin said.

"Still?" Ardis said.

His smile was lopsided. "I used the present tense, didn't I?"

Konstantin pinned the edelweiss to Ardis's lapel. It pricked her skin, but she didn't flinch. A little pain seemed worth it. She folded her lapel so she could inspect the pin, and found herself momentarily speechless.

"Thank you," Ardis said.

Konstantin dipped his head. "And now I will say goodnight."

"It's far past the captain's bedtime," Wendel said.

Himmel glowered, though he looked groggy with fatigue. Konstantin hesitated, took Himmel's elbow, and waved farewell before the two of them left the airfield. Ardis hoped he would take care of the captain.

Wendel walked to the road and hailed a taxicab. They climbed into the back.

"Where to, sir?" the driver said.

"Anywhere warm," Wendel said.

Ardis leaned forward. "Hotel Viktoria, please."

"Yes, ma'am."

Fields quilted the countryside, yielding to snow-blanketed roofs as they rode from the airfield into Vienna proper. The taxicab rumbled across a bridge over the Danube River, then turned onto the Ringstrasse, an old road that circled the heart of the city. Evergreen garlands decorated the lampposts and fences.

"I can't believe it's Christmas," Ardis said.

"How so?" Wendel said.

"We were on the road for so long, running and hiding and barely scraping by. This"—she tapped on the window— "doesn't feel real."

Wendel's eyebrows angled in a frown. "This is our reality now, as strange as it may seem."

TEN

Hotel Viktoria overlooked a street shadowed by the winter branches of trees. In the gaslamp glow of the lobby, the busty brunette behind the desk looked Wendel over and tucked a lock of her hair behind her ear.

"How can I help you, sir?" the brunette said.

Ardis leaned her elbow on the desk. "A single room, please."

"Thirty koronas." The brunette barely glanced at her. "Will you be staying long?"

"Only one night."

Ardis paid for the room, plucked the key from the brunette's hand, and climbed the stairs.

"Why was she staring at me like that?" Wendel said.

Ardis rolled her eyes. Because he was handsome beneath the dirt?

"You look like a vagabond," she said.

"I *am* a vagabond, thank you."

With a laugh, Ardis unlocked the door to their room. The bed was all but lost under a quilt flowered with cabbage roses. Lace crawled along the curtains. Her cheeks warmed. She had forgotten how dainty this hotel looked.

As expected, Wendel bent over the bed and poked a pillow in the shape of a pansy. "What a sad little pillow."

Ardis flounced into a plump armchair. She peered down at her boots, crusted with indeterminate scum from the lake. "God, I need a bath."

Ardis hopped to her feet and entered the bathroom. Wendel followed, closing the door behind them. She leaned over the clawfoot tub and twisted the tap on. He picked up a purple soap bar, sniffed it, and dropped it again.

"Lavender," he said. "A necromancer should never smell like lavender."

Ardis kicked off her boots and peeled off her clothes. She climbed into the water and let out a sigh of bliss. Heat soaked her to the bone. She slid to the bottom of the tub and watched her hair swirl on the surface of the water.

Wendel tossed his jacket on the floor and unbuttoned his shirt.

"Hand me the soap," Ardis said.

He pretended to sneer at the lavender soap and dropped it into the tub. She fumbled to catch it before it sank.

"Thank you," she said, with the necessary sarcasm.

"You're welcome."

Wendel stood over the bathtub, shirtless, and arched an eyebrow. "May I join you?"

Ardis stared up at him and smiled. Wendel needed no further invitation. He stripped naked and stepped into the tub. His feet straddled her calves. She took a moment to stare at him, then tucked her knees against her chest. He lowered himself into the tub, cupped a handful of water, and poured it over his head.

Ardis held her breath and ducked underwater. When she surfaced, Wendel leaned his head back against the tub and watched her through half-closed eyes. She rubbed the soap into a rich lather between her hands and washed her arms, then her breasts. The look in Wendel's eyes ignited with smoldering intensity.

"Give that to me," he said.

Ardis looked innocent. "You changed your mind about lavender?"

Wendel's smile was wicked. He held out his hand, and she relinquished the soap. He reached across the bath and traced the curve of her breast with his fingers. Her breath caught in her throat. Her back arched out of instinct. His thumb circled her nipple until it hardened under his touch.

"That's rather distracting," Ardis said.

Wendel looked her in the eye. "You said you wanted a bath."

He slid his hand down the hollow of her back. Her muscles felt tight with tension—and he wasn't helping her relax.

"Wendel," she said.

His hand moved away. "Should I stop?"

Ardis wasn't sure what she wanted. It was too silent in the bathroom. The quiet left space for ugly thoughts to crawl through her mind. When she closed her eyes, she saw the flames of the zeppelin, seared into her memory.

"It's not your fault," she said.

Wendel gazed across the water between them. "What do you mean?"

She waved at herself. "There's a gnawing in the pit of my stomach. Like something bad will happen and I don't know when or how or why. I don't know how to make the feeling stop. It's never been this bad before."

A crease appeared between Wendel's eyebrows. He stood, the water rushing off him, and climbed out of the bath. Ardis thought he might be leaving, but he climbed in behind her and pulled her against his chest.

"I know that feeling," Wendel said, a rasp in his honey-gravel voice.

"How do you make it go away?" Ardis said.

"It never does."

She was silent. Her eyes burned with tears that threatened to betray her. She held her breath, not wanting him to see her cry. He brushed her hair from the nape of her neck and massaged her shoulders.

Ardis let the air escape her lungs. A shaky, tentative breath. Her eyes blurred.

Here in the bath, no one could tell the difference between tears and water.

Wendel said nothing, but his silence was all she needed to hear. He washed her back, his fingers strong yet gentle. She inhaled through her mouth, then splashed water in her face to rinse away the last of her tears.

Wendel kissed her neck, and his stubble tickled her skin.

"Are you going to grow a magnificent beard?" Ardis said.

He laughed. "Would I be irresistibly rugged?"

"The jury is still out."

Wendel climbed out of the tub, toweled himself off, and dragged on his old clothes.

"Where are you going?" Ardis said.

He patted his cheek. "To buy a shaving kit."

"Come back soon."

"I will."

With that, he left the bathroom and shut the door behind him.

Ardis slid lower, all but her face underwater. Her heartbeat whooshed in her ears. She lay like that until the water went cold.

Where was Wendel?

Ardis left the tub and wrapped a towel around herself. The gnawing in her stomach was back, and worse than before. When she stepped out of the bathroom, a key clicked in the lock. The door swung open.

"I return triumphant," Wendel said.

He unpacked a shaving kit in the bathroom and flipped open a straight razor. The blade gleamed with a glossy polish.

"Solingen steel," Wendel said. "The only manliness in this hotel."

Ardis laughed and twisted her hair in the towel. Wendel dropped his coat on the floor and unbuttoned his shirt. He filled a little bowl with shaving cream, whipped it with a badger-hair brush, and spread the lather over his face. He tilted his head, frowning in the mirror, and scraped the razor over his cheek.

"Ah, damn," he said.

"Did you cut yourself?" Ardis said.

A thin line of blood welled above his cheekbone. He set down the straight razor and held out his hands—they were trembling.

"Laudanum," he said. "I had forgotten."

She bit her lip, afraid to ask what he remembered.

"Ardis." Wendel offered the straight razor to her. "I trust you with a blade."

"You want me to shave you?"

"Please."

Wendel dragged a chair into the bathroom. He sat and dabbed the cut on his cheekbone with a towel. Ardis exhaled and took the straight razor. The infinitesimal edge of the blade looked sharper than her sword.

"Are you sure?" Ardis said.

Wendel met her gaze. In this light, his eyes looked darker, like jade. He let her angle his head and bring the razor to his face.

"I trust you," he said.

Ardis touched the razor to Wendel's skin. It slid down his cheek with only the slightest resistance and subtle rasp of steel cutting stubble. She shaved his cheek and started on the other. He remained quiet and still.

"Look up," Ardis said.

Wendel tilted his head. Ardis pressed her thumb to his lower lip to tauten his skin, and shaved beneath his mouth. Her thumb lingered for a second. She shaved his chin and brought the straight razor to his neck.

"Don't move," Ardis said.

Wendel raised his eyebrows. "I wouldn't dream of it."

Ardis touched his throat, his heartbeat throbbing under her fingertips. It felt wrong to hold steel to his neck, where a single cut could kill. But this was a straight razor, not a sword, and a bathroom, not a battlefield.

Her hand steady, she scraped the blade over his throat in short strokes.

When she finished, Wendel bent over the sink to wash his face, then dipped the badger brush into the bowl of cream.

"Once more," Wendel said.

Still holding the straight razor, Ardis stared at him.

"Again?" she said.

"Against the grain," he said, "for a smoother shave. I always do."

"You look shaved enough to me." Ardis set the straight razor on the counter. "We could always test this theory."

Wendel squinted. "How—?"

Ardis silenced him with a kiss. An instant later, Wendel slipped his hand behind her neck. His other hand cradled the hollow of her back. She leaned against him, his clothes rough against her naked skin, and breathed in his scent.

Ardis smiled. "You do smell like lavender."

Wendel growled low in his throat. "I would rather be dirty."

His look was anything but gentlemanly. His kiss was anything but gentle.

He brought his lips to hers and backed her against the wall. His hands gripped her hips and held her there, as if the weight of his body wasn't enough. The hint of stubble on his jaw rasped her cheek. She sucked in a shaky breath, her breasts trapped against his chest, and ran her hands over the breadth of his shoulders.

"I want you in bed," Wendel said.

He brushed his lips down her neck, the tip of his tongue tasting her skin, then dipped lower and licked her nipple.

Ardis inhaled sharply. "Wendel."

He leaned back and met her gaze. Lust smoldered in his eyes.

"There's a slight problem," she said. "We have no—"

"Preventives?" Wendel lifted his jacket from the floor. He

retrieved a tin of preventives from the pocket and balanced it in his hand. "I'm a fortuneteller."

Ardis wrinkled her nose. "Why?"

"I predicted the future," he said, struggling not to grin.

She laughed. "The future might end badly if you act that arrogant."

"So far, so good."

Wendel tried to push her against the wall, but she ducked under his arm and escaped. She ran to the bedroom and dove under the covers. Breathless, trying not to laugh, she tucked the quilt down tight.

"Good night," Ardis said.

Wendel stalked into the bedroom with pantomimed stealth. He dropped to a crouch and crawled along the wall in the shadows. After a second of silence, he pounced onto the bed and pinned her arms to the mattress.

Ardis laughed, and Wendel pretended to glare at her.

"No laughing," he said.

She couldn't stop smiling at him. "Is this serious?"

"Very."

Wendel held himself over her and kissed her on the mouth. Softly, this time, but with an undercurrent of urgency. Tension tightened his muscles. He released one of her wrists and touched his fingertips to her cheek.

"I am serious," Wendel said, "when I say that I love your laugh."

His words touched her heart so deeply they hurt.

"I love your smile," he said.

Should she tell him she loved him? Could she?

"I love your body."

Wendel's whisper was almost lost as he kissed her neck. Ardis didn't know what to say, but knew what she wanted to feel. She closed her eyes and let him explore her skin with his lips. When his fingers loosened on her wrist, she unbuckled his belt and undid his fly. She stroked his hardness with her hand.

He let out a rough little groan. "I love it when you touch me."

"Help a girl out," Ardis said. "Take off your clothes."

Standing on the bed, Wendel tossed his clothes onto the floor. As he dropped to his knees, Ardis met him halfway. They tumbled onto the tangle of sheets together. She kissed his forehead, his cheeks, his lips. He leaned over the mattress to find the preventive, then lowered her onto a pillow.

Ardis relaxed beneath Wendel. He entered her gently. When she grabbed his buttocks, he thrust deeper. She wanted to make him sweat. She held his face in her hands and kissed him, then bit his lip; he gasped.

"Harder," Ardis said.

Wendel clutched her to himself and obeyed. He stayed like that for a second, their bodies the closest they could be, then withdrew. A moan of protest escaped Ardis. He returned to her quicker than before. They found a driving rhythm together. Tension wound tighter and tighter inside her, but still didn't break.

"Wait," Ardis said.

Wendel halted, breathing hard, reluctance clear on his face.

"It isn't enough," she said. "I—"

"Allow me."

He stood by the edge of the bed and dragged her down to him. He held her there, his fingernails biting into her buttocks. When he thrust at this angle, deeper still, she gasped at the increased pleasure. She clutched the sheets in her fists, closed her eyes, and let herself surrender to him. He brought her to the brink.

"Look at me," Wendel said, his voice rough with desire.

Ardis met his gaze, panting, her skin feverish. He never looked away as he thrust into her, and the fierce adoration in his eyes was enough to nudge her over the edge. She cried out and clung to the bed. He didn't stop until he echoed her pleasure with his own. Shuddering, he held her crushingly close.

They shared a moment of wordless bliss.

Wendel touched his forehead to hers. "I love you." Three words. So small, yet so heavy.

Ardis closed her eyes to hide the inexplicable prickling of tears. She tried to speak, but his mouth on hers left her breathless.

Late that night, Ardis blinked herself awake. She stared wide-eyed into the darkness, wondering what had disturbed her sleep.

"No," Wendel said. "Not again."

Ardis froze. Her heartbeat hammered in her ears.

"I won't do this for you," he said.

She lifted herself on her elbow and stared at him. He was talking in his sleep. His hair clung to his sweaty forehead.

Her throat tightened until it hurt. "Wendel," she whispered.

"No," he said. "No, please, no."

Ardis dragged in a steadying breath and slipped out of bed. She was afraid to touch him. The last time she had woken him from a nightmare, he almost stabbed her before he came to his senses.

She couldn't let him suffer like this.

ELEVEN

rdis reached for Wendel's shoulder and shoved him with her fingertips. He flinched but didn't wake. She clutched the sheet to herself.

Her fingers shaking, she fumbled with a match and lit the old lamp by the bed. The hiss of gas seemed deafening in the silence. When the glare touched Wendel's face, he jerked awake and lurched out of bed. His legs tangled in the sheets. He fell to his knees, scrambled against the wall, and clawed his way to a crouch.

"Wendel!" Ardis said.

"Stay away from me," Wendel rasped, his eyes glittering.

Fear clamped like a fist around her stomach. She backed away from him.

"It's me, Wendel," she said. "It's Ardis."

Inky shadows darkened his face. "Ardis?"

"Yes," she said, her mouth as dry as sand. "I'm here."

"Are they coming?"

"Who?"

"Them."

"I don't know."

Wendel slid down the wall and hit the floor. His tucked his legs against his chest and touched his forehead to his knees.

"Ardis," he said. "God, Ardis, I—" His voice broke.

She tasted sourness on her tongue. She still didn't move toward him. "You were having a nightmare."

Wendel rubbed his hands over his face and clutched fistfuls of hair. "The assassins." He said no more, but he didn't need to.

"Wendel."

Silence lengthened the distance between them.

"Did I hurt you?" Wendel whispered.

"No."

He staggered to his feet and stepped past her on his way to the bathtub. He knelt and twisted the tap, ducking his head into the water.

Ardis stood in the doorway, still clutching the sheet to herself, and stared at him. "Are you okay?"

Wendel shut off the water and stared at the drain, his hands white-knuckled on the porcelain. His nakedness bared the scars crisscrossing his back—souvenirs from his twelve years with the Order of the Asphodel.

"I'm sorry," he said, his voice quiet and hoarse.

"It wasn't your fault."

"I can't sleep like this." Wendel's shoulders tightened. "I can't live like this."

Ardis swallowed hard. "The alternative to living isn't an option."

Water plinked from the tap and echoed in the silence.

Wendel kept his head bowed. "I don't know what to do."

"Well," Ardis said, "we could start with a walk."

He twisted to look over his shoulder. His eyes looked bloodshot. "Why the hell would I do that?"

She didn't flinch under his stare. "As far as I know, that's how this life thing works. You keep moving, one step at a time."

He let out a bleak laugh. "Unless we freeze to death. It's frigid out there, Ardis."

His hint of sarcasm softened the prickling of her anxiety.

"Here." Ardis tossed him a towel. "Dry off and get dressed."

Wendel grimaced, but he tousled his hair with the towel and grabbed his clothes from the floor. By the time he finished buttoning his shirt, he almost looked like himself again, if not for the shadows haunting his eyes.

"Ready?" Ardis said.

With a glance into her eyes, Wendel dipped his head. The stairs of Hotel Viktoria creaked underfoot as they descended. They stepped into the winter night together, snowflakes whirling like white moths under the streetlamps.

Ardis shivered and hugged herself. "Damn it," she muttered. "It *is* frigid."

"And I'm vindicated," Wendel said.

Ardis turned in place and peered down the streets. She wasn't sure where they should go, so she chose their future at random.

She twisted her fingers with his. "This way."

He stared at her as if holding hands wasn't something he did. But his grip tightened, and they walked together. Their boots squeaked in the snow. Their breath clouded the cold.

"I dreamed about Budapest," Wendel said.

"Oh?" Ardis said, not sure what else to say.

"I was there to kill a man." He kept his eyes on the street. "A rich man. He lived in a mansion, with guards. And I remember his children—he had three little boys. Too little to truly understand what was happening."

Ardis stared at him. "You remember? It was a memory?"

"I never forget my work."

She shivered at the cold detachment in his voice.

"Thank you for waking me before…" Wendel glanced sideways at Ardis. "My dreams always end the same way."

She squeezed his hand. "You always dream of falling?"

"I do," he said.

"I wish you never had to fall."

Wendel looked away, his eyes glittering. He stopped at the corner and scuffed his boot in the snow. "Can you forgive me?"

Ardis dropped his hand. "For what?"

"Everything."

She studied the tension in his jaw. The vulnerability in his mouth.

"I don't do indulgences," she said. "I'm not the Pope."

He arched his eyebrows. "And I'm not Catholic." His voice softened to a velvety murmur. "I'm asking for your forgiveness."

"I'm still angry at you for Constantinople."

His eyebrows descended. "You are?"

"You fought Thorsten when you knew you would lose."

Wendel took a step back. "Do you think I wanted to die?" He sounded both hurt and scornful.

"Honestly?" She steadied her voice. "I wasn't sure."

"Christ."

Wendel looked away, his jaw clenched, his hands fisted at his sides. "I wanted to win. If I won—I thought I would be free."

Anger smoldered in his eyes, and Ardis touched his arm to calm him.

"But you are free," she said.

He stared at the snow. "Is this what freedom feels like?"

"Yes," she said. "Congratulations. It's not paradise, but at least you can run away with me to Switzerland someday."

He smiled sadly. "Will I still have nightmares in Switzerland?"

Ardis hesitated, and his smile faded.

"No," she said. "You will be too busy dreaming about chocolate and cheese and meadows high in the mountains."

Wendel's smile returned, more wicked than before. "Or dreaming about you naked in bed."

"Speaking of bed, we should go back. We need to be at the Hall of the Archmages at seven o'clock tomorrow."

His sigh drifted away as fog. "Killing time until Switzerland."

On the taxi ride through Vienna, sunrise painted the sky gold and violet. They stopped outside the Hall of the Archmages, a grand building with a stately marble façade. Wendel hopped out of the automobile and offered Ardis a hand. She thanked him with a nod.

Their footsteps echoed under a dome glittering with a mosaic of the moon and stars. The guards at the entrance stared at them, and Ardis wondered if her boots were too grimy for the marble floor. Though they seemed warier of Wendel.

The door to Konstantin's office stood ajar. Ardis rapped on the doorframe.

"Come in!" Konstantin said.

She nudged open the door and discovered the archmage standing by his desk, shuffling through papers and squinting at them.

Konstantin glanced at them. "You're here. We have to hurry."

"Are we late?" Wendel said.

Ardis spotted a clock on the wall. "It's ten until seven."

"Yes," Konstantin said, "but Margareta has scheduled a debriefing on the *Wanderfalke*, and Himmel is still in the hospital."

"In the hospital?" Ardis said. "Is he all right?"

Konstantin cleared his throat and ruffled through some papers. "I'm afraid not."

Ardis grimaced and glanced at Wendel, who looked more concerned for the captain than he would ever admit out loud.

"We can visit him later," Konstantin said.

Konstantin tucked a folder of papers under his arm and bustled from his office. He led them down a hallway adorned with portraits of archmages long dead, and shoved through a pair of wooden doors that groaned on their hinges.

A battle-scarred oak table dominated a long meeting room. Margareta leaned in a throne of a chair. Her steely gray hair glinted in the sunlight pouring through the windows. Tesla tilted his head politely as he listened to her talk. Around a dozen crewmen from both the *Wanderfalke* and the *Jupiter* sat farther down the table.

"Archmage Margareta," Konstantin said.

She waved imperiously at them. "Please, sit."

Three seats remained by Tesla. Konstantin lingered behind him, then dragged out a chair. Ardis and Wendel followed suit.

"Archmage Konstantin," Margareta said. "Please share your report."

Konstantin flipped open his folder. "On the afternoon of December 25th, the *Wanderfalke* was attacked by a clockwork dragon we believe to be an invention of the Russians. The dragon's arrival was preceded by a scouting party of clockwork wasps." He slid forward a detailed mechanical diagram. "This is a sketch of a clockwork wasp that I deconstructed in my laboratory last night. The other wasp was destroyed."

"Destroyed is an understatement," Wendel muttered.

Ardis nudged him with her elbow, sure his sarcasm was unwelcome here.

Margareta leaned forward and inspected the diagram. "Any theories on the maker?"

"Fabergé," Konstantin said. "Judging by the intricate enamel."

"Was the wasp dangerous?" Margareta said.

"Not how you might think." Konstantin thinned his lips. "Ardis, would you show us your arm?"

When Ardis stood, her chair screeched on the floor. She resisted the urge to wince and managed to look stoic, like a mercenary should. She unwrapped the bandage and raised her arm. The sting had faded to a purplish welt.

"The wasp stung me," Ardis said. "I didn't think much of it until I went to the doctor, and she cut out a clockwork larva."

The men grimaced and leaned away. Ardis was secretly satisfied by their disgust.

Konstantin cleared his throat. "I believe the larva must be a prototype tracking device. Still too painful to be stealthy. Nevertheless, it betrayed our position to the Russians. The wasps likely have a magical link to the clockwork dragon."

Margareta steepled her fingers with a look of grim scrutiny. "How large was the dragon?"

"Approximately twenty meters long."

"Airspeed?"

"Faster than our zeppelin. It hunted us down."

A man in an American uniform cleared his throat. He had an impressive beard, dark and streaked with silver.

"Yes, Captain Hobson?" Margareta said.

"By our estimate," the American said, "the top airspeed of the clockwork dragon would be about seventy knots."

Captain Hobson spoke correct German, albeit with a strong American accent.

Konstantin squinted. "One hundred and twenty-eight kilometers per hour. Roughly."

"And how was the dragon powered?" Margareta said.

"Unknown technomancy," Konstantin said, a bit breathlessly. "It must have some electrical components, since lightning from the USS *Jupiter* stunned it. But I suspect the dragon's scales shield it from most forms of interference or damage."

Tesla lifted his hand. "Would it be possible for me to examine the clockwork wasp?"

Konstantin clutched his folder to his chest. He looked rather like a student eager to please his professor. "Why, of course, Mr. Tesla."

"Is the specimen here in Vienna?" Tesla said.

"Yes, in my laboratory." Konstantin glanced at Margareta. "Though I will bring the wasp to Prussia whenever we leave."

"You leave today," Margareta said.

"Already?"

"Captain Hobson will fly you to Prussia on the USS *Jupiter*. In exchange, you will give Tesla a tour of Project Lazarus upon arrival."

Konstantin's eyebrows shot skyward. "When was this decided?"

"Earlier this morning." Margareta pursed her lips. "Do you object?"

"No, not at all!" Konstantin stammered. "I would be honored to show Mr. Tesla the prototypes. Though I may require a little time to prepare the laboratory, since I'm afraid I left it in a rather disorganized state."

Tesla leaned with his hand on his mouth, though it didn't entirely hide his smile. "Rest assured. I'm sure I will be too fascinated by your inventions."

Konstantin blushed to the roots of his hair. He seemed to be holding his breath.

"I hope the archmage doesn't faint," Wendel whispered.

Ardis shot him a look. She hoped he behaved himself until the end of the debriefing.

"On the behalf of the archmages," Margareta said, "we would like to thank Captain Hobson and the crew of the USS *Jupiter* for rescuing the survivors from the *Wanderfalke*. Your courage will not be forgotten."

"We wish we could have done more," Captain Hobson said.

Margareta met his gaze. "I can't speak for the empire, but I suspect Austria-Hungary would welcome an alliance with America."

Captain Hobson nodded. "The USS *Jupiter* casts off from Aspern Airfield at noon."

"Excellent," Margareta said. "Archmage Konstantin, you will be responsible for transferring your team to the airship." She glanced at Wendel when she said this, and Ardis knew they needed the necromancer.

"Yes, ma'am," Konstantin said.

Margareta stood. "That concludes this debriefing."

Everyone shoved their chairs from the table. Ardis lingered, biting the inside of her cheek, and watched Margareta leave.

"Ardis?" Wendel said.

"I need to talk to Margareta," she said. "Alone."

"Ah," he said. "About Constantinople?"

"Among other things."

Konstantin clapped Ardis on the shoulder. "Good luck."

Her stomach somersaulted. "You aren't coming? To vouch for me?"

"My money is on you," he said.

"I wish I shared your confidence."

Konstantin smiled for a fleeting moment before sobering.

"I'm off to the hospital," he said. "To see Himmel."

"Could you wait for me?" Ardis said. "I would like to go with you, and this shouldn't take more than a few minutes."

"Certainly. Meet me by the doors."

They walked into the hallway together.

Wendel tapped her on the shoulder. "I'll be with the archmage."

After they left her alone, Ardis straightened her jacket, combed her hair with her fingers, and squared her shoulders. She strode to Margareta's office and knocked on the door.

"Come in," Margareta said.

Ardis entered. For some reason her heartbeat thumped in her ears.

"Ma'am," she said.

"Ardis," Margareta said. "I was surprised to see you at the debriefing."

That stung, but Ardis disguised it with a nod.

"Understandable," Ardis said. "I told Archmage Konstantin why I went to Constantinople, but I wasn't sure if he informed you."

Margareta's blue eyes glinted. "Falkenrath told me everything. I know exactly why you went gallivanting off to Constantinople, though I'm not entirely sure why you left all of your common sense behind in Vienna."

Heat spread across Ardis's cheeks.

"Sit," Margareta said.

Ardis sat, though she felt rather like a disobedient dog.

"I understand the appeal," Margareta said. "The necromancer is too handsome for his own good, and his past is quite tragic."

This was awkward. Ardis tried not to squirm.

Margareta didn't blink. "But this sort of behavior brings your loyalty into question."

"Ma'am," Ardis said, "I don't—"

"One moment." Margareta lifted her finger. "Falkenrath informed me that you and Wendel journeyed to Constantinople to find a technomancer. You needed him to perform a countercurse. Is this correct?"

"Yes, ma'am."

Margareta steepled her hands. "And then you detoured to the Order of the Asphodel?"

Ardis swallowed hard. Somehow her mouth had stopped producing saliva. "Yes, ma'am."

"What happened?"

Ardis rubbed her thumbnail over her lip. She didn't see how lying would help her here, but honesty seemed like a blunt weapon.

"Wendel wanted revenge," Ardis said. "Thorsten Magnusson was at the top of his list."

"And you helped him?" Margareta said.

"I did." Ardis didn't blink. "I wasn't about to let him attack Thorsten alone."

Margareta's stare was cool but relentless. "Do you believe the necromancer wanted to die?"

Ardis curled her fingers into fists. She found it hard to look at Margareta. "I don't think so."

"So you stopped him?"

"No." Ardis pressed her fingernails into her palms. "I couldn't."

"Explain."

Ardis sucked in a slow breath. "Wendel lost the fight. Thorsten stabbed him in the heart, then threw him from the top of the tower. When I found Wendel, he was dead. Undeniably. But as you may have heard, he didn't stay dead. Earlier, without telling me, Wendel lent me some of his necromancy. I revived him myself."

Margareta's eyes narrowed to slits. "Fascinating."

Were all the archmages concerned only with magic?

"Ma'am," Ardis said. "With all due respect, I didn't come here today to talk about Wendel or Wendel's mistakes."

Margareta leaned back in her chair. "I don't see how it's irrelevant."

"I don't see how his actions should define my career."

Margareta sniffed. "You helped him every step of the way."

"I tried to stop him every step of the way." Ardis forced herself to speak in a calm voice. "I'm nobody's sidekick."

"Weren't you Wendel's companion?"

"I'm not sure what you're insinuating," Ardis said.

Margareta sighed. "Ardis, I would recommend avoiding romantic entanglements. Particularly while on a mission."

"Well, it's too late for that." Ardis tacked on a hasty, "Ma'am."

Margareta leaned with her elbows on her desk. "I don't demand chastity. This is hardly a convent."

Ardis twisted her mouth to disguise a smile.

"But don't let lust distract you," Margareta said. "Your loyalty should be to the archmages first and foremost."

"Which is why I'm here," Ardis said. "Can we talk business?"

"Will your interactions with the necromancer remain professional?"

Ardis ran her tongue over her teeth and thought for a moment. "While I'm on the job. Will that be enough?"

Margareta sighed. "I suppose it will have to be. You show promise, Ardis, and I would hate to let you go to a competitor."

"Thank you," Ardis said.

"Your work in Transylvania has been especially valuable to us."

"I appreciate the compliment, ma'am, but I don't want to go back to Transylvania. I want to go to Prussia."

"Prussia?" Margareta nodded slowly. "We do need more Eisenkrieger test pilots."

"Ma'am." Ardis sat even straighter. "I would love to be a pilot."

"Konstantin did say you showed remarkable aptitude." Margareta pursed her lips. "You do, however, have one major obstacle."

Sweat dampened Ardis's hands. "What would that be?"

"You left Natalya lying on the snow, in a cemetery, pinned by her own sword."

Ardis tried not to wince. "She pistol-whipped me on the Diesel mission."

"I remember that very well."

"Natalya and I haven't always seen eye to eye."

Margareta puckered her lips. "With such a violent track record, I'm not sure the two of you should work together."

Ardis's stomach plummeted. "Natalya will be in Prussia?"

"She already is. She commands the Eisenkrieger pilots."

God, there was no avoiding Natalya.

"I can do this." Ardis squared her shoulders. "I can work under Natalya's command. Give me a chance to prove myself."

TWELVE

Margareta stared at Ardis in silence. The corner of her mouth twitched. "You won't have to prove yourself to me. Report to Natalya in Prussia."

Ardis exhaled. "I won't disappoint the archmages."

Margareta stood and shook Ardis's hand with a firm grip. "One small thing before you go."

Margareta slid open a drawer and took out a long cloth-wrapped bundle. She set it on the desk and meticulously unwound the cloth. Ardis's breath snagged at the sight of a sharkskin scabbard and a sword with a red tassel dangling from its pommel.

"Chun Yi," she whispered.

Margareta raised an eyebrow. "I believe you misplaced this."

Ardis gripped the sharkskin hilt and drew her sword in one sweep. The steel ignited with a crackling rush of golden fire. She felt the flames not as heat, but as an electricity in the palm of her hand that hummed through her bones. The magic prickled her nose like the air after a thunderstorm.

"Thank you, ma'am."

Reflected fire danced in Margareta's eyes. "It arrived an hour ago from Bulgaria. Such a pity I didn't have more time to examine the enchantment. Quite old, quite odd magic. Perhaps, in the future, you might lend it to the archmages for study."

Ardis sheathed her sword. "Perhaps."

"Good luck in Prussia," Margareta said. "Try not to damage any prototypes."

Ardis sensed an unspoken, "This time." That little adventure with the Eisenkrieger couldn't have been too damning if Ardis had her job back.

"Thank you," Ardis said again.

Margareta granted her a rare smile. "Teach those Russians a lesson."

"I will, ma'am."

Ardis walked out with her sword in hand. Outside the office, she buckled it to her belt and adjusted it so it hung just right. She strode down the hallway with her head held high. Wendel and Konstantin waited by the entrance, loitering an arm's length apart, uneasy in each other's company.

"I take it things went well?" Konstantin said.

"Brace yourself," Ardis said. "She assigned me to be an Eisenkrieger test pilot in Prussia. I'll try not to scratch your babies."

Konstantin laughed, though he winced with his eyebrows. "I trust you more than most."

Wendel feigned innocence. "Don't look at me."

Ardis pushed through the doors to the outside. Snow whirled into her face and tossed her hair, but it couldn't blow the grin from her face.

The moment she set foot in the hospital, Ardis felt her stomach twist into a familiar knot. Even here in the grand atrium, with its potted palms and cathedral ceiling, the stink of disinfectant lingered in the air. Wendel's shoulders stiffened, and he seemed reluctant to enter. Likely due to his proximity with the dying.

"Excuse me," Konstantin said to the receptionist. "We would like to visit someone."

The receptionist glanced into his eyes. "The name of the patient?"

"Himmel."

She scanned a clipboard. "Theodore Himmel?"

"Theodore?" Konstantin stumbled over the name.

The receptionist squinted. "Your relationship to the patient?"

"Professional." Konstantin's hands left sweaty fingerprints on the desk. "Captain Himmel commands a zeppelin for the archmages. Commanded, that is. He went down with his ship and suffered injuries. Can we see him?"

The receptionist inspected his edelweiss pin and tapped her pen on the desk. "Theodore Himmel is on the first floor, in Room 102. Through those doors, down the hall, and on your right."

They followed her directions. Konstantin hesitated before rapping on the door.

"Enter," Himmel said.

The room was small and bare, with a brass bed and a single chair by the window where Himmel sat staring out at the manicured evergreens. Nobody had brought him gifts or flowers, not even notes of sympathy. His right arm hung in a sling.

He lifted his head and looked at them. "Morning."

Konstantin nodded and pressed his lips together. He didn't seem to know what to say.

"How are you feeling?" Ardis said.

Himmel grunted.

Ardis folded her arms to hide her empty hands. "You look a little better."

"Do I?" Himmel said.

She studied his face. "Less pale, at least."

Wendel dropped onto the bed, crossed his legs, and leaned back on his hands. "We were worried about you. Old Teddy, our dearest friend."

"Teddy?" Himmel nearly snarled the word. "Who told you that?"

"The receptionist," Wendel said.

Konstantin smoothed his hair, though his curls didn't cooperate. "Your name is Theodore?"

"Unfortunately," Himmel said.

"Oh." Konstantin coughed. "I rather like the name Theodore."

The captain stared at the archmage. It was hard to say whose face was redder.

"I like Teddy," Wendel said.

Himmel rose from his chair. "I can still knock you out with one arm."

Konstantin stopped Himmel with a hand on his chest. "Gentlemen! This is a hospital."

"He's no gentleman," Himmel said.

"True," Wendel said. "Technically, I'm royalty."

"You won't be anything when I'm done with you."

Wendel laughed, and Himmel glared at him. The necromancer seemed glad the captain was no longer melancholy.

"My God," Ardis said. "Everybody calm the hell down."

The three men stared at her, but she didn't blink.

"Himmel, you're supposed to be wounded. Konstantin, you're supposed to be concerned. Wendel, you're being a bastard. Again."

"Am I?" Wendel said. "I thought it was rather heroic of me to save Himmel's life."

"What?" Himmel said. "Konstantin, is this true?"

Konstantin rubbed the back of his neck. "The necromancer did revive a few dead men to rescue survivors from the lake."

Himmel blanched. "You brought my men back?"

Wendel's face flipped from sarcastic to serious. "The dead don't need to breathe. They walked in and dragged you out."

Himmel's chest heaved as he struggled to find words. "You shouldn't have done that."

Wendel stared him down. "I should have let you drown?"

"Christ." With his left hand, Himmel rubbed his jaw. "You are an abomination."

"So I hear."

Ardis stepped between them. "A suggestion? Don't start yet another vendetta. We should focus on revenge against the Russians."

"And the clockwork dragon," Konstantin said.

"I'd love to." Himmel's voice darkened. "The doctors say I'm all but useless. My arm, anyway. Too much damage."

"That's poppycock," Konstantin scoffed. "Those doctors are useless."

Ardis frowned, not sure it was a good idea to give false hope.

"I'll build you another arm." Konstantin's eyes burned with zeal. "A better one! Trust me, the technomancy will be nothing but the best. Come with us to Prussia, and you can test the arm by punching a few Russians."

"Actually," Wendel said, "I like the sound of that, archmage."

Himmel stared at Konstantin with parted lips and bright eyes. "You would do that for me?"

Konstantin locked gazes with him. "If you would allow me the privilege, Theodore. Technomancy isn't without risks."

Himmel sucked in a slow breath. "It has to be better than rotting in some hospital."

"Excellent." Konstantin broke into a smile. "It's good to have you back."

"Just don't call me Theodore."

Konstantin blushed. "Right."

Bells chimed from the cathedral and echoed over Vienna. Eleven o'clock. With only an hour before departure, Ardis and Wendel visited the marketplace for some last minute purchases. Fortunately, the archmages had paid them a stipend in advance of their work on Project Lazarus. Ardis bought a new pair of boots, since her old ones had seen better days, while Wendel spent a few coins on leftover lebkuchen.

"More cookies?" Ardis said.

"One can never have too many cookies," Wendel said, with a grandiose wave

She smiled. "You have a sweet tooth, don't you?"

"Pardon?"

Ardis guessed that didn't translate into German. "You love to eat sweets."

"Ah." Wendel raised his eyebrows. "*Naschkatze*. It means… a cat who nibbles."

She laughed. "I could see that."

A black bird swooped overhead—Krampus. The raven banked, his little feet tucked under his body, and glided to a silent landing on the cobblestones.

"Krampus!" Wendel said. "You want some lebkuchen?"

Wendel tossed a crumb to the raven. Krampus cocked his head, shuffled his feet, and glanced around the market. Bristling his feathers, he clicked his beak. He didn't seem to care about the cookie in the slightest.

Wendel snorted. "What, my crumbs aren't good enough for you?"

Krampus ducked, his wings halfway open. "*Grok! Grok! Grok!*"

Ardis frowned. The raven seemed spooked by something. Her hand strayed to Chun Yi. She scanned the marketplace, but it was too difficult to pinpoint danger in the swirl of the crowd. Anxiety prickled over her skin.

"Something feels wrong," Ardis murmured.

Wendel crouched by Krampus and held out half of a cookie. The raven tucked his wings to his body and skipped sideways.

"We should go," Ardis said.

Wendel straightened, the cookie crumbling in his hand, and squinted.

"To the airship?" he said. "Already?"

Her fingers tightened on her sword. "Yes. Now."

Ardis hunched her shoulders and threaded through the crowd, trying to be stealthy, though she knew she was terrible at sneaking.

She hated enemies who never showed their faces, always skulking in the shadows.

Which was, of course, Wendel's style. Thank God he was on her side.

"Excuse me," said a man. "You dropped this."

Ardis whirled. A man stood near enough to touch, his turquoise eyes striking against his dark eyelashes and dusky skin.

"Is this yours?" the man said.

He held out a black dagger. Ripples in the metal marked it as Damascus steel. Intricate silver engravings flowered the hilt.

Amarant.

When Ardis had last seen the dagger, it had been dripping with Wendel's blood.

She struggled to keep a straight face, afraid she stared at the blade for too long. Afraid she had no hope of bluffing.

"No," Ardis said. "That's not mine."

"My apologies," said the man.

He withdrew the dagger and turned around. He strode through the crowd toward Wendel, who stood staring at the rooftops.

Ardis sucked in air to shout. "Wendel!"

Wendel looked in her direction. But he still didn't see the man. And anyone with the black dagger had to be an assassin.

A horse and cart rumbled in front of Ardis, a mountain of turnips blocking her view.

"Damn it," she hissed between her teeth.

Ardis circled around the lumbering horse and elbowed through the crowd. She ignored the glares and the protests.

When she stumbled into the street, the man halted by Wendel.

"Excuse me," the man said.

Wendel retreated a step. His face blanched to the color of bone. "Nasir."

The man dipped his head. "You remember me."

"You know I could never forget."

Ardis edged nearer, her hand clamped on her sword. Who was Nasir? Why was Wendel looking at him with such intensity?

"Have you come to kill me?" Wendel said.

Nasir looked at him, calmly confident. "You have an incredible bounty on your head."

"How does the Grandmaster know I'm alive?"

Nasir fingered the black dagger. "The archmages aren't known for subtlety."

"Nasir"—Wendel slid his foot backward—"Don't do this."

A sigh left the man, clouding the air, and Wendel bolted into the crowd. Nasir sheathed the dagger and sprinted after him.

Ardis let go of her sword and broke into a run.

The crowd jostled and shouted as Wendel zigzagged between them. He left the market behind and crossed the street. A solid wall of apartments blocked him; he veered, running down the sidewalk. Nasir leapt into traffic and dodged an automobile, losing some speed, then swerved onto the sidewalk.

Ardis pushed herself into a sprint. Her throat ached in the bracing cold.

An archway yawned between the apartments. Wendel ducked inside and disappeared. Nasir slowed to a jog and followed.

Panting, Ardis stopped outside an ivy-shrouded archway and peered around the corner.

Evergreens rustled in an arcaded courtyard. Nasir lingered in the center, head tilted, searching the shadows between the arcades, and the stairs leading to apartments.

"Wendel," Nasir said. "We haven't spoken in so long."

Ardis let out a lungful of air. She forced herself to inhale quietly as she stole through the archway and entered the courtyard.

"I remember our time in Prague," Nasir said.

Ardis ducked behind an evergreen, and glanced left and right. She spotted Wendel lurking behind a column. He held his finger to his lips. She nodded and looked back to Nasir, who stalked along the arcade.

"When you were alone at night," Nasir said, "did you think of me?"

Ardis didn't want to hear more. Heat already scorched her cheeks. She tensed the muscles in her legs and reached for her sword.

"*Grok!*"

Wingbeats rustled over the courtyard. Krampus landed on an evergreen and bounced, fanning his wings for balance.

When Nasir glanced at the raven, Wendel darted from one column to the next, his hand inside his coat. A straight razor flashed in the shadows. He held the blade low and waited for Nasir to wander nearer.

"Don't hide from me," Nasir said.

Wendel lunged from the column and attacked. Nasir dodged, the straight razor slashing his back. Wendel twisted Nasir's arm, but the assassin tumbled into a roll and flung him onto the cobblestones.

In a heartbeat, Wendel sprang onto his feet and leapt away.

"A razor?" Nasir said.

Wendel sneered. "Better than Amarant in your hands. What a waste."

Nasir slashed at Wendel, who hit his wrist to divert the blow, then slashed again. Wendel blocked with the straight razor. The brittle blade shattered, shards chiming on the cobblestones.

Armed with a broken straight razor, Wendel backed away.

"Guess what?" Ardis said. "I'm the only one with a sword."

She unsheathed Chun Yi, enchanted flames rushing down the steel.

Nasir spared her a glance. "Stay out of this, you slant-eyed bitch."

"Brilliant." Wendel laughed callously. "Insult the bloodthirsty mercenary."

Nasir stabbed at his chest. Wendel blocked the attack barehanded, the dagger cutting his forearm, then slashed Nasir's stomach with the broken razor. He tried to slash again, but Nasir hit him in the jaw and knocked him back.

Ardis took this as her invitation to the fight. With a shout, she swung Chun Yi.

Nasir hit the ground, rolled, and scrambled out of her reach, his eyes locked on her sword.

"Next time?" Wendel said. "Try killing him silently."

Ardis growled. "I hate stealth."

Chun Yi's magic tingled over her skin and hummed in her bones. The sword wanted blood, and blood would make it stronger.

Nasir looked away, his attention on Wendel.

Ardis feinted with a swooping attack. Nasir knocked aside her sword, but she angled her blade inside his arm. She surged at him, teeth bared, and drove her sword into his shoulder.

Nasir grunted and wrenched away. He swore in what had to be Turkish.

"It's over, Nasir," Wendel said.

"Already?" Nasir said. "You never did last long."

The assassin clutched his shoulder. His hand came away red. Ardis attacked again. She cut at Nasir's leg, trying to hobble him, but he whirled and grabbed Wendel's neck, shoving him against a column and pinning him there. Nasir looked into Wendel's eyes as if savoring this instant of triumph.

"You never did think things through," Wendel said hoarsely.

Wendel raised the broken razor, but Nasir grabbed his arm and smashed it against the stone; the weapon clattered on the cobblestones. Nasir held the dagger to Wendel's throat.

THIRTEEN

Ardis," Wendel said.

She didn't know what he wanted. But Nasir shared her indecision and glanced at her. Wendel elbowed Nasir's face, kneed him between the legs, and kicked him to the ground. Nasir curled with a choked moan. Before Nasir could inhale, Wendel crushed his fingers beneath his boot and forced him to drop the dagger.

Breathing hard, Wendel took back Amarant. "I don't want to kill you."

Nasir slumped on the cobblestones. Blood darkened his shirt. "Why?"

"I know who you are," Wendel said. "I know this isn't you."

Nasir stared at him. "You're a fool."

"Perhaps."

Wendel walked from the courtyard, a faraway stare in his glacial eyes.

"Wendel," Nasir said. "Wendel!"

The necromancer never looked back.

Ardis caught up with Wendel on the street. Still breathing hard, Wendel wiped Amarant on his sleeve. He rotated his arm to look at the slash. Blood dripped on the cobblestones.

"Are you all right?" Ardis said.

"Yes. Keep walking."

"Do you think Nasir was alone?"

"I don't know."

Ardis and Wendel walked until they left the courtyard at least five blocks behind. They stopped by a fountain, where Wendel washed away the blood in the icy water. A little boy stared at them until his mother dragged him out of sight.

"How the hell did you know him?" Ardis said.

Wendel shook water from his hands. "Constantinople."

"That doesn't explain anything," she said.

He blushed, which was rare enough to explain everything.

"You slept with him," she said. "And then you left him."

"No!" His shoulders stiffened. "No, I..."

Ardis glared at him. "Are you saying Nasir pined after you like poor Konstantin, and you broke his heart?" She laughed scathingly. "Jesus Christ, don't tell me you left a trail of heartbroken assassins behind."

Wendel bowed his head. "Nasir was the one who left."

Guilt and jealousy needled Ardis. She didn't want to imagine it. "Why?"

Wendel's eyebrows angled as he frowned. He concentrated on tying a handkerchief around his arm, though he was doing a poor job of it. Ardis watched him for a moment, gritting her teeth, until she couldn't watch anymore.

"Stop. Let me."

Silently, Wendel held out his arm. She knotted the handkerchief around the wound.

"You might need stitches," Ardis said.

"It doesn't matter."

"I think it does. You don't need any more scars."

Wendel kept his head down. "Nasir doesn't matter. It was a mistake. It was over in a week."

Ardis glowered at his wound. "Why didn't you kill him?"

"It wasn't that easy."

"Do you still have feelings for him?"

"God, no." He grimaced. "But I don't want my only solution to be death."

"That's surprisingly merciful of you."

"Thank you," Wendel muttered.

"If he touches you again," Ardis said, "I'll kill him myself."

Wendel's mouth twisted into a wry smile.

"Your ferocity is touching." His smile faltered. "I can't believe he found me. I can't believe the Grandmaster knows I'm alive."

"Did you expect to stay dead forever?" Ardis said lightly.

Wendel arched his eyebrows. "An unmarked grave was nice while it lasted."

The silver skin of the USS *Jupiter* gleamed in the noonday sun. Ardis and Wendel strode across Aspern Airfield, the frosty grass crunching beneath their boots. They stopped beneath the mammoth shadow of the airship.

Konstantin waved. "Ardis! Wendel!"

He had a wild glint in his eyes, his hair already windblown, and Ardis suspected he had been too busy to sleep while tinkering with the clockwork wasp last night. She wouldn't be surprised if he were running on coffee.

"This is it," Konstantin said. "Our ticket to Königsberg."

Ardis nodded at Himmel and Ursula, the doctor from the *Wanderfalke*. Konstantin beckoned everyone and bounded onto the mooring mast. Ursula marched upstairs next, her sensible heels clicking, her doctor's bag swinging in her hand. Himmel climbed more sluggishly, his right arm still cradled in a sling.

Ardis nudged Wendel with a hand between his shoulders. "Up you go."

He dug his heels into the grass. "Forgive me if I'm not thrilled to fly to Prussia on an airship. I don't like flying. Or airships. Or Prussia."

"Tough luck."

Wendel hauled himself up the mooring mast. He gripped the railings with white knuckles. As Ardis climbed after him, she saw a raven riding the wind. Krampus circled the tower, fanned his wings, and landed on the stairs.

Directly in front of Wendel.

Wendel stared down at the raven. "Excuse me."

Krampus cocked his head. His black feathers glistened violet in the sun.

"You brat," Wendel said. "I know you want to be a stowaway."

"*Grok.*"

Wendel let out a long-suffering sigh. He held out his arm. The raven flew to his wrist, then hopped to his shoulder.

"How could you ever abandon Krampus?" Ardis teased.

Wendel scoffed. "Easily."

But he bit back a smile as the raven nibbled his hair.

When they boarded the USS *Jupiter*, Yeoman Kay, the American with the fiery hair greeted them.

"Welcome back aboard," Kay said. "Our estimated flight time is six hours."

On the observation deck, Ardis settled in a chair and indulged herself in the luxury of relaxation. The airship cast off from the mooring mast. They soared above Vienna and floated over whipped-cream clouds. The airship's engines droned in her ears, and her eyelids slipped shut.

At the sound of footsteps, Ardis opened her eyes. Wendel walked to the windows, Krampus hopping behind him.

"Were you sleeping?" he said.

Ardis blinked. Sunset painted the clouds pink. "What time is it?"

"Six o'clock."

"Already?" She hid a yawn behind her hand. "Where are we?"

Wendel tapped his finger on the glass. "East Prussia."

Ardis moved to the window, gazing out at a vast stretch of steely water. Ice frosted the coast and fragmented into shards farther from shore. The temperature had fallen by several degrees. Krampus shivered and puffed his feathers to twice his normal size.

"The Baltic Sea?" Ardis said.

"No. The Frisches Haff. A freshwater lagoon." Wendel pointed across a thin spit of sand. "There's the Baltic."

She nodded, though she had never been to Prussia before.

"Look," he said. "You can see the castle in Königsberg."

Ardis peered down the lagoon. At the opposite shore, if she squinted, she could make out the reddish stone towers of a castle.

Her heartbeat did a strange little skip. "Your castle?"

"It was never mine." Wendel rested his hand on the glass. "Though I have entertained the thought of liberating my inheritance."

She rolled her eyes. "You can't steal a castle."

A smile curled his mouth. "But you can conquer it."

"Really?"

"I wouldn't. I'm not that evil."

"Thank goodness," Ardis deadpanned.

She straightened the collar of his shirt. Judging by his eyebrows, Wendel was bemused by her efforts to tidy his clothes.

"Are you ready for this?" she said.

Wendel looked at her with a bastard's smirk, but his eyes betrayed his fear. "Prussia? I doubt they are ready for me."

The USS *Jupiter* glided low over the lagoon on its final descent. It hovered over a pebbled beach and silenced its engines. Landing lines dropped, and men on the ground walked the airship into an immense shed.

Ardis and Wendel disembarked from the airship together. Krampus perched on Wendel's shoulder. The raven gurgled like a pigeon, the feathers at his throat bristling. Konstantin halted them at the bottom of the stairs.

"Your minion stays outside," Konstantin said.

Wendel managed to look worthy of a halo. "Who? Krampus?"

A crimson blush colored Konstantin's face. He jabbed his finger at the raven, but Tesla strode down the stairs on his lanky legs.

"Mr. Tesla!" Konstantin said. "Ready for the tour?"

Tesla smiled. "Quite."

When they stepped from the airship shed, a bitter wind whipped their hair and stung their eyes. Ardis squinted and lowered her head. Krampus leapt into the air and sliced sideways through the wind. The raven vanished in the trees. They hurried across a gloomy field to a shipyard on the lagoon. A giant industrial building dominated the scene. As they walked closer, Ardis realized it had to be a roofed drydock.

Two guards bundled in furs saluted them at the doors.

"Archmage," one of the guards said. "Welcome back."

Konstantin squared his shoulders. "Mr. Tesla will be touring the facilities."

The guards hauled open the door with the groan of heavy steel. Tesla glanced at Ardis and waved her onward like a gentleman. She stepped into the drydock, but didn't make it far before stumbling to a halt.

A gargantuan Eisenkrieger dominated the space.

It towered over thirty feet tall, its massive metal feet planted on the concrete, its hollow head nearly bumping the rafters. A sputtering of sparks glittered from the Eisenkrieger's face as an engineer welded steel in the cockpit. It looked like a brutally effective work of engineering, still all raw wires and rough steel.

Tesla stroked his mustache. "Remarkable!"

"Isn't it?" Konstantin said.

The archmage ran across the floor, his coat flying behind him, and patted the Eisenkrieger's foot like an adoring father.

"Our latest prototype," Konstantin said.

Wendel sneered it with obligatory disdain, though the widening of his eyes betrayed his wariness. Ardis judged Wendel to be six feet tall, but his head had no hope of reaching the Eisenkrieger's knee.

Tesla stood with his hands on his hips and looked the Eisenkrieger up and down. "Is this prototype operational?"

"Yes, sir," Konstantin said. "Care for a demonstration?"

"Please."

Konstantin sprang into action. He signaled for the engineer to stop welding in the cockpit, then flagged down another man. "Find Commander Volkova."

The man saluted and scurried away.

"Pardon me," Wendel said, "but isn't Volkova a Russian name?"

Konstantin glared at the necromancer. "Natalya Volkova has worked for the archmages for years. Her loyalty is absolute. She would never sabotage the prototypes, not even to protest an army of mechanical men."

Wendel coughed, since he had done exactly that.

"I'm not looking forward to this," Ardis said. "Not after the cemetery."

"Speak of the devil," Wendel said.

Ardis gritted her teeth and turned around.

Natalya Volkova advanced on them. She had a tailored black uniform, and a look colder than a glacier. Her blonde hair gleamed blue beneath the fluorescent light. Her hand closed on the hilt of her rapier.

Ardis touched her cheek, remembering that blade's paralyzing sting.

"Archmage." Natalya saluted somewhat casually. "Reporting for duty, sir."

Konstantin returned the salute. "Commander Volkova."

"You again?" Natalya challenged Ardis with a stare. "Are you lost, darling?"

Damn. This wasn't going to be easy, was it?

"Commander," Ardis said. "I realize we didn't part on the best of terms—"

"You pinned me with my own sword." Natalya's lips thinned in a smile. "It would have been convenient to kill me in the cemetery."

Ardis grimaced. "You didn't kill me on the *Dresden*."

"Sorry for pistol-whipping you. That wasn't part of the plan."

"Are we even?"

"Maybe." Natalya flicked her eyebrows upward. "Are you back for more?"

"I'm here to work for you, Commander." Ardis kept her voice level. "Archmage Margareta assigned me to be an Eisenkrieger test pilot."

Natalya threw back her head and laughed. "You? Working for me?"

"Yes, ma'am."

"Sweetheart, I like your style." Natalya smirked. "You remind me of myself when I was your age. And I could use another underling."

Ardis exhaled. "Thank you."

Konstantin smoothed his hair. "We don't want to keep Mr. Tesla waiting. Natalya, I want you to pilot the prototype."

"Which one?" Natalya said.

"The Colossus."

Natalya had a crooked smirk. "Yes, sir."

Commander Volkova swaggered to the prototype, climbed a stairwell in the scaffolding, and crossed a gangway to the cockpit. Konstantin sat in a chair and wheeled himself over to a desk with a wireless telegraph.

Tesla clasped his hands behind his back and bent over the archmage's shoulder. "How do you control the Eisenkriegers?"

"Technomancy." Konstantin's face reddened. "Though the control systems in the Eisenkriegers still have a slight issue with interference. As a consequence, we can't operate more than one prototype at the same time."

Tesla gazed at the Colossus. "And the power?"

"Hybrid," Konstantin said. "Electricity and technomancy."

With a rumble, the Colossus hummed to life. A light shone inside the barebones cockpit, illuminating Natalya's face. Konstantin telegraphed a message and held the wireless receiver to his ear.

"Ready?" Konstantin said. "Everyone clear the way."

Ardis hurried to stand by the archmage. Wendel lurked behind Tesla.

Pneumatics hissed and steel groaned in protest as the Eisenkrieger disengaged from the scaffold. Its first footfall boomed against the concrete. It crossed the room in three easy strides and towered over them. Ardis backed away out of instinct. The Eisenkrieger saluted, naked gears whirring in its arm.

High in the cockpit, Natalya waved down at them.

"A most impressive demonstration," Tesla said.

Konstantin's face flamed. "Thank you," he stammered. "It would be my pleasure to show you more of Project Lazarus."

Tesla nodded. "I'm particularly interested in your control systems."

Konstantin fished a pocketwatch from his coat and clicked open the case. "Perhaps we might talk more at the castle?"

"Certainly," Tesla said.

His eyes shadowed, Wendel stepped between the two of them. "The castle? Why?"

Konstantin picked at a thread on his sleeve. "We were invited to dinner."

"We were?"

"Everyone, that is, except you."

Hurt flashed across Wendel's face.

"Your family still believes you to be dead," Konstantin said. "You should be the one to inform them of the truth."

Wendel stared at his boots and failed to find a sarcastic retort.

Night fell on Königsberg. Hail bounced off the cobblestones and rattled on the roof of their sleek black automobile. Ardis peered out the window at the brick buildings, wrought-iron lampposts, and townspeople shielding their heads with umbrellas or newspapers. It hardly looked like a city under threat of invasion.

Wendel sat with his eyes shut, his cheek resting against the leather of the seat.

Ardis admired how handsome he looked in a black swallowtail coat and white waistcoat. They had both bought eveningwear suitable for tonight, though she was less fond of her gown. She smoothed the tangerine silk across her lap, then tugged her shawl around her shoulders. Gowns always felt too flimsy. She hadn't bothered with gloves, jewelry, or heeled shoes, but had brought her sword in its scabbard.

To hell with the latest fashion.

"How close are we to the castle?" Ardis said.

Wendel didn't even look. "Close."

"Don't be sarcastic."

Wendel's jaw tightened, and he opened his eyes to give her a cool look. "Go on without me."

Ardis snorted. "You know Konstantin won't like that. And he won't leave you alone with Project Lazarus. Not after last time."

Wendel glared out the window. "You know why I did it."

"That doesn't make it right."

He drummed his fingers on his knee. "Sabotaging the Eisenkriegers accomplished nothing. I was foolish to think it would slow the war."

"With the Russians knocking," she said, "now we need the Eisenkriegers."

"Need?" He stared into her eyes. "Do we need to find new ways to die?"

She didn't look away. "That's bleak even for you. I prefer to think of ways to survive."

"Suit yourself."

"Breathe," she said. "Tonight won't kill you."

Wendel worked his jaw like he was chewing on his words. "I don't want to go home. It isn't home anymore."

She reached across and clasped his hand. "I know."

The automobile rolled to a stop. They glanced out the window.

Königsberg Castle loomed over the city. Its towers disappeared in the underbelly of the clouds. Ardis almost expected lightning to flash. The driver opened the door, and they stepped into the wind and the hail.

Ardis tucked her sword into the sash of her gown and faced the weather. "There's Konstantin."

The archmage hurried toward the doors of the castle. Himmel and Tesla followed him.

"Pardon?" Wendel said by her ear.

He obviously hadn't heard her over the weather. She grabbed his hand and dragged him toward the castle's doors. The closer they walked, the tighter his grip became. Finally, she twisted her fingers free and winced.

Wendel didn't notice, his stare locked on the castle. He faltered by the door, then pressed his hand to the wood and pushed it open, holding it for Ardis. She stepped inside, glancing at him as she passed.

She could see it in his eyes—the urge to run and not stop running.

"Wendel," she said.

He blinked, lowered his head, and followed her into the castle. The door shut behind them with a resounding thud.

When Ardis looked around, she gasped.

She had been in one or two castles before, but none nearly as grand as Königsberg. The entrance hall stretched before them with walls paneled in mahogany and floors carpeted in Turkish rugs. Candles glowed like a constellation of stars. The air felt warm on her rain-chilled skin, scented with beeswax and an aroma like faded rose perfume.

"What a beautiful castle," Ardis whispered.

"Why are you whispering?" Wendel said. "This isn't a church."

He glanced around with supreme disinterest. Even with his scars and his ragged hair, she could see he had belonged here once, long ago. It wasn't hard to imagine him as a prince, wearing a prince's regalia.

Wendel's eyebrows descended. "Why are you looking at me like that?"

Ardis didn't know how to tell him any of it without sounding hopelessly sad. He touched her arm with his fingertips.

"Are you all right?" he said.

His concern, and his complete disregard for his own feelings, made her smile.

"Don't worry about me," Ardis said. "We have to find the dining room."

Wendel didn't seem convinced, but he looked away. "The castle has more than one dining room."

"I should have known."

"We should go to the drawing room. Guests gather there before dinner."

Wendel walked down a hallway to the right guarded by suits of armor. Ardis traced her fingers over the engraved and gilded steel. It must have cost a king's ransom only a few centuries ago. Wendel halted outside a closed door. Light slivered underneath and shone on the toes of his shoes.

Ardis tilted her head toward the murmur of conversation. "I hear them."

Wendel's hand closed on the doorknob. He stood that way for a silent moment, his eyes distant, and rubbed his thumb over the polished brass.

He opened the door and stepped aside with a bow of his head. "Ladies first."

Ardis rolled her eyes. "I'm hardly a lady."

She tugged her shawl straight and walked into the drawing room.

A chandelier shimmered like a cascade of crystal from a ceiling adorned with plasterwork angels. Tesla leaned against an ornate fireplace, his elbow on a dragon carved from granite. Konstantin and Himmel sat shoulder to shoulder on a gilded loveseat, talking with a raven-haired lady in a tiara—Juliana, Princess of Prussia. Wendel's sister. Behind her stood Wolfram, Prince of Prussia. Wendel's little brother.

Wendel lingered on the threshold. All but invisible to his family.

"Introduce yourself," Ardis murmured.

Wendel sucked in a slow breath, then strode into the center of the drawing room and brought the conversation to a halt.

Perhaps that wasn't such a good suggestion.

"Good evening, everyone," Wendel said. "I'm back."

FOURTEEN

glass shattered. Wine darkened the floor like a bloodstain. Juliana sprang to her feet as if stung, her earrings swinging. "How are you still alive?"

Wendel sneered. "Pardon?"

"You burned that ballroom in Vienna to the ground."

"I walked away." Wendel spread his arms. "Don't look so disappointed."

Wolfram clutched the back of a couch, then walked to Wendel and held out his hand. Wendel stared down at Wolfram, who wasn't quite as tall, then grabbed his little brother's hand and dragged him into a crushing hug.

"I knew you would come back," Wolfram said, his words muffled.

Wendel's face tightened, and he closed his eyes for a moment. He stepped away and clapped his brother on the back.

"Where are Mother and Father?" Wendel said.

"You didn't tell them you were coming, did you?" Wolfram whistled. "Christ, Wendel."

Behind Ardis, a breeze drafted from the door. Someone cleared their throat.

Ardis sidestepped. "Sorry."

A lady regarded Ardis with jade green eyes and a flawless smile.

Diamond earrings quivered by her slender neck. Silver glinted throughout her black hair, the color echoed in her shimmering gown of silk and lace.

"Are you here for the dinner?" said the lady.

She spoke English with an accent reminiscent of British royalty.

"Yes, ma'am," Ardis said. "I should be the mercenary on the guest list."

The lady inclined her head. "Lady Cecelia. Welcome to Königsberg."

Wendel stared at the carpet like he wished for nothing less than invisibility. His face was no more than a blank white mask.

Cecelia frowned at him, then touched her gloved fingers to her mouth.

"Oh, good God," she whispered.

Wendel looked at her with a distant sadness in his eyes.

"Mother," he said. "It's me."

With a quivering smile, Cecelia reached for him. Wendel's shoulders stiffened, but he allowed her to embrace him. He stooped to her height, patted her shoulder like she was porcelain, and retreated from her touch.

"My poor Wendel." Cecelia touched his cheekbone. "What have they done to you?"

Wendel closed his eyes. When he opened them again, he had buried his emotions deep. He stared at his mother with nothing but haughty disinterest on his face. Like he didn't give a damn what she thought about him.

"You know what they did to me," Wendel said. "You sent me there."

Cecelia sighed. "Wendy, dear, we had no choice."

"Please don't call me that." His fingers curled into fists. "Wendy died a long time ago."

Cecelia flared her nostrils, her chest heaving against her corset. She seemed to be struggling to keep a stiff upper lip.

Ardis coughed, aware of everyone in the room staring at them.

The door swept open, and a man marched into the drawing room. Uniformed in Prussian blue, he had polished boots and a salt-and-pepper beard. A plethora of ribbons and medals decorated the front of his jacket.

He stopped dead and stared at Wendel. The color drained from his face.

"My God," the man said.

"Waldemar," Cecelia said. "Our eldest son has returned."

Waldemar's mouth hardened. "He wasn't invited."

"Isn't this my home?" Wendel said. "No, wait, I'm sorry. For one heartwarming moment, I forgot I was disinherited."

Father and son stared at each other with eyes cold enough to rival the winter.

Konstantin climbed to his feet and cleared his throat. His hands looked a little shaky, and he clasped them behind his back.

"I must apologize," Konstantin said. "I have neglected my introductions."

Waldemar looked at Konstantin, who quailed under his glacial stare.

"Archmage," Waldemar said. "Were you the one who invited him here?"

"Yes, your highness," Konstantin stammered. "Wendel has agreed to work with the archmages on Project Lazarus."

"Explain."

Konstantin dipped his head. "His necromancy has proved invaluable."

"Has it?"

Waldemar curled his lip, looked Wendel up and down, then turned his back on him. "Dinner is served." He offered his arm to Cecelia with stiff formality.

The couple swept from the drawing room, and their guests followed suit.

They crossed the hall to a dining room. It looked even grander than the drawing room, with walls paneled in carved mahogany, but Ardis found it hard to appreciate the furnishings. Wendel had a dark look in his eyes, and she hoped he didn't intend to do something drastic. She touched the taut muscles in his arm.

"Wendel," Ardis said quietly. "We can go."

He lowered his gaze. "No."

Elegant ivory cards marked their places. Waldemar stood at the head of the table and waited for the guests to find their seats. Just as everyone bustled into the dining room, two more guests arrived breathlessly—Natalya and Ursula. Both of them looked windblown, raindrops glittering in their hair.

"Sorry for our late arrival," Natalya said. "We encountered a delay."

Waldemar dismissed her comment with an imperious wave of his hand.

As Ardis reached her chair, Natalya intercepted her. The blonde caught her by the wrist and whispered in her ear.

"Darling," Natalya said, "can you keep a secret?"

Ardis put on her poker face. "Why?"

"Trouble."

"What kind of trouble?"

"A man in black was lurking behind the airship shed," Natalya said. "He got away."

Ardis would bet money on an assassin. Her stomach twisted into a knot. "Understood."

With the grace of blissful ignorance, Cecelia glided to the foot of the table. Tesla, as the guest of honor, sat to her left. He drew out Cecelia's chair, and she thanked him with a nod. Tesla, Natalya, Wolfram, and Juliana sat on one side of the table, while Konstantin, Ardis, Himmel, and Ursula sat on the other.

There was, of course, no place for Wendel.

"Wendel," Cecelia said, "I'm afraid we weren't expecting an eleventh guest."

Juliana had a chiming laugh. "At the eleventh hour."

Wendel waited by the doors, his cheekbones stark in the

shadows, and clenched his hands. He looked as though he wanted to knock a candelabra from the table and burn down the dining room. Which wouldn't be the first time.

Konstantin lingered behind his chair. "Wendel, you are welcome to sit by me."

Wendel blinked as though surprised by the archmage's kindness. "Thank you."

A footman carried another chair into the room and placed it at the corner of the table, between Konstantin and Cecelia. Wendel sat tentatively, as if this might be a trap. He leaned sideways to allow the footman to set his place.

Himmel smoothed his napkin in his lap. "I could use a drink."

"Wine will be served with dinner," Waldemar said.

Wendel ran a fingertip over his glass. "Alcohol might make this tolerable."

Waldemar's mustache bristled, but he didn't take the bait.

Juliana's lips curved into a little smile. "Why return, Wendy, if you find us so intolerable? Are you suffering from amnesia?"

"Anyone would suffer in your company," Wendel said.

His sister gifted him with an icy smile. "I missed your witty little remarks."

Footmen entered the dining room and delivered a first course of beetroot soup. Sour cream swirled in the purple. Ardis swallowed a spoonful. It tasted rich and savory, but she wasn't sure her stomach could tolerate it.

Why was an assassin stalking them? Who was his target?

It could be anyone. Wendel, for defying Thorsten. Konstantin, for building Project Lazarus. Waldemar, for fighting the Russians.

Ardis pretended to straighten her napkin and touched the pommel of Chun Yi.

She wasn't sure who to protect, but was ready to fight.

"Wine, madam?" said a footman.

He leaned over her elbow and held out a bottle of white wine.

"Yes, please," Ardis said.

The footman poured her half a glass. She brought it to her lips and rolled it over her tongue. The wine tasted like honeycomb, apricots, and lemon blossoms. Its fleeting warmth felt like sunshine under her skin.

"A 1890 Riesling," Waldemar said. "One of my favorite vintages."

Wendel rested his cheek on his knuckles and watched a footman pour him a glass.

"The same vintage as me," Wendel said. "Though I'm clearly not as favored."

Ardis gripped her wineglass. "Wendel. Please."

His smirk didn't convince her. She could see the hurt in his eyes, since he wasn't nearly as good at hiding it as he thought, but being a bastard wouldn't win anyone's heart.

Tesla sipped his soup. "Konstantin, I have been pondering the control systems of your Eisenkriegers. I may be able to help."

Konstantin perked up. "Your help would be most appreciated."

"Have you heard of my work on teleautomatons?"

"No, Mr. Tesla."

Tesla smiled. "Please, call me Nikola."

Konstantin's eyes looked starry. "Yes, Nikola."

Himmel harrumphed, but the archmage didn't seem to hear.

"By all means," Konstantin said, "tell me more about your teleautomatons."

Tesla dabbed his mustache with a napkin and dropped a cracker into his soup. "At the Electrical Exhibition of 1898, my invention caused quite a sensation in New York City. I floated a miniature boat in a pool at Madison Square Garden. I could control this teleautomaton by radio waves."

Tesla blew on the cracker, which floated across his bowl of soup.

Wolfram, who had been silent, piped up. "How did it work?"

"Wireless telegraphy," Tesla said. "I transmitted signals to the teleautomaton, which responded by changing its course."

Cecelia cocked her head, her diamond earrings glittering in the candlelight. "Oh, how marvelous!"

Tesla smiled with a faraway look in his eyes. "I found the invention marvelous myself, though I never interested the Americans in my idea for wireless torpedo boats. They didn't understand the science. But my work might benefit the archmages now."

"Please, Nikola," Konstantin said. "Go on."

Tesla nodded. "I would like to perform some experiments with the necromancer."

Wendel, who had been drinking, sputtered and wiped his mouth with a napkin. "Excuse me?"

Tesla managed to look mild. "Konstantin and I talked on the way. I understand your necromancy inspired the control systems of the Eisenkriegers. The archmage's technomancy mimics how your magic commands the dead."

Waldemar reddened at the mention of necromancy.

Wendel narrowed his eyes. "Correct."

"Then you will allow me to experiment," Tesla said, "for the good of Project Lazarus."

"How can I refuse?" Wendel deadpanned.

Konstantin glared at him. "Not in the light of recent events."

Wendel sighed and fidgeted with his spoon.

The footmen whisked away the bowls from the table and served a second course. Ardis stared at the tiny filet of salmon on her plate, the fish drowned in hollandaise sauce and decorated with thinly sliced cucumber.

"More wine?" said a footman.

"Please," she said.

She was going to need it to get through this dinner.

Himmel took his knife in his left hand and clumsily tried to cut the salmon. It slid to the edge of his plate. He sawed off a sliver of fish, dropped the knife, and grabbed his fork. Konstantin watched with worried eyes until Himmel caught him staring. Konstantin looked away and ate a forkful of salmon.

Ardis wanted to help, but didn't want to insult the captain.

"Archmage," Wendel said, "you might want to help Teddy."

Himmel gave him a deadly glare. "No, thank you, Wendy."

"Are you sure, Teddy dearest?" Wendel said through clenched teeth.

"Quite sure, Wendy."

Konstantin stared at his plate, unblinking, and heaved a sigh.

Cecelia pursed her lips. "Captain Himmel, I couldn't help but notice your arm. Were you injured in the line of duty?"

Himmel inspected the tines of his fork. His face looked blank. "I lived, but I lost a lot of good men."

Cecelia touched her throat. "You have our condolences."

"Thank you."

A muscle twitched in Wendel's jaw. "Condolences won't bring back the dead."

Juliana laughed. "That's your privilege, Wendel."

Waldemar slammed his fist on the table and rattled the silverware. "Enough. There will be no necromancy at this dinner."

Wendel stared at him with blatant hostility. "Then I should go."

"You should have never returned."

Wendel tossed down his napkin and shoved his chair back.

"Waldemar!" Cecelia said. "Wendel!"

The volume of her voice startled everyone at the table.

Cecelia's earrings quivered. "Sit. Down."

Silence reigned.

Konstantin coughed and drank some wine. He choked, swallowed, and held a napkin to his mouth. His fingers trembled.

"Archmage?" Wendel said. "Konstantin?"

Konstantin tried to speak, but he was silenced by a hacking cough.

Himmel's eyes flashed. "Doctor! He's choking."

Ursula leapt to her feet and ran to Konstantin, who crumpled the napkin in his fist. He sucked in a shuddering breath.

"No," Konstantin said hoarsely. "Not choking."

Ursula held his wrist and took his pulse. Her mouth hardened. "Look at me."

Konstantin blinked and met her gaze. His eyes looked dark.

"Your pupils are dilated," Ursula said, "and your heart rate is too high. Konstantin, are you allergic to anything?"

He furrowed his brow and nodded.

Ursula thinned her mouth. "Allergic to what?"

Konstantin tried to reply, but that triggered another coughing fit.

"Get my bag," Ursula said. "Quickly."

A footman ran out and returned with the doctor's bag. Ursula readied a syringe of adrenaline, rolled up Konstantin's sleeve, and stabbed the needle into his arm. Wincing, Konstantin managed a single word.

"*Solanum,*" he rasped.

"Solanum?" Waldemar said. "Is he speaking in tongues?"

Ursula ignored him. "Konstantin, are you allergic to all solanum species?"

He stared at the table, his face as pale as parchment.

"Think," Ursula said.

"Never this badly." He exhaled. "Slight reaction to tomatoes."

Cecelia twisted her napkin in her hands. "But there were no tomatoes in tonight's dinner. I planned the menu with our chef."

"I abhor tomatoes," Waldemar said.

"Tomatoes aren't my concern at the moment," Ursula said. "Solanum is the proper name for the nightshade family."

Nightshade. Ardis clenched her hands, her fingernails biting into her palms.

Himmel blanched. "Doctor, is the archmage poisoned?"

"Yes." Ursula remained remarkably calm. "Who ate any of the second course?"

Juliana shoved her plate away. "I did. Am I poisoned as well?"

"Nightshade poisoning takes one to two hours. You have time

for the antidote."

"And the archmage?" Himmel said.

"Konstantin has a weakness to nightshade," Ursula said, "thanks to his otherwise slight allergy to solanum species."

The captain clenched his jaw. "Will he be all right?"

"The adrenaline will counteract the anaphylaxis."

Himmel squinted. "Meaning?"

"He should be fine."

Konstantin managed a smile. "Only ate one bite."

Wendel stared at his untouched plate. Then he turned on his heel and advanced on the four footmen who stood by the table.

"Father," Wendel said, "have you hired any new servants lately?"

Waldemar's eyes darkened. "No."

Wendel stalked down the row of footmen. All of them stood at attention, and each looked equally anxious. The first was sweating; the second had a twitch in his eyelid; the third and fourth stared into space.

"Untie your cravats," Wendel said.

The first footman glanced at the lady of the house. "Your highness?"

"Do as he says," Cecelia said.

He loosened a crisp white cravat knotted in a bow at his neck. The others followed his lead.

"Turn around," Wendel said.

Each of the footmen faced the wall. Wendel stared at the backs of their heads. He pinched the fourth footman's cravat and whisked it away, then grabbed a fistful of the footman's hair and yanked his head toward the floor.

A double-headed eagle blackened the man's neck.

Ardis gasped and grabbed her sword. That very tattoo darkened Wendel's neck, a mark from the Order of the Asphodel.

"This man is an assassin," Wendel said.

FIFTEEN

The footman struggled, but Wendel slammed his face onto the table and wrenched his arm back at a sickening angle.

Waldemar lunged to his feet. "Gustav? Preposterous!"

The other three footmen stood petrified along the wall.

"When did you hire him?" Wendel said.

"Over a year ago. He's a good Hessian lad!"

Gustav squirmed and groped for a knife on the table. Wendel hauled him away and held the black dagger to his throat.

"Give me an excuse," Wendel murmured.

Gustav swallowed, his Adam's apple bobbing close to the blade. He looked like a lad, as Waldemar had said, not more than eighteen years old. Or perhaps his cornflower blue eyes granted him a deceptive innocence.

"Sir," Gustav said. "Please. Let me speak."

Wendel's eyes burned with fire. "Do you know who I am?"

"Yes." Gustav blinked rapidly. "The princeling assassin."

"I hate that nickname."

Gustav flinched. "It's what they all say."

"You trained with the assassins in Constantinople?"

Gustav nodded. "It was either this or the army. They recruited me and sent me to infiltrate the castle at Königsberg."

Wendel bared his teeth and took a step back. "Tell the Grandmaster not to send boys."

"Wendel!" Waldemar bellowed the word. "Don't you dare let him go. This worm of a coward betrayed our family."

A dark look shadowed Wendel's face. He angled his dagger.

"Our family?" he said, with frosty precision.

Waldemar reddened, his face blotchy. "He tried to poison us all."

"He *did* poison us all," Himmel said, and he touched Konstantin's arm.

Ardis drew her sword and advanced on Gustav. "Wendel. We can't let him leave."

Gustav's eyes glistened. "Please. I should have never agreed. It was a mistake."

The necromancer inspected him with cold scrutiny. "The only mistake was you being such a terrible assassin."

Wendel raised Amarant. The black dagger gleamed in the candlelight.

Cecelia muffled a shriek. "No!"

Wendel halted. "Would it be bad manners to kill a footman in the dining room?"

"Stop," Cecelia said, flying to her feet. "Someone, call for the police."

Wendel lowered his dagger. Gustav eyed him, then muttered under his breath.

"What?" Wendel said.

Gustav raised his voice. "I wasn't the only assassin."

Wendel swore and hit Gustav's head with the pommel of his dagger. Gustav crumpled, his eyelids fluttering shut.

Ursula crouched by Gustav. "He's unconscious. I could have sedated him."

"Right, doctor," Wendel said, with immense sarcasm. "Remind me of that tactic the next time we face an enemy."

Natalya sprang to her feet. "How many assassins?"

"How should I know?" Wendel said.

"Sweetheart. You could have asked him before you knocked him out."

Waldemar's chair screeched across the floor. "Everyone remain calm. I will order the drivers to bring your cars around, and then we will exit the dining room together."

Ardis shook her head. "There might be assassins waiting."

Waldemar glared as if this would silence her, but she didn't blink.

"We better not walk into an ambush," Ardis said. "Wendel and I can scout ahead and make sure the coast is clear."

"I'll stay here," Natalya said. "Didn't think I'd need my rapier at a dinner party."

Tesla, Juliana, and Wolfram sat at the table like statues. Himmel stood behind Konstantin, his hand on the back of his chair.

"Hurry," Himmel said. "Konstantin is still poisoned."

"I'm feeling much better," the archmage said, rather feebly.

Himmel looked down at him. "I don't want to take any chances."

"He's right," Ursula said. "We need the antidote to nightshade."

"Wait here," Ardis said.

She sounded more confident than she felt. Her stomach wormed with fear. Wendel took her by the elbow and walked her from the dining room. In the hallway, he bent down by her ear and spoke in a hushed voice.

"The archmage isn't the only target," Wendel said.

"I know," Ardis murmured. "If the Russians hired the assassins, they would benefit by killing the entire dinner party."

He smiled thinly. "Shall we kill them first?"

Ardis nodded, though she still wondered why Wendel had shown mercy to Gustav, the assassin with such young eyes.

Maybe he didn't want his little brother Wolfram to see him as a murderer.

"This way," Wendel said.

Ardis followed him down the hallway. She held her sword at a low angle, Chun Yi smoldering and spitting cinders.

"Where should we look?" Ardis said. "This castle is so damn big."

Wendel furrowed his brow. "Gustav was hired over a year ago. Likely as more of a spy than an assassin. It would be a waste to force anyone decent to work as a footman for that long. Which means he wasn't alone."

"Gustav already told us that," Ardis said.

Wendel stopped by a window. He peeked through the curtains at the darkening clouds. "I wonder who brought him the nightshade."

"The real assassin," Ardis said. "I assume Gustav would report back to him. Shouldn't we check with the butler?"

Wendel arched an eyebrow. "The butler?"

Her cheeks warmed. "Don't butlers keep track of footmen?"

"They do. Though I'm surprised you know."

"We had rich people in San Francisco."

Wendel's smile came and went within an instant. "I remember a shortcut."

He walked no more than few paces down the hallway, then stroked the wood paneling. His fingertips lingered on a twisted carving. Under his touch, a hidden door clicked open. A dim corridor stretched both left and right.

"A secret passageway," Wendel said. "The castle is riddled with them."

"What for?" Ardis said.

He looked at her like this was obvious. "So the servants won't be seen."

"Where does this one go?"

"Downstairs to the kitchen. Eventually."

Wendel stepped toward the shadows, but Ardis caught him by the arm.

"We don't know who's in there," she said.

"Servants?"

She grimaced. "If you wanted to poison an entire dinner party, wouldn't you hide in the walls and wait for them to die?"

"No." He had the gall to sound offended. "I'd kill them myself."

"Wendel."

"Poison is chancy. Particularly in the hands of an idiotic footman."

"Wendel! I get it. In your professional opinion as an assassin, this nightshade business was a complete fiasco. But we need to think like someone who wants to stay hidden. Someone who doesn't mind sacrificing Gustav."

"Gustav was unnecessary."

Wendel stared into the shadows. He still seemed to care about Gustav's fate.

"Thorsten Magnusson will do anything," Ardis said, "for a price."

"I would kill him for free," he muttered.

She sighed. "I know."

After a heartbeat of indecision, Ardis sheathed her sword. She hated to do it, but Chun Yi's magic was anything but stealthy.

"Wendel." Ardis found his hand and laced her fingers between his.

"Yes?" he said.

"Shadows, please."

Wendel dipped his head in a bow. "My pleasure."

He slipped Amarant from his coat pocket. The icy fire of his necromancy tingled over her skin as his fingers tightened around hers. Darkness swirled from the black dagger like ink clouding water. The shadows unfurled and shrouded Wendel, then spiderwebbed from his hand to Ardis. She held her breath as the magic cloaked her. It felt like a thin veil over her mouth. All but invisible, she let herself inhale.

"Ready?" Wendel whispered, his breath warming her ear.

Ardis nodded, then wondered if he could even see her. "Let's go."

Together, they stepped into the secret passageway. Wendel's footsteps were soundless, and Ardis tried to muffle her shoes. Stone cooled the mildewed air. The passageway narrowed and turned within the castle walls.

"I can barely see," Ardis said.

"Quiet," Wendel whispered.

His grip tightened on her hand. Through the wall on the left, faint voices murmured. The dinner party. Ardis shivered, wondering if the assassin was waiting for silence. Light outlined the shape of a secret door.

The door stood opposite the dining room. Where did it go?

Ardis wanted to ask Wendel, but didn't want to betray their position. She waited for him to walk, but he stood motionless.

Holding his breath.

The shadows moved. The shape of a man separated from the darkness.

An assassin.

Wendel lifted his foot and placed it with care. Ardis tiptoed after him. Her boot scuffed the stone. She froze, her heartbeat hammering, and swore in her head. Wendel clamped her hand so tight that her bones ached.

The assassin in the darkness bolted for the door.

Wendel lunged after him and dropped Ardis's hand. Shadows evaporated from them as they ran and leapt into a dark study. The assassin dodged around a writing desk. Wendel vaulted over it and landed behind him.

Only seconds ahead, the assassin shoved through the door.

Wendel and Ardis chased him down the hall. The assassin darted through another door and slammed it behind him.

A deadbolt lock clicked.

Wendel swore. "There's another passageway by—"

Ardis hitched up her gown and kicked down the door.

It splintered open to reveal a dimly lit library that looked deserted. Moonlight glimmered on the gilded spines of books.

Ardis drew her sword. She stalked to the velvet curtains and poked them with the point of her blade. Nothing. She checked the latches on the windows. Locked. Wendel stared at the bookshelves, then snapped his fingers.

"*The History of Fishes*," he said.

"What?" Ardis said.

"That book. Find it."

"Why?"

"Trust me."

Ardis went to the nearest bookshelf and craned her neck sideways to peer at the books. One shelf over, Wendel skimmed his fingertips over their spines. He muttered under his breath, then found a tome bound in red leather.

"Here."

Wendel tilted the book forward. With a clunk, the bookshelf swung forward to reveal yet another secret passageway.

"Where does this one go?" Ardis said.

"To the cellars." Wendel glanced at her burning sword. "Are you planning to walk down there with that on display?"

She scowled and put away her sword. "No."

Wendel took her wrist with a gentleman's touch. His necromancy reawakened the magic of Amarant, and darkness cloaked them again.

Together, they walked downstairs into the underground.

The cellar beneath the castle stretched into shadows. The sweet musty scent of wine and oak steeped the air. A flickering candlestick burned atop a wine barrel, illuminating an elderly man who sat bound and gagged in a chair. Blood trickled from his temple and dripped onto his immaculate white shirt.

The butler, judging by his age and uniform.

Whispers echoed in the cavernous space. Wendel and Ardis stole nearer. They huddled behind a rack laden with wine and peeked beyond the bottles. The assassin stood there, talking to a man hidden in the shadows.

"We should go," said the assassin. "The necromancer is here."

The hidden man was silent for a moment. "Did he eat the poison?"

Ardis knew his voice—Nasir.

"I don't know," said the first assassin. "He's looking for me. He's not far behind."

Wendel pushed Ardis behind an oak barrel and held his finger to his lips. He let go of her hand, lifting the shadows from her skin, and crept toward the assassins. She gripped her sword's hilt and braced herself for a fight.

Ardis lost Wendel as he prowled into the darkness.

"We didn't come here to kill the necromancer," Nasir said.

A shadow sidestepped behind the nameless assassin. Swiftly, Wendel muffled the man's scream and slit his throat.

"I came here to kill you," Wendel said.

Nasir bolted to the butler, cut him free from the chair, and dragged him to his feet. The butler grunted with pain.

"Show yourself," Nasir said, "or the butler dies."

Wendel laughed from the darkness. "You think you know me."

Ardis tensed. Wendel had to be bluffing. But blood from the dead assassin pooled on the stone and crawled toward her toes.

"Nasir," she said.

Ardis straightened and strode out from behind the barrel. Nasir backed away and pressed a knife to the butler's throat.

"Wendel won't spare your life a second time," she said.

Candlelight glittered in Nasir's eyes. "Stay where you are. Unless you want the blood of an innocent on your hands."

The butler let out a strangled whimper.

"How do you want this to end?" Ardis said. "How do you plan to drag that hostage with you all the way upstairs?"

Nasir glanced to the left. There had to be another passageway there.

"Let him go," Ardis said.

Nasir shuffled back and yanked the butler with him. A shadow flitted behind Nasir—Wendel, trying to surprise him.

Ardis knew she had to distract the assassin.

"Why did you leave Wendel?" she said.

Nasir blinked. "What?"

"How did it end?" She stared straight at him. "How did it even start?"

Nasir had no time to reply. From the shadows, Wendel lunged for the assassin's knife, but Nasir flung out his arm, dragging the blade through flesh. Blood spurted from the butler's neck and splattered Wendel's eyes.

Blinded, Wendel staggered back.

Nasir abandoned his hostage and fled into the darkness. Ardis ran to the butler. Scarlet pulsed from his throat and poured down his shirt. She tore the gag from his mouth and pressed it against his wound, but knew he was dying.

The butler gasped and met her gaze. His hand fumbled at her own.

A small eternity later, he shut his eyes.

Wendel blinked away blood, wiped his face on his sleeve, and chased Nasir.

Ardis leapt to her feet. "Wendel!"

He didn't stop running, so she ran after him.

Wendel dodged down yet another secret passageway. Stairs climbed toward the surface. Ardis struggled to keep up. Ahead, Nasir's footsteps echoed off stone. Fading fast. A door slammed. Wendel burst through the door, and Ardis stumbled after him into the night. They stood in an alley behind the castle.

No sign of Nasir.

Gasping, Wendel dropped into a crouch. He stared at the cobblestones.

Ardis sucked in air. "We lost him."

Wendel straightened, his head bowed, and paced up and down the alley. With a snarl, he punched the nearest wall. Then he leaned his forehead on the stones and stayed like that until he wasn't breathing so hard.

"Wendel," Ardis said.

He lifted his head. He had smeared blood on the stones.

"Damn," he said, his voice gravelly. "Remind me not to punch a castle again."

"Are you all right?"

His jaw tightened. "Yes."

Physically, perhaps, but emotionally… self-loathing simmered in his eyes.

"Do you think there are any more assassins?" Ardis said.

"I know Nasir. He wouldn't run away unless he was alone." Wendel's nostrils flared. "God, Nasir was right."

"What?"

"I am a fool."

She shook her head. "Nasir just wanted you to doubt yourself."

"He didn't deserve my mercy. I should have slit his damn throat. He's so blinded by the Order, he would never defy them."

Ardis was silent for a moment. "Maybe you see too much of yourself in him."

He raked his fingers through his hair, but said nothing.

"We should go back," she said.

Wendel glanced at the secret passageway. "Through there?"

Past the pair of dead bodies in the cellar. She winced. How could they explain that to the hosts of their dinner party?

"Is it the fastest way?" Ardis said.

"No."

Wendel started walking. He obviously expected her to follow. She hurried to catch up, holding the stitch in her side.

"The main entrance is quicker," Wendel said.

"But you're covered in blood."

"I don't care who sees me."

His words sounded so hollow, she believed him.

But he took her hand and at least granted her the anonymity of Amarant's shadows. They walked unseen among the residents of Königsberg. When they crossed the threshold of the castle, Wendel let the shadows fade.

He hid his dagger in his coat and marched into the dining room.

SIXTEEN

P redictably, Cecelia shrieked at the sight of blood. Wendel was drenched in it—from the man he had killed, and from the man he hadn't saved. He stood by the doors of the dining room and stared right back at them.

"You may need another butler," Wendel said.

Waldemar spoke in a subterranean growl. "What have you done?"

A muscle in Wendel's jaw twitched. "I saved you from the assassins lurking like vermin in your walls. You're welcome."

"And the butler?" Waldemar said.

"He blundered upon an assassin in the cellar. Which usually ends badly."

Waldemar lowered his head like a bull about to charge. "How dare you speak of these matters in such a disrespectful manner."

Ardis stepped between them and tried to salvage the situation. "We couldn't save the butler. The assassin slit his throat."

Judging by their grimaces, perhaps that was overly descriptive for her audience.

"I'm afraid I feel rather faint," Juliana said.

She backed against the table and clutched the tablecloth.

"Darling!" Cecelia caught her by the shoulder. "Juliana, sit down."

Juliana avoided the sight of Wendel. She wilted into a chair and fanned herself. Ardis suspected this was all for show.

"Please, Wendel," Cecelia said. "You're upsetting your sister."

Cecelia touched the back of her hand to Juliana's forehead as if taking her temperature, the picture of maternal concern.

Wendel's face darkened with longing and disgust. He feigned a formal bow. "Good night."

Cecelia and Juliana acted as though they hadn't heard him. Waldemar glanced at him with such shame in his eyes that Wendel looked away almost immediately. Wolfram, the last of his family, sat at the table in silence.

"Ardis?" Wendel said. "After you."

She grabbed the doorknob, her bloodstained fingers stark against the brass. They stepped from the dining room together.

"Where do you want to go?" Ardis said.

Wendel kept his head down. "It doesn't matter."

The door clicked open. Wolfram slipped into the hallway. He looked at his brother, his eyes bright in the candlelight. "I'm sorry."

Wendel's eyebrows angled into a frown. "Why?"

"You saved us, and they still treated you so badly."

Wendel's frown softened into something much more fragile. He touched his thumb to his mouth and inspected the carpet. "I'm never the hero."

Wolfram stared defiantly at him. "You're my brother."

When Wendel met his gaze, his eyes looked luminous with sadness. "Wolfram. You don't know me."

"Then tell me what happened to you."

Wendel retreated a step. "No."

"Don't treat me like a child." Wolfram folded his arms. "I deserve to know."

"Wolfie. No."

"Why not?"

"I can't." Wendel sounded hoarse. "I don't even know how to tell you."

Ardis backed away from the brothers, not wanting to intrude, but Wendel glanced into her eyes. She thought she saw a hint of desperation in his eyes, as if he wanted her to save him from having this conversation.

"Excuse me," Ardis said, "but you seem to be dripping blood on the carpet."

It wasn't a lie—a few drops speckled the floor by his feet.

"Mother will be thrilled," Wendel said dryly.

"You need a bath," Ardis said. "I'm a bit dirty myself."

Wolfram dipped his head. "I will tell the servants. I'm sorry, I meant to do so sooner."

He spoke with polite formality. Like a prince. Like Wendel, in fact, despite the necromancer's tendency to be a bastard.

Wendel ran his tongue over his lip. "I would appreciate a change of clothes."

"I have some clothes you can borrow," Wolfram said.

"That should suffice." Wendel had a shadow of a smile. "I'm still taller than you."

Wolfram sniffed. "Not by much."

Konstantin joined them in the hallway, followed by Himmel.

"Pardon me," the archmage said. "I didn't mean to interrupt."

"It wasn't important," Wolfram said. "Please, go on."

Konstantin thinned his lips. "Are there any more assassins in the castle?"

"No," Wendel said.

"He killed one," Ardis said, "but the other got away."

Konstantin blew out his breath. "Good work, regardless."

"Pardon?" Wendel said.

"We were meant to die before the last course. You both saved lives tonight."

Wolfram glanced at Wendel with a look that clearly said he agreed with the archmage, but Wendel responded with a grimace.

"The antidote to nightshade." Himmel furrowed his brow. "We still need it."

Konstantin waved his hand. "Details."

"I never ate the second course," Wendel said.

"Neither did I," Ardis said, "which means we can go."

Wendel looked down at his bloodstained shirt. "And take a bath."

Ardis locked the door to the bathroom and let her gown slither to her ankles. She stepped out and dropped it by her sword, where the tangerine silk puddled on the floorboards. Blood lingered under her fingernails.

It wasn't much, and it would wash away. Though the memories never did.

Ardis climbed into the clawfoot tub and lowered herself to the bottom. Warmth embraced her body. She tipped back her head. Underwater, her heartbeat echoed in her ears, and the rhythm soothed the tension in her muscles.

A sharp cramp made her wince. She sat upright and pressed her hand to her stomach.

Ardis realized she couldn't remember the last time she had her period. Her mind raced backwards through time. She should have started bleeding five days ago. Maybe more. She hadn't thought much of it until now.

Her dream. Where she was…

Ardis worked the soap into a lather. She washed herself, trying to scrub away the fear clinging to her skin. Her breasts felt tender to her touch. She froze, her fingers cupping herself, and sucked in a shuddering breath.

Was her dream an omen? Was she pregnant?

The heat of the water went cold. Ardis shivered and tucked her knees against her chest. She had to talk to Wendel.

Not that she had any idea how.

A rap on the door startled Ardis. "Yes?" she called.

"When you have a minute," Ursula said, "I would like a word."

"Coming!"

Ardis stepped from the tub, dried hastily, and wrapped the towel around herself. When she opened the door a crack, the doctor looked her over with complete disinterest. Doubtless she had seen worse than a little nudity.

"Sorry to intrude," Ursula said, "but I'm worried about Wendel."

"Why?" Ardis said.

There were a lot of things to be worried about, but she wanted to know which one.

Ursula nudged her glasses up her nose. "Laudanum. He asked me for a prescription, and became angry when I declined."

Another cramp panged through Ardis, and she bit the inside of her cheek. "That sounds like Wendel."

"Laudanum can be addictive if abused," Ursula said.

Ardis nodded. It wasn't like nobody knew this.

"Does Wendel drink?" Ursula said.

"Obviously."

The doctor's eyebrows descended, so Ardis explained quickly.

"Wendel isn't a drunk," she said. "A glass of absinthe now and then."

Ardis rubbed her belly. She wasn't sure why she was cramping.

"Is something the matter?" Ursula said.

Ardis averted her gaze. "Can we talk in private?"

"Of course."

Ursula stepped into the bathroom and shut the door behind her. Ardis gulped a deep breath and went straight for the jugular.

"Doctor," she said. "I'm afraid I might be pregnant."

Ursula blinked. "When was your last—?"

"November, which means it's late."

"That's not unusual. Stress can delay menstruation."

Ardis's face burned. "By five days?"

"Yes."

"But doctor, it's been like clockwork before."

Ursula clucked her tongue. "Are you aware of preventives?"

Now Ardis was sure her face was crimson. She clutched her towel closer.

"It's not like we didn't," she said. "But they aren't perfect."

Ursula sighed. "You shouldn't be particularly paranoid. Even if you were pregnant, it's still too early to tell."

"When"—Ardis swallowed hard—"would I know?"

"Wait another week for menstruation. If not, come back to me."

Ardis hoped nobody outside the bathroom overhead them. It wasn't like *menstruation* was a word for polite company.

"In the meantime," Ursula said, "you may want to find Wendel."

Ardis almost choked on her own spit. "Why?"

"The laudanum." Ursula arched an eyebrow. "He left the castle."

"He did?"

"To find something superior to laudanum. His words, not mine."

"Jesus Christ." Ardis blew out her breath. "Doctor, you won't tell him about this?"

"I wouldn't dream of it."

Ursula reached for the doorknob, then glanced over her shoulder.

"And Ardis?" she said. "Good luck."

Ardis gave her more of a grimace than a smile. "Thanks."

With that, the doctor left.

Ardis dragged her gown over her damp skin. She cursed the delicate silk and hoped it wouldn't be utterly ruined after tonight. She wished she had something more practical to wear, but needed to hunt down Wendel.

And figure out just how angry she should be at him.

The streets of Königsberg looked sparse at this time of night. But Ardis still attracted the attention of passersby. She wished, once again, she wasn't wearing a tangerine silk gown, and muttered curses under her breath.

Admittedly, the sword tucked under her arm didn't help.

"Blackbird Lane," she said. "Where the hell is Blackbird Lane?"

That's where Wendel had gone, or at least what he had told Konstantin. The archmage hadn't seemed particularly concerned, although Ardis had neglected to mention the laudanum. Or anything superior to laudanum.

If Wendel didn't get himself killed, she would kill him herself.

At the street corner, Ardis hurried toward a gentleman in a top hat.

"Excuse me," she said. "Where can I find Blackbird Lane?"

The gentleman stared at her as if she had escaped from a mental asylum. Ardis frowned and started to rephrase her question, but he ducked his head and hurried across the street. She glared at the back of his hat.

"*Grok!*"

Thank heavens. Ardis had never been so happy to see that abominable raven.

Krampus flew from a rooftop and landed on a lamppost. The light glimmered off his inky feathers. He cocked his head.

"Krampus!" Ardis called in a singsong voice. "Here, Krampus!"

Now everyone on the street stared at her like she had escaped from an asylum.

"*Grok?*"

Ardis didn't speak raven, but that sounded like a question.

"Krampus," she said, "I lost Wendel. Help me find him."

The raven pumped his wings and flew from the lamppost. Ardis gathered up her gown and ran after the bird. He led her away from the castle, into the western outskirts of the city. Moonlight gleamed on the lagoon as it lapped at the earth. The buildings on the water looked medieval, rickety and swaybacked.

A burly man blocked the sidewalk. His urine splattered the wall.

Ardis tightened her grip around her sword and crossed to the other side of the street. The man turned and whistled at her, then grabbed himself in a rude gesture. She gritted her teeth and convinced herself not to emasculate him.

That would definitely ruin her gown, and she was already sick of blood tonight.

Krampus landed above a door and croaked. Ardis approached him and spotted a wooden sign painted with a black bird.

"Thank you, Krampus," she said.

The raven blinked.

Ardis opened the door and stepped into a gloomy room. Candles guttered in the wind. She shut the door, then blinked as her eyes adjusted to the darkness. A woman in a yellow dressing gown climbed from an armchair.

"Good evening, madam," said the woman.

A whiff of sweet smoke curled out from beneath a door. Ardis breathed in the aroma, and her stomach tightened into a knot.

It wasn't a smell you could forget.

Opium.

The woman eyed Ardis with wary politeness. "May I help you?"

"I would love to smoke," Ardis lied. "I'm having a bad night."

The woman's smile bared snaggleteeth. She shuffled to the door that led deeper inside. Ardis followed her into the opium den.

Lanterns hung overhead like overripe fruits. Their golden light glowed through fever dreams of swirling smoke. Ardis covered her mouth, but the perfume of burnt poppies still invaded her lungs. She crossed Turkish rugs and stepped around smokers who reclined with pipe in hand, many of them lost to the world.

"A pipe, madam?" said the woman who had brought her here.

"No," Ardis whispered, because she saw him.

Wendel sprawled across the pillows on a couch. His hand hung over the edge, his fingers loosely curled around an ivory opium pipe. His face had the innocence of sleep, his eyelashes black crescents on his cheeks.

Ardis touched his hair, still damp from the bath. "Wendel?"

He stirred but didn't wake. She shook his shoulder, and his fingers tightened on the pipe. He blinked open his eyes.

"Ardis," Wendel said, smoke roughening his voice.

"You can't do this," she said.

A frown disturbed the tranquility of his face. He lifted himself on his elbow and dragged a lacquered tray closer to the couch. He reached for a bowl of raw black opium, skewered a lump on a needle, and heated it over a lamp.

"Can't I?" Wendel said.

Ardis dug her fingernails into her palms. "This isn't your first time."

Wendel scraped the opium into the pipe, then offered it to her. "Is it yours?"

She swallowed past the anger choking her throat. "Yes."

"Please," he said. "Join me."

Wendel's words sounded languid, his eyes glassy with pleasure. She took the pipe from him and cradled the warm ivory. She had seen opium dens before, in San Francisco, and had seen people lose themselves to the poppy. Their lives shriveled as their faces grew gaunt and their money faded away like smoke.

"No," Ardis whispered.

Wendel swung his legs over the edge of the couch. He slung his arm around her shoulders and tugged her closer.

"One breath," he said. "One breath, and you forget it all for one glorious moment."

"Like you forgot me?" Ardis said.

Wendel looked sideways at her, and a pinprick of pain sharpened his eyes. "I told the archmage to tell you."

"You didn't tell him where," she said. "You didn't tell him about the opium."

"I'm sorry."

Wendel tilted his head and kissed her on the cheek. His clumsy lips met her mouth. She tasted the bittersweet opium on him.

"No." Ardis shoved him away. "Get up. Now."

Wendel let himself fall against the couch. He scowled at her as if it were her fault. "And go where?"

"Anywhere but here," Ardis said.

Wendel strained to reach the opium pipe in her hand, but she tossed it away like garbage. The woman in the yellow gown scrambled after it, crouching to pick the sticky opium off the carpet.

"Madam!" said the woman. "I must ask you to leave."

"He's coming with me," Ardis said.

She seized Wendel by the wrist and hauled him to his feet. He stumbled and almost knocked over the lamp on the tray.

"Ardis!" Wendel said.

But he didn't fight her as she towed him from the opium den. The winter night hit her face like a splash of ice water. She coughed, the sickly opium smoke still lingering in her lungs. Wendel twisted his wrist free.

"Let me go back," he said.

She stared him down. "Absolutely not."

"But I haven't paid them."

She laughed harshly. "You don't have any money, remember?"

Wendel frowned, but a moment later, his face smoothed into a placid look. He leaned back his head and stared at the sky. "The stars are beautiful tonight."

Ardis narrowed her eyes. "When did you start smoking opium?"

"Years ago." He looked down to the cobblestones. "Never often."

That didn't reassure her.

"Promise me," she said, "that you will never smoke opium again."

Wendel met her gaze. His eyes looked distant and dark. "I dream only with opium. Without it, I only have nightmares."

Ardis blinked away sudden tears. "Opium dreams aren't real. You know that."

"I want to dream again."

"And you will. But not like this."

His gaze wandered back to the stars. "What's wrong with me, Ardis?"

She bit her lip. "You died, for starters."

"And I can't use that as an excuse?"

"Hell no."

He let out his breath in a long sigh. "You won't let me go without promising, will you?"

"Not a chance."

When he met her eyes, his mouth looked soft and vulnerable.

"If I do," he said, "will you help me?"

Ardis's throat tightened with an exquisite ache. She had to catch her breath. "I promise."

"And I promise no more opium." He glanced away. "Though I will miss it."

Ardis squeezed his hand tight. She didn't know how to help him, or how to tell him this, and it scared her half to death.

She would be damned if she didn't try.

SEVENTEEN

The glow of a golden morning crept through the curtains. Sighing, Ardis rolled over in bed and reached for Wendel. He wasn't there.

Ardis sat upright and squinted through her hair. There, on the couch, was Wendel. She didn't remember him falling asleep there. Quietly, she kicked aside the sheets and slid out of bed. She didn't want to wake him.

"Good morning." Wendel had a rasp in his voice. "Did you sleep well?"

He held her gaze for a second too long, and knew he was worried about last night.

"I did," she said. "Did you?"

Wendel rubbed the bridge of his nose. "More or less."

Ardis sat by him on the couch and touched the back of his hand. "You don't have to sleep alone."

His eyes looked luminous in this light. "Are you sure?"

She knew he was asking her to forgive him. For last night. For his nightmares.

"Yes."

A smile stole over Wendel's face, and in that moment, he looked beautiful in the sun. "Shall we head down to breakfast? I'm starving."

Ardis couldn't help but return his smile. "Me, too."

They dressed and went downstairs. The restaurant hummed with chatter and the clink of silverware. Their hotel overlooked the icy river and the cathedral of Königsberg. Seagulls squabbled over a fish in the street.

At a table by the window, he pulled out a chair for her. She smiled to thank him, but a knot tightened in her gut.

She still hadn't told him. It was only an uncertainty, a dream, but if she was pregnant...

"Ardis?" Wendel said.

She whistled something tuneless. "I have a question for you."

"Then ask," he said.

If only it were that easy. Ardis wondered if she should write him a letter, but was better with a sword than a pen.

"We haven't talked about this before," Ardis said.

Wendel gazed across the table and stroked his thumbnail across his lips.

"But it's not impossible," she said, "that it might happen to us."

He cocked his head. "Us?"

God, she was absolutely awful at this. She chewed on the inside of her cheek.

A waitress hovered by their table. "Can I get you anything to start?"

"Coffee, please," Wendel said.

The waitress looked to Ardis. "And you, ma'am?"

Words. Articulate words. That would be nice.

"Coffee." Ardis folded and refolded her napkin. "Could I see your menu?"

With a nod, the waitress bustled away.

"Continue," Wendel said. "I'm morbidly curious."

Ardis grimaced. Why did she feel like she might be sick?

The flippancy on his face vanished, replaced by something far more serious. And that was somehow a thousand times worse.

"What is it?" Wendel said.

Ardis curled her fingers into fists and stared at her knuckles. "I'm sorry. This is harder than I thought it would be."

Wendel reached for her hand, then froze, his fingers hovering over the table. "Ardis."

She glanced into his face. God, no, she could see the questions in his eyes. And a glimmer of what had to be alarm.

He held her gaze. "Are you—?"

The waitress flitted back to their table. She scooted a menu across the table and poured them each a cup of coffee.

"What brings you both to Königsberg?" the waitress said.

Wendel gave her a tight smile. "Business."

"Königsberg is beautiful in the winter." The waitress tucked a lock of hair behind her ear. "I love the castle around Christmas."

Ardis curled her toes inside her boots. A blush burned her face.

"I'm from here," Wendel said.

The waitress touched a menu to her mouth. "Are you?"

"Yes."

"What part of Königsberg?"

Wendel stopped smiling and drank his coffee. Slowly. "The middle."

Ardis cleared her throat and opened her menu at random. "Can I have a Berliner? Thank you."

The waitress pursed her lips. "Certainly, ma'am." She scurried away.

Wendel leaned on the table with his knuckles against his mouth. "You had a question. Tell me. Please."

Ardis looked him in the eye, since she owed him that much. "What would you think if we had a baby?"

Wendel went deathly white. He drank some coffee. The cup clattered on the saucer, betraying his trembling hands. "What?"

Ardis forced herself to inhale. Unspent tears burned in her eyes. "You heard me the first time."

He looked dazed. "But we—"

"I know."

"Are you sure?"

"No." She shook her head. "Not yet."

It sounded so foolish; she stared into her untouched coffee.

Wendel didn't speak for an eternity. "I owe you an answer."

Ardis hid her face behind her hands. Panic crashed against her ribs like a caged bird. "I'm afraid it's true."

With gentle fingers, he moved her hands from her face. "If it's true, then we can be afraid together."

His voice gave her the courage to look at him. He had a hint of a smile.

"Truthfully," he said, "I'm terrified."

Ardis laughed, and it brought her dangerously close to tears.

"It could be nothing," she said.

"It could be something." He raised his eyebrows. "I've always wanted a tiny minion."

"Wendel!"

He struggled not to smile. "Did I say that? I meant baby."

"You've always wanted one?"

"That's a lie." His smile faded. "Not always."

"Oh."

He met her gaze. "Not until you told me."

The sincerity in his eyes left her breathless. She let out a shuddering sigh.

"Stop looking at me like that," she said.

"What? Like what?"

"So hopefully." She drank her lukewarm coffee. "It's a long shot."

Wendel rubbed the back of his neck. "How long of a shot?"

"I'm five days late. That's all."

"Late...?" Understanding cleared his face. "Ah."

"I asked the doctor," Ardis said, "and she told me to wait a week."

Wendel squinted at the dregs of his coffee.

"Should you rest?" he said. "Should you even be piloting an Eisenkrieger?"

"She didn't say."

"You should ask."

She sighed. "Wendel. Don't worry."

He stared out the window and bounced his leg with excess energy. "Do you want a baby?"

Ardis shrugged, her shoulders tight, since she honestly didn't know.

"I'd make a terrible mother," she said. "I'm a mercenary."

Wendel glanced back at her. "You might have to set down your sword," he said lightly. "Just long enough to hold the baby."

Ardis smiled. "I would make you hold it."

She imagined him carrying a baby—their baby—and felt a little flutter in her heartbeat. Damn, these were dangerous thoughts.

What was it about the idea that made her so giddy?

The waitress returned. "Your Berliner."

"Thank you," Ardis said, a bit more charitable toward the waitress.

Ardis bit into the German doughnut and savored how sweet it was. Though everything tasted a lot sweeter at the moment.

"Need anything else?" said the waitress.

"I'm fine," Ardis said, because she was.

"The eggs." Wendel closed the menu. "And today's newspaper."

Ardis devoured her pastry and licked her fingers clean. Her appetite was back with a vengeance. This couldn't be morning sickness. But could she be eating for two? The possibility of being pregnant consumed her thoughts.

The waitress returned with the eggs and a newspaper. "Here you are, sir."

Wendel spread the newspaper flat on the table and absently stabbed the eggs with his fork. Ardis tried not to stare at his food.

"Could I have a bite?" she said.

"Of course." Wendel scooted the plate across. "We can order more."

Ardis ate a forkful of eggs and helped herself to a second one. Wendel didn't seem to be as hungry as she was. He frowned over the newspaper. His thumb rubbed the words, back and forth, until ink blackened his skin.

"The Russians," Wendel said.

"What about them?" Ardis said.

The newspaper crumpled under his hand. "They are a day's march from Königsberg."

The lagoon glimmered like quicksilver. Wendel loped along the waterfront, and Ardis ran to match his long stride. He noticed her breathing hard and slowed, though he hadn't stopped scowling since the newspaper.

At the doors to the drydock, the guards waved them inside.

"Archmage!" Wendel shouted.

Several people stared at him, none of them Konstantin.

"Have you forgotten his name already?" Ardis said.

Wendel wrinkled his nose. "I haven't a clue what you mean."

"You called him 'Konstantin' last night."

"Did I?"

"When you thought he was choking."

"That was a mistake."

Wendel seemed even more on edge, and it was sharpening his words.

Ardis recognized someone, though it wasn't Konstantin. A woman jogged along the wall, her white coat flying behind her.

"Archmage Carol!" Ardis said.

Carol waved. "Aren't you one of the test pilots?"

"Yes, ma'am. We met in Vienna."

"That's right." Carol cocked her head. "You scratched up one of the Eisenkriegers."

Ardis winced. "Konstantin told you?"

"No, but he's a terrible liar. Brought back one of the prototypes after a little expedition. Those marks didn't buff out."

Wendel scoffed with impatience. "Is he here?"

Carol gave him a once over. "And you must be the necromancer,. Pleased to meet you."

"Charmed," Wendel said. "Perhaps we can chat later over drinks."

"Why not?" Carol didn't blink. "Never had drinks with a necromancer. Or a disinherited prince, come to think of it."

Wendel arched an eyebrow. "Count on the Russians arriving uninvited."

"Let them." Carol folded her arms. "We have some party favors for Saint Petersburg." She jerked her chin toward the biggest Eisenkrieger.

Wendel glowered at its metal knees. "Not nearly enough."

"That's why we're here." Ardis nudged him in the ribs. "To help Konstantin."

This provoked a long sigh and a dark look from Wendel.

"Konstantin should be in back," Carol said, "working with the captain."

Ardis tried to be especially polite to counteract Wendel's rudeness. "Thank you, archmage."

Carol nodded. "Come back so I can outfit you for the Eisenkriegers."

"Will do."

Ardis hurried after Wendel, who was already walking. They found Konstantin and Himmel sitting together by a workbench. Himmel's arm rested on top of the workbench. Bandages didn't entirely hide the raw, red scars zigzagging across his skin.

Konstantin pushed a pair of goggles over his head. "Good morning!"

"You seem chipper, archmage," Wendel said.

Himmel grunted. "The antidote cured him completely."

The captain looked considerably less awake, his hair rumpled from sleep.

"Myself," Himmel said, "I need more coffee."

Konstantin's sky blue eyes twinkled. "I'm on my third cup."

"Good God," Ardis said.

"Woke early to work on *this*."

Konstantin spoke with a sort of reverence. He hopped off his stool and fetched something from a table. He held it in both hands.

"My mechanical arm," Konstantin said.

It was a work of beauty. Raw, with naked gears, but still beautiful. Konstantin had taken an armored gauntlet, the steel intricately articulated and engraved, and outfitted it with technomancy to power its movement.

"Theodore," Konstantin said. "Would you care to demonstrate?"

The captain coughed. "Himmel."

"Yes! Sorry."

With an unintelligible grumble, Himmel lifted his arm. His tried to straighten his hand, but his fingers curled like claws. With his left hand, he dragged the mechanical arm across the table and fumbled with the buckles.

Konstantin bit his lip. "Let me help—"

"No," Himmel said. "I need to do this alone."

"Of course."

Himmel tugged the mechanical arm over his own and tightened the buckles. Grimacing, he stared at the metal fingers. They clenched into a fist, tiny gears whirring, then twitched open. He groped for a wrench and grabbed it.

"There." Himmel attempted a smile. "That wasn't impossible."

"I realize it's rough," Konstantin said, his gaze downcast, "but I can adjust—"

"Thank you."

Himmel said it so gruffly that Ardis couldn't help but smile, and Konstantin's blush reached legendary proportions.

"Bravo," Wendel said.

Both Konstantin and Himmel glared at him.

"I'm genuinely impressed." Wendel held up his hands. "Don't look at me like that."

The archmage checked his pocketwatch. "We should get to work."

"Exactly my thoughts."

"You seem rather eager to help," Konstantin said.

"I find myself motivated by an army of Russians."

Konstantin clicked his pocketwatch shut. "Mr. Tesla will arrive shortly. Then we can start his experiments in the field."

"Oh, joy," Wendel said.

Himmel dropped the wrench with a clank. "Losing your nerve?"

"Experiment away," Wendel said. "Just try not to break your one and only necromancer. I hear they can be hard to find."

Konstantin looked coolly at him. "We will do our best."

"For my sake." Ardis arched her eyebrows. "And I'm waiting for your orders."

Konstantin wasn't joking when he said experiments in the field.

Ardis swigged metallic water from a canteen. Her hair clung to her sweaty forehead. She rubbed it away with her sleeve, glanced around to see nobody watching, then flopped back on the grass.

Above her, an Eisenkrieger knelt, its steel skin rippling with reflected clouds.

Her Eisenkrieger, she supposed.

Ardis had piloted it before, in Vienna, and recognized the gouge on its knee. The consequence of an assassin's blade, from that time when she and Konstantin marched it into a coffin factory to rescue Wendel.

"You need a name," Ardis said.

Technically, the smaller Eisenkriegers were designated Knight class, while the single large Eisenkrieger was a Colossus.

"Fritz?" she said. "You look like a Fritz."

Ardis breathed in the brisk scent of crushed grass, then let out her breath. After a few hours in the cockpit, the heat felt smothering. Thank God they had stopped for a lunch of cheese and rye bread.

Overhead, a zeppelin hovered under the clouds. A man leaned from the gondola and waved at them. His metal arm flashed in the sun—Himmel. He wasn't wearing a captain's hat, but he was well enough to scout.

Ardis sat upright and waved back. She glanced across the field.

A second Knight Eisenkrieger knelt in the grass. Konstantin and Tesla bent over a panel in its back, still tinkering with wires.

"Damn!" Konstantin said. "We need to recalibrate it again."

Tesla stood with his hands on his hips. "I'm positive this should work."

Wendel wandered away from them and tossed a breadcrumb to Krampus. The raven swooped and caught it in midair.

"Wendel!" Konstantin said.

Wendel didn't look back. "Yes?"

"We need you."

Wendel laughed dryly. "I'm in high demand."

He sprinkled the breadcrumbs onto the grass. Krampus landed and strutted across the muddy footprints of the Eisenkrieger.

"Come here." Konstantin flapped his hand. "Help us with the harmonic transmitter."

"I have absolutely no clue what that means," Wendel said.

Tesla brushed away his comment. He hadn't bothered to be irritated by the necromancer, not even when Wendel complained.

"If each Eisenkrieger has its own frequency," Tesla said, "there will be no interference."

"Your necromancy functions on the same principle," Konstantin said.

Wendel held up his hands. "I will take your word for it."

Nearby, another pilot leaned against a tree. She spotted Ardis staring and crossed the field. Ardis brushed crumbs from her trousers, stood, and held out her hand. The other pilot had a firm handshake.

"You must be Ardis," said the pilot. She spoke English with an Australian accent.

Ardis nodded. "I didn't catch your name."

"Steph," the pilot said.

"Australian?"

"I am."

"You're a long way from home."

Steph smiled. Sunlight brought out golden glimmers in her brown hair. "Takes one to know one."

Ardis glanced at her Eisenkrieger and patted his hip. "This is Fritz."

"You named him?" Steph laughed. "I hadn't thought of that. I suppose it's best not to get too attached to a prototype."

Ardis was no stranger to losing things in battle, but battle seemed so far away today.

"Have you heard about the Hex?" Steph said.

"What about it?" Ardis said.

"Rumors say the magic is creeping into Russia." Steph folded her arms. "Gunpowder doesn't work for a few miles beyond the border. They say the archmages planned this all along, and the Tsar is less than thrilled."

Ardis rubbed the back of her neck. "It won't end the war."

"Right." Steph snorted. "I hear the Russians have swordsmen on horseback. Cossacks."

"Swords can still kill you."

Steph nudged the Eisenkrieger with her boot. "But wait until they see the Eisenkriegers."

Ardis didn't mention the clockwork dragon. She wasn't sure if the archmages wanted everyone to know about it. To fear it.

Carol came running across the grass. "Gear up. Both of you."

"At the same time?" Ardis said.

Carol grinned. "Cross your fingers. The control systems should be working."

"Yes, ma'am." Steph sprinted across the field.

Ardis clambered into her Eisenkrieger's cockpit. She reached for the ignition by her chest and twisted the key. The Eisenkrieger rumbled to life.

"Come on, Fritz," Ardis whispered.

Carol cupped her hands to her mouth. "On my mark!"

Ardis braced herself—any interference would wrench her arms and legs.

"Stand!" Carol said.

Ardis tensed her legs, the muscles in her thighs already aching, and braced herself with giant metal knuckles on the ground. She brought the Eisenkrieger to its feet. The pneumatics in its joints hummed and hissed.

Steph lumbered upright and waved.

Ardis waited for a delayed command, a yank to her arm, but her Eisenkrieger didn't budge. Tentatively, she lifted her foot and crunched the grass. The machine across the field stayed motionless. Which was a first.

"Archmage?" Ardis managed to sound cool and calm. "It appears to be working."

Carol gave her two thumbs up.

A boom shook the ground. Her heartbeat thudding, Ardis turned around.

The Colossus thundered onto the field, every footfall a minor earthquake, and towered over them all. From the cockpit, Natalya saluted the archmages. Awe tightened Ardis's chest, and she saluted back.

Konstantin punched the air in victory and did a little dance.

Tesla hid his smile behind his hand. "I was right."

His eyes glistening, Konstantin looked like he wanted to hug the man.

"Yes, Nikola," he said, "you were. And I'm forever—"

"Sir!" Carol bent over a wireless receiver. "A telegram from the zeppelin."

Konstantin's smile wilted. "Yes?

"The Russians are advancing."

EIGHTEEN

Ardis curled her hands into fists. The Eisenkrieger's knuckles glinted in the sun.

"How many Russians?" Konstantin said.

"The zeppelin reports a scouting party," Carol said. "At least two dozen men."

Konstantin's mouth thinned into a grim line. He glanced at the zeppelin. "Any sign of the clockwork dragon?"

"None."

"Commander Volkova," Konstantin said. "I want you to lead the Eisenkriegers into battle. Drive the Russians back."

"Yes, sir," Natalya called down.

The Colossus thudded across the field. Ardis followed in the Eisenkrieger's footsteps, Steph marching alongside them. The zeppelin floated above like a silver sentry, though it could do little to help in combat.

Natalya held up a hand. "Wait."

They hesitated at the edge of the field. Dry winter grasses rattled in the wind. Dark-needled pines bristled ahead.

"Split up," Natalya said. "Try to flush them out of the forest. I will be waiting."

"Yes, ma'am," Ardis said.

Steph saluted and marched into the forest. Twigs crashed underfoot. Branches whipped back into place as she passed. Ardis swallowed, her mouth dry, like she hadn't drunk a drop from her canteen. The Australian seemed overeager to meet the enemy—an Eisenkrieger wasn't a ticket to invincibility.

Ardis lowered her head and strode into the forest.

She pushed aside branches with her arms. Needles rained to the ground, and a pinecone pinged off the metal shoulder. The scent of pine sap crept into the cockpit. Even from this height, she couldn't see far through the gloom.

Ardis stopped and peered through the mist.

There. Ahead. A man in a gray jacket lay on his stomach under the bushes. A Russian. He thought he was hidden.

Ardis wondered what he intended to do, but wasn't sure she wanted to find out.

She grabbed a fallen branch—more of a log—and held it like a baseball bat. Back in San Francisco, she had never played baseball. None of the boys wanted a girl on their team. Today, however, she had other plans.

When Ardis walked past the Russian, he surged to his feet and unsheathed his sword. Ardis swung the wood and knocked the blade clean out of his hands. He staggered and braced himself against a tree.

She swung again and hit him in the head. He crumpled to the ground.

Ardis dropped the wood and stared down at the Russian. Had she killed him? She waited until his breath clouded the air.

So the Eisenkrieger wasn't quite *that* powerful.

"Hey!"

Ardis straightened, her heartbeat kicking into a higher gear, and turned her head.

Another Russian stood between the trees, brandishing a sword. Even from here, she saw freckles speckling his cheeks.

He had copper hair and the barest wisp of a beard. More of a boy than a man.

The Russian hefted a stone and hurled it at her. It bounced off the cockpit and left a spiderweb crack in the glass.

Konstantin wasn't going to like that.

Ardis swung her arms and lunged at the Russian. He bolted through the trees. He was fast, but no man could outrun an Eisenkrieger. As she closed the distance between them, he glanced over his shoulder, the whites of his eyes flashing. They crashed through the forest. He zigzagged and bolted through the bushes.

She wouldn't kill him. Just teach him not to run with—

The Eisenkrieger's foot jerked forward. Ardis stumbled onto her knee and caught herself on her hand. Her fingers sank into mud. When she looked down, she realized she had blundered straight into a murky swamp.

Breathing hard, the Russian broke into a grin.

He had lured her here. She should have killed him when she had the chance.

When the soldier shouted in Russian, three of his comrades stepped from the trees. Ardis struggled upright, but mud clung to the Eisenkrieger. Dragging her deeper. She didn't want to know how far down it went. A log lay halfway across the swamp. She groped for it, but the rotten wood crumbled into dust.

The Russians advanced, swords gleaming dully in their hands.

Ardis hadn't taken Chun Yi with her. If she left the Eisenkrieger, she would be unarmed, and didn't know how the Russians would treat her as a prisoner. She was an Eisenkrieger pilot, an American, a woman—

The copper-haired man tossed another stone. It clanged off the metal, though she stopped worrying about dents. The more she struggled to escape, the more the soldiers lost the fear in their eyes.

Mud crept around her. Cold invaded the cockpit.

Think. There was always a way out.

Ardis stopped fighting and lowered her head. She watched the Russians through the corner of her eye. They edged closer. The copper-haired soldier, the boldest, reached out to jab at the Eisenkrieger with his sword.

That was his mistake.

Ardis lunged and caught the sword. The soldier didn't let go of the hilt quickly enough. She yanked him within reach. Her fist connected with his chest. He flew back and crashed into bushes, which quivered and stilled.

The Russians stared. They had stopped smiling.

Ardis glanced at the sword, like a toothpick in the giant metal hand, and threw it at them. The blade cartwheeled and buried itself in a tree. Too much power, not enough finesse. Yet again. Ardis raised her fists in a defensive stance.

Time to see how many men she could take on at once.

The three Russians circled Ardis. She twisted, trying to keep them in her sights, but when she saw two of them, the other stalked behind her back. And every move dragged her deeper, murky water sloshing past her chest.

Her heartbeat hammered. The cockpit had gotten pretty damn claustrophobic.

She waited for a Russian to blunder within reach, but they kept back, waiting for her to drown or abandon the Eisenkrieger.

Mist swirled through the forest. Disturbed by a shadow.

Wendel.

He stepped from the darkness and sliced open a Russian's throat. The soldier dropped. Blood mingled with mud. Wendel never looked back. He dodged a sword blow, kicked a man, and stabbed the other in the back. One opponent left. Wendel waited for him to attack, then finished him with a slash to the neck.

Ardis waved at him. "Wendel!"

He sheathed his dagger and crouched by the swamp. "Take my hand."

"What? You can't—"

Wendel grabbed the Eisenkrieger's wrist and strained to drag Ardis from the swamp. His feet slipped out from beneath him. He braced himself against a root, but he had no hope of budging the metal beast from the mud.

"Climb out," Wendel said.

"I can't," Ardis said.

His eyes narrowed. "Climb out of the Eisenkrieger."

Ardis shoved at the cockpit door, but the thick muck trapped it shut.

"I can't!" she said. "Find Steph."

"Steph?"

"The other pilot. We split up."

Wendel nodded, his jaw taut, and ran back through the forest.

The Eisenkrieger sank deeper into the swamp. Water lapped at the glass and trickled through the crack into the cockpit. Ardis pressed her hand flat against the fracture, though she knew that was hardly a solution.

Footsteps boomed on the ground. Steph had arrived in her Eisenkrieger. Wendel ran after Steph and halted her with a shout.

"Watch out for the swamp!" he said. "Let's not replicate this predicament."

Relief flooded Ardis. "Give me a hand?"

"My pleasure," Steph said.

Steph sidestepped nearer to Ardis and crouched. Ardis grabbed her hand, and with Steph's help, hauled herself out of the muck. Once she was free, she brought the Eisenkrieger to its knees and climbed out. Her legs shaking, she dropped to the ground.

Wendel was at her side in an instant. "Are you hurt?"

"No." Ardis sucked in a lungful of air. "Christ, don't tell Konstantin."

She looked sideways at her Eisenkrieger, the steel caked with stinking mud.

"I think we have to," Steph said.

Ardis rubbed her eyes with her knuckles. "Later."

Wendel touched her shoulder. He waited for her to meet his gaze. "Are you sure you are all right?"

"Yes," she said, which wasn't entirely a lie.

Overhead, a rustling sound rushed over the treetops. Like giant wings. Ardis looked in time to glimpse a flash of red.

"The clockwork dragon," Wendel said hoarsely.

Ardis scrambled to her feet and climbed back into the cockpit. "Time to get the hell out of here."

"The dragon can't attack us in the trees," Wendel said. "Remember?"

Ardis slipped her hands into the Eisenkrieger's gauntlets. "It can attack the others."

They skirted the swampland and charged through the forest. When they returned to the field, they found Natalya waiting for them in the Colossus. They didn't stop running, and she fell in step with them.

"What happened?" Natalya said.

"The clockwork dragon," Ardis said. "We saw it over the forest."

Natalya scanned the horizon. No sign of the dragon, though the zeppelin hovered above the field like a bumbling target.

"We have to warn them," Ardis said.

"I will telegraph them," Natalya said. "Protect the archmages."

Ardis sprinted across the field towards where Konstantin waited by a truck. She didn't see Carol or Tesla.

"Konstantin," Ardis said. "The clockwork dragon."

The archmage stared at the sky. His face looked pale and frozen. "Not again. Not the zeppelin. Himmel is up there!"

"Down here isn't safe, either."

Konstantin jumped into the truck and slammed the door. The growling engine didn't mute the thundering of hooves. Calvary galloped across the field, a dozen or more men, their coats an unmistakable crimson.

Cossacks.

Ardis had her orders. *Protect the archmages.* And yet she stood her ground.

Where was Wendel?

She hadn't seen him since the forest. The field granted him no place to hide. If the Cossacks caught him in the open—

"Ardis!" Natalya towered over her in the Colossus. "Follow Konstantin."

Ardis blinked back to reality. "What about Steph?"

"Moving to Carol's position. You need to protect Konstantin."

"Yes, ma'am," Ardis said.

Natalya maneuvered the Colossus to face the charging Cossacks. Clouds darkened the sky with the promise of a storm. A horse skittered back and reared, shying away from the metal giant. Its rider fell from the saddle and rolled away from hooves. The rest of the Cossacks charged onward, their sabers gleaming.

Ardis forced herself to look away. That wasn't her fight.

She sprinted after Konstantin and caught up with his truck. He glanced at the mirror. Ardis gave him a thumbs up, and he nodded with a grim smile. When Konstantin looked in the rearview mirror, his eyes widened. He gripped the wheel and gunned the engine.

The clockwork dragon soared over the forest, its scales glistening blood red.

Time slowed to the space between heartbeats. Ardis watched the dragon shadow the field. The Cossacks reached the Colossus—Natalya swung her arm and knocked them aside. Horses and men scattered like toys.

The dragon swerved around the Colossus and swooped lower.

Ardis stared into its golden gemstone eyes. The dragon flared its wings, slowing its descent, its talons raking the air before they screeched across the roof of the truck. Konstantin ducked down inside.

Ardis seized her chance. Literally.

She jumped at the dragon and grabbed its tail as it whipped by. The lurch knocked the Eisenkrieger off balance and the dragon off course. Scales clattered through Ardis's hands. Gritting her teeth, she gripped even harder.

The dragon careened earthward and dragged Ardis across the grass. Its tail arced through the air, and for a second, she was flying. Her heart lurched into her throat.

They both hit the ground.

The impact knocked the wind from her lungs and rattled her teeth. She lost her grip, rolled across the mud, and skidded to a halt. Her muscles screaming, her ears ringing, Ardis staggered to her feet.

The fallen dragon writhed on the grass, then flipped itself upright.

God, Ardis wished she had a sword. She would slay this bastard right here and now.

The dragon snaked its neck and looked sideways at Ardis. It bared steel fangs with a serpent's hiss. Steam curled from its jaws. When it straightened, she realized how much bigger the dragon was than her Eisenkrieger.

Maybe making it angry wasn't such a smart move.

Ardis squared her shoulders and braced herself for an attack. The dragon coiled, then lashed out with its claws. She dodged as talons whistled past her head. Before the dragon attacked again, she backed away.

Pain stabbed her knee whenever she took a step. Her body ached with bruises.

Limping, Ardis retreated. The dragon hissed and spread its wings, scrambling across the field toward the forest, its tail slithering through the grass.

Where was Wendel? Lurking in the trees?

Hooves drummed the earth. Her heart pounding, Ardis turned around. The Eisenkrieger weighed on her like ponderous armor.

A rider on a pale horse galloped nearer. Blood trickled from the horse's white neck.

Wendel. He had revived a dead horse from the battlefield. Judging by his bloody hands, that hadn't been all he had done.

"Ardis!" Wendel reined in his undead steed. "Need any help?"

Hardly a chivalrous knight, but at least he had come to her rescue.

Ardis surveyed the forest. The canopy shivered as the clockwork dragon disappeared. The Cossacks, however, hadn't yet retreated. They swarmed around the Colossus and tormented it with sabers. Natalya swatted at them as they attacked the vulnerable pneumatics behind the Eisenkrieger's knees.

"Natalya looks like she needs help," Ardis said.

Wendel spurred his ghoulish steed toward the Cossacks. The horses still alive flattened their ears, whinnied, and skittered away from the necromancer. Wendel galloped behind them, herding them away from the Colossus. Lumbering into the fray, Ardis hurled a boulder at the Russians. It boomed on the ground and rolled across the grass.

Spooked, the horses bolted and took the Cossacks with them.

Wendel watched them go. "Should we finish them?"

"No," Natalya said, and marched to the road.

Ardis followed. She trembled as adrenaline faded from her blood.

Konstantin stood on the running board of the truck and ran his fingertips over the gashes carved by the dragon's claws.

"Archmage," Natalya said. "We should return to Königsberg."

Konstantin peered over the truck. He paled at Wendel's dead horse. "Not with *that*."

Wendel sneered. "It was a nice horse."

Despite his flippant tone, his eyes simmered with anger. Ardis suspected he found it abhorrent to kill animals.

"Let it go," Konstantin said. "The battle is over."

NINETEEN

Ardis knelt in the back of the truck. Her kneecap ached. Biting the inside of her cheek, she checked the straps tying down her Eisenkrieger. She tightened the buckles, straightened, and gave a thumbs up to Konstantin.

Wendel waited for her behind the truck. "Ardis."

She leaned on his arm and let him help her down.

"How badly are you hurt?" he said.

"Not badly."

Wendel's fingers tightened on her elbow. "Spare me the bravado."

Ardis escaped from his grasp as they climbed into the cab.

Konstantin waited behind the wheel. "Why the devil did you wrestle that dragon?"

"I caught it by the tail." Ardis shrugged. "One thing led to another." She tasted blood on her tongue, and touched her split lip. "Luckily, I didn't knock out any teeth."

"Luckily," Wendel said, "you didn't die."

Ardis glowered at him, but he stared out the windshield. "You *are* the expert."

He didn't blink.

Konstantin looked between them. "The Eisenkriegers performed admirably. Thank you."

"You are most welcome," Wendel said, in the most sardonic way possible.

Ardis sighed. "There's no need to be a bastard."

Wendel didn't say another word on the way to Königsberg. Ardis pressed her hands between her knees. She didn't want to sit so close to Wendel, not with this tension in his muscles. Not with this sickness in her stomach.

At the drydock, she marched the Eisenkrieger inside and got out.

"Himmel is here." Konstantin peered through the window, trying to hide a smile, and darted outside.

Ardis followed. "Are we done for the day?"

"Of course." Konstantin gazed at the zeppelin. "Get some rest."

Ardis walked from the drydock and found Wendel by the lagoon. He fractured the ice with his boot and dipped his hands into the freezing water. Bloodstains slipped easily from his hands, but he kept scrubbing.

He would never wash away his memories of touching the dead.

"I'm walking back to the hotel," Ardis said.

She didn't wait for Wendel, but he followed regardless. Gravel crunched beneath his boots. Snow drifted from the sky and dusted her hair. The cold stiffened her muscles, and her knee throbbed more sharply.

Ardis stopped by a park and leaned against a wrought-iron fence.

Wendel was at her side in an instant. "Ardis?"

"I want to sit," she said.

He took her elbow without asking and walked her to a bench. She sat with a sigh.

"I'm okay," she said.

Wendel sat by her. "I don't believe you."

"You don't have to."

"I can see the bruises on your skin."

Ardis tilted her face skyward and let snowflakes fall on her cheeks.

"We should go," Wendel said.

"My knee is killing me," Ardis said. "Can we take a taxi to the hotel?"

"Not the hotel," he said.

"Where?"

Wendel leaned with his elbows on his knees. Shadows darkened his eyes.

"Away from Königsberg," he said. "Away from Prussia."

"You would abandon your family?" she said.

Wendel shrugged, his shoulders tight. "I'm returning the favor."

"Don't you want to fight the Russians?"

Wendel dug his fingernails into his legs. "Perhaps you shouldn't."

"It's my job."

"Then resign."

She laughed. "We need the money."

"Money is worth nothing. You are the only thing of value to me."

Wendel looked fiercely at her, as if daring her to disagree. Ardis found herself speechless. Tears stung her eyes, though she blamed the wind.

"I don't want to lose you," Wendel said.

A lock of her hair blew across her face, and he brushed it aside with his thumb.

"You don't have to protect me," Ardis said.

"But—the baby."

She looked away, blinking hard, and willed herself not to cry. "We don't know that yet. There might never be a baby."

Wendel curled his fingers around hers. "Never?"

The hurt in his voice underlined the finality of the word. She stared at their hands, twisted together, and sucked in a breath.

"Can I admit something?" Ardis said.

"Anything," Wendel said.

"I never daydreamed about babies or husbands or weddings."

Wendel frowned. "Who does?"

"Girls." She smiled at his confusion. "All the girls in America, I think, except me."

"Why not?"

"I blame growing up in a brothel. And then learning how to fight for a living. My point is, I don't think I'm a normal woman."

Wendel wrinkled his nose. "A normal woman? Why would I want that?"

"Because one of them would be more than happy to have your babies and get married and sweep some little cottage in Switzerland."

"I don't see how sweeping matters," he said.

She snorted. "Somebody has to keep the cottage clean."

"I would rather have a dirty little cottage with you." Wendel's eyes twinkled. "And rest assured, that isn't a euphemism."

"God, Wendel," she said, "now you ruined Switzerland."

"It doesn't have to be Switzerland."

She hesitated. "Where else would we go?"

"Wherever you want."

Ardis pretended to sigh. "You can be very persuasive."

"I know." A smile crept over his face. "Is that a yes?"

"To what?"

"A future together. With the possible addition of a baby."

She looked him in the eye. "Consider me persuaded."

Wendel kissed her with gentle certainty. His hand curled around her neck and held her closer. Snow fell and hushed the sound of all but their heartbeats. Ardis melted in his arms, all her bruises and fears forgotten. He kissed her until she could only cling to him, and then he kissed her again, on the curve of her neck.

"Are you cold?" Wendel said.

"A little," Ardis said.

He drew back and arched an eyebrow.

"A lot," she admitted.

Wendel stood and clasped her hands. "Inside with you, woman."

"You can't call me that."

His smile looked like it should accompany a halo. "Wife?"

Ardis grimaced. "Husband."

"Darling," he said.

"Sweetheart."

"Little honeybee."

She burst out laughing. "What the hell?"

Wendel tugged Ardis to her feet. She stumbled against him, and he held her there.

"No one has ever called you that?" he said.

"Not ever."

"Good."

Ardis rolled her eyes. "Jealous of hypothetical German men?"

"Should I be?"

"Let me think." She paused. "No. You win."

Ardis started to walk—or limp, rather—and Wendel supported her weight.

"You must be my prize," he said.

She laughed. "Don't act prehistoric."

Wendel raised his eyebrows. "There must have been prehistoric necromancers."

"That's no excuse."

"I wonder if they revived woolly mammoths? Or saber tooth tigers?"

Ardis tried hard not to laugh. "Please don't ransack a museum."

"That's a brilliant idea." Wendel grinned. "We can fight the Russians with bones."

"Back to fighting the Russians?"

His grin faded. "For the time being. Before we decide on our future."

Ardis didn't like to see sadness in his eyes. She leaned her head against his shoulder. "We can scheme more at the hotel."

Wendel kissed the side of her head, then blew on her hair.

"What?" she said.

"Snowflakes."

"If you treat me like a china doll," she teased, "I'll break you."

"You are Chinese."

"Half." She faked a glare. "And no part of me is delicate."

"I beg to differ."

She touched her belly. "Maybe a baby."

Wendel frowned. "That would certainly require you to be careful."

"I know, I know."

They arrived at the hotel together. The moment Ardis stepped into their room, Wendel tugged her jacket from her shoulders. She suspected he was still being more than polite, but found his attention sweet.

"I will have a maid tend to the fire," Wendel said.

Ardis glanced at the log in the fireplace. "I can do it."

She grabbed a box of matches and a few sheets of hotel stationary. Within a few minutes, she had kindled a crackling fire.

Ardis set down the matches. "Anything else?"

Wendel bent over the bed and yanked back the quilts. "Take off your clothes."

She stared at him. "Is this you as a prehistoric necromancer?"

"The snow on your clothes is melting."

Ardis realized he was right. She kicked away her boots and peeled off her clothes.

Wendel watched her undress. "Get in bed."

"Yes, little honeybee."

As she limped to bed, he smirked. She climbed under the covers and snuggled down into the pillow.

When Wendel joined her, he was naked.

"Your feet!" Ardis slid away from him. "They feel like ice."

"My apologies." Wendel didn't sound too apologetic.

He brushed her hair from the nape of her neck and massaged her shoulders. His fingers brought a sigh to her lips. He pressed himself against her back, his body hot and hard along hers. She ran her hand over his buttocks.

"You feel nice," Ardis murmured.

"Nice?" Wendel laughed. "Is that all?"

He kissed her on the neck, then traced her spine with his lips. She shivered at his touch, his kisses sparking electricity on her skin. The soreness in her muscles melted, but the ache of unspoken words built behind her ribs.

A sigh escaped Ardis. "Wendel."

He stopped kissing her. She took a breath, just enough air to voice her confession.

"I love you."

"I wondered when you would say that." Wendel sounded like he was smiling.

"I already did," she whispered. "You didn't hear me."

Wendel tensed behind her. He must have known she was talking about the night he died, the night she brought him back with borrowed magic. Ardis hated that she had reminded him. She turned to him and kissed him to make him lose sight of his memories. He returned the kiss gently, then fiercely, his fingers weaving in her hair. She closed the inches between them, craving no space between their skin.

She wanted to show him her unsaid feelings, beyond the inadequacy of words.

"You know I love you," Wendel said, a rasp in his voice.

"I do." Ardis smiled. "You told me. Many times."

"I meant it every time."

Wendel leaned on his elbow and looked into her eyes. She studied the sharp shadows of his cheekbones, the questioning set of his mouth, and the quiet green clarity of his eyes. He was so beautiful it almost hurt to look at him. Of course, her opinion may have been swayed by him lying naked beside her.

Wendel's eyebrows furrowed. "Why are you smiling?"

"You are so ridiculously handsome," Ardis said.

"For a moment," he said, "I thought you might say *pretty*."

Ardis laughed, since she had called him that before. She rested her head in the crook of his arm and breathed in his scent. The spice of pines clung to his skin. He curved his hand down the hollow of her back. She waited for him to do more, but he seemed content to lie there and look at her with a smile shadowing his face.

"Come closer," Ardis said.

Wendel dragged her against him, his fingertips firm on her spine.

"Closer," she said.

He flicked his eyebrows upward. "How close?"

She could feel how hard he was against her hip, and slid her hand down to stroke him. His lips parted. He closed his eyes, tilted back his head, and surrendered to her touch. A groan escaped from deep in his throat.

"Wait," Wendel said.

He slid off the bed swiftly. He hunted for his coat, found it on the floor, and reached into the pocket. Sprawled on the sheets, Ardis admired the view.

Wendel caught her staring at him and gave her a smoldering look. "Are you ogling me?"

"Absolutely," she said.

Wendel returned with a preventive. He leaned against the bed and looked her up and down. His jaw taut, he tilted his head. She would have loved to know what he was thinking. Her heartbeat thudded in anticipation.

"I'm still cold," Ardis said. "Come to bed."

Wendel sat on the edge and caressed her breast. He rubbed his thumb over her tight nipple, and her breath snagged.

"Cold?" he said, like he didn't believe her.

Ardis smoothed the sheets. Inviting him. But he stood beside the bed and ran his hand down the hard planes of his chest, along the dark trail of hair, even lower. He touched himself and watched her watching him.

Ardis crossed her ankles and curled her toes. "Don't be so bad."

Wendel smiled, devilishly, as he slid on the preventive. Then he climbed into bed and grabbed her by the waist. He dragged her down and held himself over her, his weight denting the mattress, his hands clutching the sheets.

"That's better," Ardis said.

Wendel kissed her on the mouth. She licked his lip, then nipped him, just hard enough to make him moan. She couldn't stop kissing him, her heartbeat thumping as if she had been running and finally caught him.

"I want you," Ardis said.

Wendel had a wicked glint in his eyes. "Be more specific."

"I want you inside me." Her cheeks heated. "Obviously."

"I'm happy to oblige."

Ardis wanted to knock the smirk from his face, but Wendel distracted her by nudging her legs apart with his knee. He slid inside in one long stroke. She groaned and gripped his buttocks, her fingernails marking his skin.

"What do you want?" Wendel said, his voice like dark velvet.

"Your cock," she whispered.

He started slowly, every stroke a delicious torment, then quickened his pace. She hooked her legs behind his and took him even deeper. He kissed her on the collarbone, his breath hot on her skin, and sucked on her nipple.

Ardis ground against him. She ached with unspent desire. "More."

Wendel thrust even deeper, filling her completely, but she still felt a hollow ache. She kissed his neck and tasted the salt of his sweat. He reached under her and gripped one of her buttocks. His groan spiked her lust.

"Let me," Ardis said.

Wendel glanced into her eyes. "What?"

She hooked her leg behind his and flipped him onto his back. He fell against the pillows. Straddling him, she stroked him in her fist. His hardness felt slick in her hand. He sucked in his breath, a shuddering intake of air.

"Ardis—"

"What do you want?" she said.

Wendel narrowed his eyes, but he looked disoriented, his face flushed.

"You," he said.

She kissed him and whispered, "Be more specific."

Wendel glowered halfheartedly. She sank down and took all of him. When he angled his hips upward, she bit back a moan and reached down to touch herself. He watched her through his eyelashes, his gaze scorching, then lifted himself on his elbows. He kissed her on the mouth, his tongue darting between her lips.

Ardis quickened her fingers, the pleasure on the brink of excruciating.

"Come," she said.

"What?" Wendel sounded drunk with lust.

"I want you to come."

He didn't need to be told twice. He pounded into her with uninhibited pleasure. She rode him until he clutched her close, every muscle in his body stiffening. He let out a stuttering groan. The sound thrilled her in primal ways.

When he came, Ardis came with him.

Her tension spent, she lay in the crook of his arm and closed her eyes. He smoothed her hair from her face. She rested her head on his chest, breathless, his heartbeat thumping against her ear. Her body glowed with joy.

This, she decided, was what love felt like.

"I love you," Ardis whispered.

Wendel answered her with a kiss.

Ardis lay beside Wendel, daydreaming, as the sky darkened to the color of a blackcurrant. A knock on the door startled her.

Wendel sat upright. "Wait here."

He dragged on his trousers and answered the door. A maid looked him up and down, none too subtly. Ardis clutched the sheet to her chest. Likely the maid thought Ardis was a prostitute, and Wendel was fair game.

"Sir," the maid said, "you have a guest waiting for you in the lobby."

"Who?" Wendel said.

"He said his name was Wolfram."

"Wolfram?" Wendel scowled. "What does he want?"

"I'm afraid he didn't say, sir." The maid brushed a lock of her hair behind her ear. "Do you require anything else, sir?"

Ardis thought she might vomit if she heard another *sir*. God knows what the maid would do if she knew Wendel was once a prince.

"No, thank you," Wendel said.

He shut the door in the maid's face, much to Ardis's satisfaction.

Ardis swung her legs over the edge of the mattress. "Should I come?"

"You already did." Wendel gave her a thoroughly evil smile.

She rolled her eyes. "Should I go downstairs with you?"

"It's nearly dinnertime."

Ardis dressed and braided her hair. She hoped she didn't look feral, though there wasn't much she could do without a bath. Wendel raked his fingers through his hair and splashed water from the sink onto his face.

They descended to the lobby together.

Wolfram was waiting in a chair. He leapt to his feet when he saw them.

Wendel arched an eyebrow. "If Mother and Father have invited us to dinner at the castle, you already know my answer."

A crease appeared between Wolfram's eyebrows—a look Ardis knew well.

"I'm inviting you both to dine with me," Wolfram said.

Wendel blinked. "Where?"

"Here."

Ardis wasn't sure Wendel would say yes, so she took matters into her own hands.

"I would love to," she said. "I'm famished."

Ardis had wanted to sound more ladylike, but her stomach grumbled rather spectacularly. Wolfram hid his smile behind a polite cough. Wendel echoed the smile, but he still had a hard unyielding look around his eyes.

"Very well," Wendel said.

Wolfram's smile widened. "Shall we?"

TWENTY

Their footsteps clicked across the marble floor of the lobby. Gaslight burned at a dim glow in the restaurant. Ardis chose a corner table, and Wolfram pulled out her chair. Wendel frowned as if he had been usurped.

Which, in a way, he had been.

A waiter arrived with their menus, and Ardis flipped hers open. She was distracted, however, by another waiter delivering a plate of meatballs in white sauce, with a side of boiled potatoes. Her mouth ached fiercely.

"What are those?" Ardis asked Wendel, quietly enough not to be rude.

Wendel followed her gaze. "*Königsberger klopse.*"

"It's a traditional dish," Wolfram said. "Meatballs, cream, capers."

Wendel wrinkled his nose. "I can't stand the anchovies in the sauce."

Ardis wasn't fond of anchovies herself, but today her stomach disagreed. It looked delicious. She closed her menu decisively.

"That's what I want," she said.

Wolfram nodded. "I'll have the haddock with the mustard butter. Wendel?"

Wendel scanned the menu with apparent disinterest. "The waiter isn't back yet."

"He will be," Ardis said. "Make up your mind."

Wendel drummed his fingers. "You weren't joking about being famished?"

Ardis smiled and kicked his shin under the table. To his credit, he only barely flinched.

The waiter returned on cue. "Have you decided?"

"The haddock, please," Wolfram said.

"Meatballs," Ardis said, "with cream and capers."

"The Königsberger klopse? Very good, madam." The waiter looked expectantly to Wendel. "And you, sir?"

"Roast duck," Wendel said. "You do have roast duck, don't you?"

"Certainly, sir."

As the waiter whisked away their menus, Ardis glared at Wendel. He arched his eyebrows, but didn't look so innocent.

Wolfram put on a polite face. "How have you been, Wendel?"

Wendel slid his thumbnail along a faded scar on his arm. He thinned his lips slightly. "When? Since Vienna? Since Constantinople?"

Wolfram didn't blink, his eyes blue like the sea on a sunny day. "Since you left."

"That was twelve years ago." A thin smile bent Wendel's mouth. "Would you like the abridged version of events?"

"I would."

Ardis drank a long swig of water. This might take a while, but she was curious how Wendel would tell his story.

"They said you died," Wolfram said. "That you drowned in the lagoon and your body wasn't fit for an open casket."

"Damn," Ardis said softly.

Wolfram glanced at her. "I apologize for the details. That was coarse of me."

She shrugged.

Wendel laughed. "That's how I died? Drowning? I'm a better swimmer than that."

"I know," Wolfram said. "But whenever I asked questions, Father said nothing. Mother... Mother had such sadness in her eyes, and it made me hate myself for ever mentioning it. Eventually, I stopped asking."

"Sadness?" Wendel's face looked emotionless. "And you believed her?"

"We all mourned you, Wendel."

Wendel stared into his glass. He hadn't drunk a drop. "I'm sorry. I didn't want to leave."

Ardis wanted to reach across the table and touch his hand, but wasn't sure she should.

"What happened to you?" Wolfram said.

The waiter returned at that inopportune moment. He gave Wolfram his haddock, Wendel his roast duck, and—finally—Ardis her meatballs and potatoes. She spread her napkin in her lap and speared a meatball on her fork. She devoured it in a single bite and resisted the urge to wolf down the rest like a wild woman.

"I take it you like them?" Wendel said dryly.

"Is it that obvious?" Ardis said. "And keep talking."

Wendel sighed and leaned back in his chair. Steam wafted from the roast duck on his plate, but he neglected his knife and fork.

"Do you remember Maus?" Wendel said. "The cat?"

Wolfram frowned and chewed a mouthful of fish. "No."

"He died, and that's how I first discovered my necromancy."

Wolfram leaned away. "You revived Maus?"

Wendel's eyes glimmered a cool green. "I never intended to do that. I only wished Maus wasn't dead, and then he wasn't."

Wolfram said nothing, but he wouldn't look away from his brother's face.

"I mistakenly brought him to Mother and Father," Wendel said.

"What did they do?"

"Nothing. Not that night. But a man came for me a month later. At the time, I didn't know he was an assassin."

Wolfram held his knife and fork suspended in midair. "They hired a hit man?"

Wendel laughed entirely without humor. "No, Wolfie, the assassin brought me to Constantinople. Where I was trained."

Wolfram studiously sliced his haddock into smaller and smaller pieces. Silence overshadowed the table. Ardis finished her last meatball and pushed a potato around her plate until she couldn't bear the silence, and ate it.

"Are you an assassin?" Wolfram asked, as if questioning his preference in tea.

Wendel dipped his head. "One of the very best."

Ardis glanced at Wendel. His face betrayed none of the pain she knew he had endured, none of the scars still marking his skin.

"Not by choice," Ardis said. "You tried to escape the Order."

"I did escape them." Wendel sipped his water. "With your help."

"How many—" Wolfram coughed. "How many men have you killed?"

"Honestly? I can't remember."

Wolfram's nostrils flared. "And your necromancy?"

"What about it?"

"How many men have you brought back?"

"Similar quantities."

Wolfram dabbed his mouth with his napkin. He stared at the food left on his plate and didn't look his brother in the eye. "Should I be horrified by you?"

Wendel sawed at his duck with more vehemence than necessary. "I have done horrifying things."

"You sound as if you don't care."

Wendel shrugged and ate a forkful of duck.

Ardis pushed away her empty plate. "Of course Wendel cares. He doesn't like to talk about what happened to him."

Wolfram's face tightened. "I meant no offense."

"I'm not offended." Wendel cut another slice of duck. "My mere presence offends most."

"Why?"

Wendel stared at his brother. "People don't consider raising corpses a parlor trick."

Wolfram frowned. "Someone has to touch the dead. Morticians and gravediggers do. And doctors, they learn from cadavers."

Wendel shook his head. "Constantinople wasn't medical school."

Wolfram let out an impatient breath, picked up his glass, and set it down again. "I don't understand."

Wendel tapped his fingernail on his glass. "Clearly."

"Why did Mother and Father send you away? They could have helped you. They—"

"Helped?" Wendel's eyes flashed. "I'm hardly an invalid. Spare me the asylum."

Ardis crumpled her napkin and tossed it on the table.

"Pardon me," she said. "I need to... powder my nose."

She strode toward the ladies' room. Best to give them time alone.

After the toilet, Ardis lingered by the mirror. She *did* look feral, with a blush in her cheeks and rebellious hair escaping from her braid. She turned on the faucet, cupped water in her hands, and splashed it into her face.

The door whisked open. Natalya strode in and raised her eyebrows. "Bruised, darling?"

Ardis shrugged. "That dragon tossed me around a bit."

"I would say more than a bit."

Natalya met her gaze in the mirror. "Come join me for drinks in the bar."

Ardis hesitated. "Sure. Thanks."

"I'll see you out there in a minute."

Ardis strolled from the ladies' room. She glanced at Wendel and Wolfram, who still seemed to be absorbed in conversation. The lighting was dim inside the bar, and a mirror gleamed dully behind the bartender.

"A drink, madam?" the bartender said.

Ardis touched her belly for a fleeting moment. She had been lectured on the evils of alcohol, and how it could hurt an unborn baby, by her mother. At the time, Ardis had rolled her eyes and said it would never happen.

"The soda water," she said. "Thank you."

Natalya sidled up to the bar next. "Get me a vodka on the rocks."

The bartender slid their drinks across to them. Natalya downed her shot while Ardis sipped her fizzy soda water.

"Do you always drink alone?" Natalya said. "Where's that necromancer of yours?"

"Occupied," Ardis said.

She didn't want to give Natalya any ammunition.

Natalya toyed with her shot glass. "You did a fine job today."

"Thank you, ma'am." Ardis squared her shoulders. "I only wish I could have done more. The dragon destroyed our zeppelin."

"I heard," Natalya said. "Honey, you have ambition. I like that."

Ardis blushed. "Thank you."

"What made you leave America?"

Ardis felt her mouth go dry, and sipped her drink. "Why did you leave Russia?"

"You first."

"A man wouldn't listen when I said no."

Ardis omitted the part about running him through with a sword, and how she was an outlaw in America as a result.

Natalya caught the bartender's eye and raised her finger for another shot.

"I ran away from a man," she said. "My father wanted me to marry this disgusting old relic pickled in vodka."

Ardis grimaced. "That sounds miserable."

Her mother had never pressured her to marry—though she was busy running a brothel.

"I shouted with my father for months," Natalya said. "Back then, I had only been on the marriage market for a year. I finally agreed on the condition they would send me to a finishing school first. The one with the fencing academy." She grinned. "Once I learned how to master a blade, I never looked back."

She must have come from a rich family. Ardis never had formal lessons in fighting.

"When was this?" Ardis said.

"Darling," Natalya said, "a lady never reveals her age."

Ardis smirked. "Before the Hex?"

"Definitely." Natalya knocked back her second shot. "I worked the fencing circuit for awhile. Then I had a stint as an aviatrix."

"Really?" Ardis said.

Natalya smiled. "A little red biplane. Did stunts until it almost killed me. Then the Hex came along, and I decided to die another way."

No wonder Natalya was the commander of the Eisenkrieger pilots.

Ardis raised her glass. "A toast to your colorful career."

"Is that soda water?" Natalya laughed.

Heat stole over Ardis's face. "Maybe."

"Bartender, get this girl some vodka."

Ardis held up her hand. "I shouldn't."

"Why, sweetheart?"

Ardis chewed on the inside of her cheek. Time to think of a cover story.

"Doctor's orders," she lied. "Said not to drink. My liver got a bit bruised."

"God damn," Natalya said. "You must have hit the ground harder than I thought."

"No broken bones," Ardis said.

"Good." Natalya clapped her on the shoulder. "I need my pilots in fighting form."

Natalya had a strong arm, and her hand hit a bruise. Ardis managed to look stoic.

"Why are all the pilots women, anyway?" Ardis said.

Natalya grinned. "We're some of the toughest bitches around."

Ardis laughed, then winced at her aching ribs.

"There's a height limit on the cockpit," Natalya said. "Women are smaller. At least, that's what I heard from the archmages."

"You ever worry about fighting for the archmages?"

"I have no loyalty to Russia." Natalya snorted. "And anyone who thinks I'm a turncoat can take a bayonet to their backside."

Ardis arched her eyebrows at this rather vivid imagery. "I'm not doubting you, but it's strange not to fight for home."

"Lucky for you, America isn't in this war."

"Yet."

Natalya toyed with her shot glass. "You learned how to fight in America?"

"Yes and no." Ardis stared at her knuckles. "When I was a girl, we didn't live in a nice part of town. When I got myself into trouble, I learned how to get myself back out of trouble. With my fists or my sword."

"You brought your sword to street fights?"

"I wish." Ardis laughed. "I didn't learn how to swing a sword until I went across the pond. Worked with a swordswoman for a year. I did all the carrying and cooking and cleaning, and she did all the teaching."

Natalya pursed her mouth. "Where is she now?"

"Dead."

"I'm sorry."

Ardis shrugged. "She died fighting."

"Somebody always wants to kill somebody," Natalya said, slurring a little. "And they can hire us if they want better killing."

A slow grin spread on Ardis's face. "I'll toast to that."

"With your paltry soda water?" Natalya scoffed.

"Take it or leave it."

Someone tapped Ardis on the shoulder. She turned and found Wendel there.

"Were you derailed on your return to dinner?" Wendel said.

"I already ate dinner," Ardis said.

"I'll take that as a yes." Wendel cocked his head. "Wolfram and I are returning to the castle. You are welcome to join us."

Ardis glanced into his eyes. His face looked smoother. Calmer.

"Don't mind me, darling," Natalya said. "Enjoy your evening."

Ardis smiled. "Try not to drink too much vodka. Konstantin might ask for more field testing first thing in the morning."

Natalya groaned and pretended to knock her forehead on the bar. "Heaven help us."

"See you in the morning," Ardis said cheerfully.

Wendel raised his eyebrows, but he didn't comment as they walked through the restaurant to the doors. Outside, Ardis breathed in the crisp night air. A glittering of stars sprinkled the sky. Wolfram waited by a taxi.

"Why the castle?" Ardis said.

Wolfram reached for her door, but Wendel beat him to it and smirked. Wolfram laughed. The brothers seemed to be on better terms.

"I left something," Wendel said, "and Wolfram tells me I can have it back."

Ardis climbed into the taxi. "Can I guess?"

"Go ahead," Wendel said.

The brothers climbed into the taxi, and it rumbled over the cobblestone streets of Königsberg. Ardis wondered what Wendel missed from home. Besides his family, though he would never admit to being so sentimental.

"Is it valuable?" Ardis said.

"Yes," Wendel said.

"Of course it is."

Wendel poked her in the ribs, which tickled.

She bit her lip. "Is it a crown?"

Wolfram and Wendel both laughed.

"You think I'm so greedy?" Wendel said.

"Well, yes," Ardis said. "Is it a painting?"

Wolfram smirked. "Have you developed an appreciation for art, Wendel?"

"Only nudes," Wendel said.

Ardis slid her finger down the window. "Is it a fainting couch?"

Wolfram laughed. He looked delighted by his brother's grimace.

"Your guesses are increasingly horrible," Wendel said.

"Give me a hint," Ardis said.

Wendel, sandwiched between her and Wolfram, did his best to look pensive. "It once led to Juliana calling me talentless."

"Oh?" Ardis teased. "And here I thought necromancy was your only talent."

Wendel narrowed his eyes, smirking.

At the castle, Wolfram didn't linger inside the entrance hall. They followed him to a room wallpapered in emerald damask. A grand piano dominated the space, as big and slick as a black whale. It seemed to be a music room, though Ardis had never been to a home grand enough to afford such an indulgence.

Wendel looked around the room, then detoured to a walnut cabinet. "Is it still here?"

"Yes." Wolfram handed him a small brass key.

Wendel unlocked the cabinet and found a pear-shaped case. He freed a violin from its velvet coffin. The violin's wood gleamed a rich chestnut, and he caressed its curves with soft wonder in his eyes.

"Has it been tuned?" Wendel said.

Wolfram wiggled his hand. "Mother does, on occasion, though she claims she can't bring herself to play it anymore."

Wendel grunted more than a little derisively. He tucked the violin under his chin and dragged the bow over its strings.

A terrible screech split the air. Ardis winced.

"Juliana was right," Wolfram said. "It does sound like a tortured cat."

Wendel scowled. "I would never torture a cat. The bow simply needs more rosin."

Wendel put down the violin, as gently as if it were a baby, and found a little metal tin containing an amber cake of rosin. He rubbed it over the hairs of the bow, his lips pursed with devoted concentration.

"Allow me to prove you wrong," Wendel said.

He touched his bow to the strings, then narrowed his eyes. "Did anyone hear that?"

"Hear what?" Ardis said.

Wendel opened his mouth, closed it again, and shook his head. "Nothing."

Wendel tugged the bow across the violin and played a single clear note. He fingered the strings as he climbed through one scale, then another, and another. With every repetition, his playing softened and sweetened.

Wendel lowered the violin and laughed. "I tried to play in Constantinople. I even bought a questionable violin from a merchant in the bazaar. Only to have it taken away from me by the assassins, once they realized that would punish me."

"That's a shame," Wolfram said.

Wendel looked down. "I have forgotten so much."

Wolfram went to the walnut cabinet and found a battered book of sheet music. Wendel flipped through the old pages, his eyebrows angled in a frown, then flattened the book on a table. He lifted the violin to his chin.

"Bach's Partita Number Two," Wendel said.

Ardis held her breath. Wendel began to play, the notes hesitant, not always harmonious. He frowned at the paper, then closed his eyes. After a minute, the tension in his shoulders melted. The melody shimmered like quicksilver. Soaring and falling, a swallow in the wind, a storm unfurling across the sky. Wendel's face tightened with bliss as he lost himself in the music. Lightning shivered down Ardis's spine.

Clapping echoed from the other end of the room. Startled, Wendel lowered the violin.

A lady in red lingered by the door. Ornate beadwork glittered across her crimson gown, her black hair twisted in a sleek bun. The lady's eyes reminded Ardis of her own, and Ardis recognized her when she smiled.

"Lady Maili!" Ardis said.

"Please," Maili said, "keep playing. I didn't intend to interrupt."

Wendel fidgeted with his bow. "I'm very much out of practice."

"Such modesty," Maili said. "And I'm glad to see you both after that tragedy in Vienna. Ardis, are you entirely all right?"

Ardis hugged herself and shuddered at the memory of the inferno. "I am now. What brings you to Königsberg?"

"I'm visiting with my husband, Lord Max Weissman, on our way to London."

Wolfram smiled. "Maili and Max are quite the world travelers."

Wendel fussed over a string, then placed his violin in its case. He clasped his hands behind his back and bowed his head. "I will spare your ears any further torment."

"If I didn't know you better," Ardis said, "I would call you shy."

Wolfram smirked at Wendel. "Are you?"

Lady Maili settled in a gilded chair and smoothed her gown over her legs. "Please, play for us."

Wendel arched an eyebrow and glanced at Ardis, as if he needed her approval.

"You play beautifully," Ardis said. "What else can I say to flatter you?"

Wendel turned down the corners of his mouth as if trying hard not to smile. "Let me think."

She looked him in the eye. "Play."

Wendel cleared his throat and took back his violin.

A rumble crawled across the sky. Thunder. At least, it sounded like thunder until the shriek of metal on stone interrupted. Wendel ran to the window and yanked aside the curtains. His hand gripped the cloth.

"Christ," he said. "Time for an intermission."

TWENTY-ONE

rdis sprang to her feet and ducked under Wendel's arm. She pressed her hand against the cold glass and peered outside.

The clockwork dragon clung to the highest tower of the castle. It flared its wings as it clawed at the roof, its talons scattering tiles and splintering the wood beneath.

Wendel swore under his breath. "It's going to tear down the castle."

"What will?" Wolfram said.

Wendel turned from the window and let the curtain fall, but it was too late to shield his brother from the sight outside.

Wolfram leaned against the wall, his jaw slack, and gawked out the window. "What an enormous monstrosity!"

Wendel shook his head. "Now isn't the time for polysyllabic exclamations."

"We have to get out of here," Ardis said.

Lady Maili hovered behind them. "What is it *this* time?"

"You don't even want to know," Ardis said.

Wendel closed his violin in its case and cradled it under his arm. He strode to the door and held it open. Lady Maili took the hint and hurried through, but Wolfram lingered by the window.

Ardis tapped his shoulder. "Wolfram."

The clockwork dragon whipped its tail and smashed a window. Glass rained onto the courtyard as the monstrosity snaked its neck and stared at them. Ardis yanked the curtains shut and ran, Wolfram following at her heels.

A collision shook the ceiling. The windows shattered in a symphony of broken glass. Ardis stumbled and glanced over her shoulder. The clockwork dragon swiped at the window like a cat reaching into a mouse's hole. Its claws gouged the windowsill and snagged the curtains, shredding the velvet into tatters.

"Ardis!"

Wendel's hand clamped on her arm, and together they bolted into the hallway.

Flustered, Lady Maili fanned herself. "We're safe inside, aren't we?"

"No," Wendel said.

Wolfram frowned. "This castle is solid stone."

"That dragon is solid destruction."

As if to underscore his point, the dragon attacked the broken window. Its claws raked across the stone with a grating screech that prickled the little hairs on Ardis's arms. She retreated from the ruined music room.

"Stay away from the windows and doors," Wendel said.

"My husband." Lady Maili sucked in a breath. "I left Max in the conservatory."

Wendel frowned. "What? Why?"

"We were invited to a dinner party."

Wendel swore and ran. Ardis followed him, the others in pursuit.

The conservatory proved to be clear at the other end of the castle. Panting, Ardis clutched the burning stitch between her ribs. She straightened and looked around. A glass dome arched above, frosted by the cold, though the air felt muggy, scented with the rich aroma of rot and green growth. Potted palms arched over the lily pads floating in a small tiled pool. Candlelight glimmered in the water.

The dinner party, lords and ladies alike, mingled in this bottled oasis.

"Max!" Lady Maili said.

A gentleman in a tailcoat strolled across the conservatory. He rumpled his brown hair and gave Maili a bemused smile. "I wondered where you disappeared to."

"Max." Maili rested her hand on his arm. "Let's go home."

"So soon?" Max glanced between their faces. "Prince Wolfram, why is everyone so breathless? Been playing a game?"

Wolfram shook his head. "Hardly."

"Wendel!" Juliana's voice chimed across the party. "Have you come to play for us?"

Wendel glanced at the violin under his arm, then handed it to Ardis. "I trust you to keep this safe."

"You're welcome." Ardis sighed. "Though I wish it were a sword."

She had left Chun Yi at the hotel. There never was a safe time to let down her guard.

Juliana glided between the palms, shoving their fronds aside with her slender arm. Her jasmine perfume clashed with the wine on her breath.

"Hello, Wendy." Juliana's eyes glittered darkly. "Uninvited, yet again?"

"I'm here to save you," Wendel said, "yet again."

She pouted. "With what? Your pitiful violin?"

Wendel stared icily at her. "Now isn't the time to be a bitch."

Juliana gasped with more authenticity. "How dare—"

"Everyone needs to leave. Immediately."

"Why?" Juliana sipped her wine. "Assassins?"

"Actually, no."

"Wendel isn't lying," Wolfram said.

She puckered her lips. "Oh, shut up, Wolfie."

"Fine," Wendel said. "Die. See if I care."

Juliana looked like she wanted to strangle him.

Wolfram, glowering, strode past them both and stopped by the pool. He cleared his throat and clinked a fork on a wineglass.

"May I have everyone's attention?" he said. "Please, exit the conservatory."

"Why?" someone called. "This party is just getting started."

Laughter echoed under the glass dome.

Wendel touched his brother's shoulder. "This party is over."

More laughter.

"Aren't you the bastard prince?" shouted a drunk.

"Disinherited." Wendel sneered. "There's a difference."

Waldemar shoved through the crowd, the medals on his chest clinking. "What the hell is this commotion about?"

"The clockwork dragon," Wendel said.

"Where?"

Wendel looked him in the eye. "Here."

His timing couldn't have been more perfect.

The clockwork dragon landed on the conservatory, scrabbling its claws on the dome, flaring its wings for balance.

Cracks spiderwebbed through the glass and raced to the edges.

Waldemar stared skyward. "Holy—"

The dome yielded under the dragon.

Shattered glass rained on the guests. Ardis ducked and shielded her head with her arms. Shards rattled on the floor. She stole a glance as the dragon bent into the conservatory, delicately, and gaped its jaws over Wolfram.

Steam drifted between the dragon's fangs and misted Wolfram's hair.

Wendel tackled his brother into the pool. Water splashed out and wet the dragon's snout. Snorting, the beast recoiled. Wendel and Wolfram climbed to their feet. The pool sloshed at their knees.

"You saved my life," Wolfram said, drenched.

"Don't bother—"

Juliana shrieked.

The dragon lunged for Wendel. He saw it coming from the corner of his eye and flung himself sideways. Steel teeth clashed on a mouthful of air. With a hiss, the beast slithered down between the steel beams of the shattered dome.

Spitting water, Wendel staggered to his feet.

The dragon swatted him back into the pool. It pinned him, holding him underwater.

Ardis ran for the pool. "Wendel!"

Wild-eyed, Wolfram smashed a chair on the dragon's arm. The wood splintered, but did nothing to hurt the clockwork.

Wendel groped at the dragon's claws. Bubbles of air broke the surface.

Ardis's heart hammered so hard it deafened all thought. She dropped Wendel's violin by a palm and vaulted into the pool. The dragon tilted its head to watch her, but let her advance. As if she was no threat at all.

Ardis waded to Wendel, scattering lily pads, and ducked underwater.

Wendel lay pinned to the bottom of the pool, his eyes open, his hair drifting like seaweed. Still holding his breath. Barely. She reached under his arms and yanked, but had no hope of budging the dragon's weight.

Ardis reached into Wendel's coat and found his black dagger.

She surfaced, panting, and stared at the scales armoring the dragon's arm. Even the biggest enemies had a weakness.

There.

Ardis stabbed the dagger behind the dragon's wrist. Oil gushed like blood.

The dragon hissed and jerked back, lifting its claws from Wendel. He burst from the water with a gasp. Ardis grabbed Wendel by the arm and dragged him away from the dragon. They scrambled from the pool together.

"Run," Wendel rasped.

"Not without you," Ardis said fiercely.

The clockwork dragon reared back, its wounded arm lame, and bared its fangs.

Waldemar, tipsy and armed with a rapier, marched to the dragon. He didn't bother with a heroic pose, like Ardis thought he might, and stabbed the dragon's armored belly. The rapier stuck between a crack, and the dragon scuttled away. Waldemar released the blade before it pulled him off balance.

Guests screamed and scrambled from the conservatory.

Ardis hauled Wendel to the hallway. Lady Maili and Lord Max waited there, braver than most, and they both steadied Wendel when he doubled over. A cough wracked his body.

Wendel wiped his mouth with a shaking hand. "Where's Wolfram?"

"I don't know," Ardis said.

Maili stared at wreckage. "There are still people in there."

Ardis knew Maili had to be remembering the downfall of the ballroom in Vienna, when it was a miracle no one died.

Well, no one but the assassins sent to capture or kill Wendel.

"Let me go," Wendel said. "I can fight."

He shrugged off Max and Maili's helping hands and straightened.

"You nearly drowned," Max said, though he sounded more impressed than horrified.

"Wendel," Ardis said. "We need to retreat."

"Where?" Maili said.

Max pressed his hand to Maili's back. The protective ferocity in his eyes made Ardis wish Wendel would do the same.

"The cellar," Ardis said.

Determination steeled Wendel's voice. "My dagger, please?"

Cathedral bells tolled an alarm. Ardis glanced at the black dagger in her hand. Dragon's oil slicked the blade like iridescent blood. She returned the dagger to Wendel. His cold fingers lingered on hers, and he met her gaze. His eyes betrayed the tenderness of concern that he so carefully kept from his face.

She wanted to drag him into an embrace, but settled for a nod.

Wolfram scrambled into the hallway. "Wendel!"

"Wolfie." Wendel exhaled. "Stay close. Don't do anything stupidly heroic."

Dripping wet, Wolfram looked between them with bright eyes. "How is the dragon so *smart*?"

Wendel grimaced. "You're as bad as Konstantin."

"Is it entirely clockwork? Or is it—"

Talons scraped the floor, followed by the rustling of steel scales. Wolfram's back stiffened, and his face went bone white.

"Wolfram!" Wendel said. "Get—"

The clockwork dragon lunged from the conservatory and sank its fangs into Wolfram's shoulder. Wolfram screamed and tried to break free, but it jerked him off his feet and shook him like a dog with a rabbit.

Bile soured Ardis's throat. It wanted to snap his neck.

The dragon flung Wolfram across the conservatory. He crashed through a window and crumpled on the lawn. Wendel sprinted toward him, heedless of danger, and Ardis followed. Shards of glass clung to the window like crooked teeth. Wendel kicked them away, climbed through, and stumbled into the night.

Outside, Wolfram lay facedown on the lawn.

The dragon snapped at the heels of the fleeing guests. Ardis stepped through the broken window and sprinted into the night.

Wendel skidded to his knees and flipped Wolfram over. Wolfram's head lolled.

"Oh, God," Wendel said. "Wolfie."

Ardis stared down at them. "Is he…?"

Trembling, Wendel touched Wolfram's neck. "He isn't dead."

Juliana hobbled across the lawn, her heels sinking into the grass. "Wolfram?" she called. "Wendel?"

Glass chimed in a cascade. The dragon smashed through another window and clambered from the conservatory. Starlight glimmered off its scales, the red so dark it looked black. It crunched across the broken glass, driving shards into the earth, and lowered its head with a hiss. Ardis looked into the dragon's gemstone eyes. A strange intelligence lurked behind their glow, transcending clockwork and magic.

"Take my hand," Wendel said.

The shadows of Amarant rippled over the necromancer, staining his skin with darkness. He disappeared against the night sky, no more than a patch of missing stars. He gripped her hand, and shadows bled from his skin to hers.

"Don't let go," Wendel said.

"I won't," Ardis said.

Wendel dragged her down to Wolfram. He touched the flat of the dagger to Wolfram's hand and let the shadows blanket him.

The dragon crawled from the wreckage.

Ardis held her breath so it wouldn't fog the air. She huddled by Wendel, who was shivering from the cold—or from the strain of hiding the three of them. She didn't know how much the dagger drained his magic.

"Bloody hell," Juliana said.

Juliana stared at the dragon for no more than a second, then did the sensible thing and kicked off her shoes. The dragon cocked its head. Juliana hurled her shoe at it. The heel hit it square in the eye. The dragon jerked back, blinking, and Juliana bolted for the castle. Barefoot, she zigzagged around broken glass.

The dragon snarled at Juliana, then slinked across the lawn.

Ardis sucked in a quick breath. Wendel clutched her hand so hard it hurt her bones. Wolfram stirred and moaned softly.

The dragon halted and tilted its head. Listening.

Across the river, the cathedral bells still tolled. The gonging echoed over the water.

Wolfram stirred. "Did I fall?"

Wendel hushed him with a hand over his mouth.

The dragon bent over them and sniffed the air. Ardis froze. The hot steam of its breath filled her nostrils. It smelled like brimstone, and an unearthly perfume—black cherries and smoke—that could only be magic.

Still shivering, Wendel struggled to stay motionless.

Wolfram opened his eyes. He let out a startled yelp, muffled by Wendel's hand. The dragon hissed and bared its fangs.

Ardis tensed the muscles in her thighs. Ready to run.

Footsteps shook the earth. The dragon recoiled and faced its new opponent.

The Colossus.

Natalya tromped over the bridge and across the river, the bridge quaking under the weight. She stopped at the edge of the lawn and shouted in Russian. Ardis hoped she wasn't still drunk.

The dragon leapt into an attack.

Metal met metal in a deafening crash. The dragon reared for the cockpit. Natalya blocked, and the beast bit the Eisenkrieger's arm. Fangs gouged the steel. Natalya braced herself, the Eisenkrieger's feet digging muddy gashes.

The dragon clamped down, but Natalya didn't yield.

She wedged her armored hand between the dragon's jaws, prying them open, hinges screeching, and yanked her arm free. Her punch knocked the dragon reeling; it staggered, found its balance, and rushed her again. Natalya sidestepped, though not nimbly enough.

The dragon tackled the Colossus with the force of a small earthquake. The cockpit's glass shattered under its claws. Natalya wedged an elbow under the dragon and forced it away, then staggered to her feet and charged.

With a burst of speed, Natalya caught the clockwork dragon by its wing.

The dragon hissed and writhed, biting at her legs, but she didn't let go. She dragged it down to the river and hurled it in. The dragon thrashed, its tail churning the water white, until it sank to the river bottom. The light in its eyes sputtered out.

Ardis and Wendel stood by Wolfram. Natalya turned to them, parked the Colossus on one knee, and climbed down.

"Still in one piece?" Natalya said.

Ardis nodded, then shook her head.

Wolfram looked at his brother. "Did I fall?"

"You did," Wendel said.

Natalya grunted and touched her ribs. She stared at her hand, red with blood.

"You aren't in one piece yourself," Ardis said.

She sounded much braver than she felt, her stomach sick with fear.

"Dragon's claw," Natalya muttered. "Stabbed me through the cockpit."

Natalya swayed and sat on the ground. Ardis hoped some of that was thanks to the vodka, and not the severity of the wound.

Wolfram blinked. "Did I fall?"

"What's wrong, Wolfie?" Wendel said.

Wolfram didn't seem to understand the question. His eyelids fluttered shut, and his back arched. His body began to convulse.

"Ardis!" Wendel said.

Her heartbeat thundered in her ears. "He's having a fit."

"Help him. Please."

The anguish in Wendel's voice tore at Ardis.

"I can't," she said. "We have to wait for it to end."

Wendel cradled his brother's head in his hands, shielding Wolfram from the dirt, but he looked so powerless to help him.

TWENTY-TWO

Candlelight couldn't chase the shadows from Königsberg Cathedral. Wendel waited just inside the doors, a hollow look in his eyes, and Ardis squeezed his hand. He startled, then squeezed back and lifted his head.

"We don't have to do this," Ardis said quietly.

Wendel shook his head. "I gave my word."

He looked down the length of the cathedral. Ardis sucked in a slow breath. The sweetness of beeswax lingered in the air.

Juliana rose from a pew. "Thank you for coming."

Wendel said nothing, but his mouth hardened.

"Please," Juliana said, "pray with us."

Ardis furrowed her brow. She didn't tell Juliana she didn't believe in prayer, and didn't know if Wendel believed in anything anymore.

Juliana returned to the pew. Wendel joined her, his back stiff, and Ardis sat by him.

"Where are Mother and Father?" Wendel whispered.

Juliana glanced at him. "They will be here soon."

The princess looked away, and her lips moved soundlessly in prayer.

Wendel lowered his head and let his eyelids close halfway. Ardis slid her hand to his knee, and he caught her fingers in his own. An ache burned in her throat. She didn't know what to tell him, how to comfort him.

They all knew that Wolfram might never wake.

"You won't let me go without promising, will you?"

"Not a chance."

"If I do," he said, *"will you help me?"*

Wendel's words echoed in her mind. When she looked at him now, she could see the despair simmering in his eyes.

He didn't think he could be helped, because he couldn't help anyone.

A cough echoed in the sanctity of the cathedral. Waldemar and Cecelia walked down the aisle. They traversed the rainbow light slanting through the stained glass windows. Waldemar's eyes looked red around the edges, his face frozen in a solemn grimace, and Cecelia kept a handkerchief close to her mouth.

"Wendel," his father said.

Wendel stood and stepped past Ardis into the aisle.

"Is he awake?" Wendel's voice sounded hoarse.

Cecelia's mouth quivered. "Not yet."

"Try not to upset your mother," Waldemar said.

"Should I say nothing?" Wendel spread his arms. "Should I pretend it never happened?"

Waldemar spoke in an intense murmur. "I saw you try to protect Wolfram."

Wendel's arms dropped. "I failed. Forgive me."

Cecelia reached for her son, the handkerchief crumpled in her hand. Her face wavered as if she wanted to smile, but couldn't.

"I know you must feel terrible," she said, "but please don't blame yourself."

Wendel stared at his mother and his eyes glittered in the candlelight.

"Is it so easy?" he said. "To feel blameless?"

Cecelia's mouth thinned into a pale line. "We mustn't linger in the past, Wendel. We must pray for Wolfram's future."

Wendel cleared his throat, looked down, and ran his hand over the back of his neck. When he glanced up, his mouth was twisted. "Does Wolfie have a future?"

Cecelia stifled a sob with her handkerchief.

Waldemar glared at his son. "Enough."

Juliana stepped between them and lifted her hands. "Please don't fight. I asked Wendel here, as part of the family."

Wendel tightened his jaw. "I'm no longer part of this family."

Ardis stood. She caught Wendel's gaze, waiting for him to say they could go, but his eyes looked faraway.

"I'm sorry." Grief roughened Wendel's words. "I couldn't save him."

With that, Wendel clenched his hands into fists and turned his back on his family. He walked from the cathedral, his face hardened by bitterness. When Ardis followed him outside, his expression looked fragile. He blinked fast in the morning.

"It was my fault," Wendel said. "I failed. I couldn't—" He sucked in shuddering breath. "Everyone I know gets hurt."

Ardis said nothing, because there was some truth to it.

Wendel leaned against the wall, his hands splayed on either side, and touched his forehead to the stone. The muscles in his arms tightened, the veins standing in stark relief. He said nothing, his breath fogging the air.

"You asked me what I remembered," Wendel said.

"When?" Ardis said.

"When I fell from the Serpent's Tower." He held his breath. "I remember dying. But I remember nothing of being dead."

She exhaled. "I'm not sure what I expected."

"There was no heaven. No hell."

"Isn't that a relief?"

"No."

Wendel's fingernails scraped the stone of the cathedral. "If there's nothing after death, there's nothing waiting for Wolfram."

Something broke inside Ardis, the shards hurting her heart. "Wendel"—she said his name as almost a sigh—"Wolfram isn't dying."

"We don't know that."

"He might wake at any moment. We have to hope for that."

"I'm not sure I can hope anymore."

His voice sounded bleak, already caught in the undertow of despair.

"Yes, you can." She gripped his arm. "And you will."

Wendel leaned back from the cathedral and looked down at Ardis. His eyes glittered with emotion he couldn't contain.

She didn't want to leave him alone, and was desperate to distract him. "Your violin."

He narrowed his eyes. "What about it?"

"You left it in the castle."

"Did I?"

"In the conservatory. When the dragon attacked, I hid it under a potted palm."

He blinked. "I suppose we should rescue it from the rubble."

They left the cathedral and walked the streets of Königsberg to the castle lawn, glittering with thousands of glass shards. The river rippled like corrugated steel.

"Both of you, please stay back."

A boyish soldier in Prussian blue clutched the hilt of his sword like he might have a reason to use it. At least two dozen other soldiers guarded the castle. On the river, the Prussian Navy dredged the bottom with a barge.

Ardis frowned. "Did they find the dragon?"

"That's classified, ma'am." The soldier licked his lips. "I have to ask you to leave."

Ardis wondered how she should educate him, but was saved the trouble.

Wendel smiled thinly. "We won't be more than a moment."

He walked into the conservatory. Ardis blocked the soldier's path long enough for Wendel to return with his violin.

"How is it?" Ardis said.

Wendel took out his violin and traced his fingers over the glossy wood. He frowned, his lips pressed together pensively. He wandered downriver, tucked the violin under his chin, and drew the bow over its strings.

"It may be a little off," he said.

Wendel played a simple melody, his eyes closed, his face tight with concentration. His sadness bled through the music and shivered into the air. After the song quieted, he lowered the violin and opened his eyes. He sucked in a slow breath and let it out even more slowly. The tension faded from his stance.

"There you are!"

His boots rapping on the bank, Konstantin hurried along the riverside.

"Archmage," Wendel said, by way of greeting.

Konstantin had shadows under his eyes. He looked like he hadn't slept, not that Ardis had slept much, either. Not with Wendel tossing and turning the whole night, and her worrying about the return of his nightmares.

"Did they find the dragon?" Ardis said.

Konstantin shook his head. "I'm afraid not."

"Unsurprisingly." Wendel's mouth hardened. "I'm not waiting here for its grand entrance. See you back at the hotel."

Before Wendel could go, Ardis kissed him on the cheek. He squeezed her shoulder, then strode away, violin under his arm.

"Ardis," Konstantin said, "I have something to show you."

She waved him onward. "Lead the way."

With a brisk nod, Konstantin started walking. Ardis followed him back to the drydock.

Engineers scrambled over the Colossus as they worked to repair the damage done by the clockwork dragon.

"This way." Konstantin led them to a small office.

It wasn't crammed nearly as full of books as the one he had in

Vienna, but it still had a haphazard décor. Konstantin settled in a chair behind the desk, slipped on a pair of glasses with magnifying lenses, and dragged a lamp closer to the desk, where he had pinned a bug to a piece of metal.

Ardis shuddered. "Is that a clockwork wasp?"

"Yes," Konstantin said. "Please, sit."

The only other chair was a high-backed leather armchair in the corner by the door. Ardis sank into the cushions and let out a puff of air. It was damn comfortable.

She wasn't sure she ever wanted to get up again. "What did you want to show me?"

Konstantin stared intently at the clockwork wasp. He prodded the insect's guts with a screwdriver, and a mechanical leg twitched. Ardis slid further away and rubbed the faint scar on her arm where she had been stung.

"I have been studying this specimen," Konstantin said, "and trying to understand what makes it tick." He laughed quietly at his own joke. "Though it doesn't seem to be powered so much by clockwork as it is by magic."

"Technomancy?" Ardis said.

"Yes and no," Konstantin said. "Looking at the wasp in more detail, I believe that the magic must be psychothaumaturgy."

Ardis blinked. "What? I can't even pronounce that."

Konstantin flipped up the magnifying lenses. "Powered by a soul."

A knot tightened in her gut. "There's a soul in the wasp?"

"There was."

"And the clockwork dragon?"

"An infinitely more powerful soul."

Ardis stared at the dissected clockwork wasp. "How do we kill the dragon?"

"There should be a crystal in the dragon's heart," Konstantin said. "That would contain the soul and act as a battery."

Ardis imagined tearing into the dragon and grabbing a fistful of magic. "How big?"

Konstantin bent over a piece of paper and scribbled down figures in the margins of what already looked like an extremely complex equation. "According to my calculations, the dragon would require a crystal the size of a loaf of bread. Approximately."

Ardis pinched the bridge of her nose and laughed. "So I'm looking for an enchanted baguette?"

"An enchanted crystal as big as a baguette," Konstantin said, missing the joke completely. "Tesla agrees with my theory. I'm trying to convince him he should stun the dragon first, but he insists the USS *Jupiter* must remain an observer."

Ardis blinked. "America is still neutral? Even after the dragon attacked them earlier?"

Konstantin mimicked Tesla's accent. "That was self-defense."

Ardis sighed and let her head fall back against the chair.

"This crystal possesses immense power," Konstantin said, "and may damage you or the Eisenkrieger. So please use caution."

She grunted. "I'll try."

A quick knock sounded on the door.

"Who is it?" Konstantin said.

The door swept open and Himmel marched in. "Falkenrath. We need to talk."

Konstantin pursed his lips. "I'm afraid I'm rather busy right at the moment."

Himmel let out a short laugh and rubbed the stubble on his chin. "God. You're always busy. Don't you ever sleep?"

Ardis arched her eyebrows, since Himmel hadn't seen her sitting behind him.

"I haven't had much time for sleep," Konstantin said.

Himmel looked him in the eye. "They assigned me to another airship."

"Oh?" Konstantin's blue eyes brightened. "That's wonderful news."

"I don't want to go."

Himmel closed the distance between them. Frowning, Konstantin stepped out from behind his desk, his hand on his hip.

"But why?" the archmage said.

Himmel lowered his voice. "You."

The frown melted from Konstantin's face. "Oh."

"I've waited too damn long to do this," Himmel said.

Himmel grabbed Konstantin by the shoulder and yanked him into his arms. Konstantin sucked in a breath, but only that one before Himmel kissed him with unrestrained passion. Konstantin let out a quiet cry, his hands empty at his sides, then reached behind Himmel's neck. Himmel dragged him closer and deepened the kiss.

Her ears hot, Ardis cleared her throat. Loudly.

Himmel and Konstantin broke apart, both of them panting. Himmel looked at Ardis, and his eyes rounded with shock.

"Don't worry about me," Ardis said. "I was on my way out."

Konstantin touched his lips "Theodore," he managed to mumble.

Ardis showed herself out. As she turned the doorknob, Himmel spoke.

"Well?" he muttered.

"The mustache tickled a bit," Konstantin said faintly.

Ardis bit back a laugh and slipped through the door.

"You know what I mean," Himmel said, even gruffer then before.

Ardis glanced back, just a peek, and saw Konstantin reply with another kiss.

With Natalya out of commission, Ardis spent the rest of the day training to pilot the Colossus. The controls were nearly the same as the Knight class, though with an Eisenkrieger this big, the feedback from the limbs wasn't as responsive. Ardis had to put some brute strength into controlling them. Never mind the wireless telegraph in the cockpit—there wasn't enough time to learn Morse code.

By sunset, Ardis was tired and more than ready for a bath.

She climbed from the cockpit and descended the scaffolding on aching legs, and said goodbye to Konstantin, who barely noticed. He had been sleepwalking through work with a dreamy smile ever since Himmel left his office. Ardis grinned, glad the archmage and the airship captain had finally kissed.

Out in the streets of Königsberg, wind rattled the bare branches of trees together.

So many soldiers had been stationed in the city over the past few days. Ardis saw Prussian blue on every street corner. She tugged her jacket closer and shivered at more than the cold. War was almost upon them.

Golden gaslight spilled from the hotel. Prussian army officers lingered in the lobby. They wore spiked helmets called *pickelhauben*, the steel and gilt polished to a high shine. Ardis appraised the cavalry sabers at their sides.

Not bad, though she doubted they knew what they were up against.

She trudged upstairs, her muscles sore, and her stomach grumbled. Hopefully, Wendel was back at the hotel. They could have dinner together, something with buttered bread. That sounded delicious right about now.

She stopped outside their room and turned the key.

It was already unlocked. She hesitated, hand on the door, then shoved it open.

Wendel lay on the bed with his arm over his eyes. He was barefoot, his shirt unbuttoned, the quilt wrinkled beneath him.

Well, he needed the sleep, after—

The sheets rustled. A woman lay behind Wendel. A naked woman.

Ardis stood in the doorway, her legs locked. Heat rushed into her face, then drained and left her feeling ice cold.

What the hell was going on? Who the hell was she?

The woman lifted herself on her elbow and traced her fingernail along Wendel's cheekbone. The intimacy of the gesture hit Ardis like a kick in the gut. Nausea twisted her stomach. Saliva filled her mouth.

The naked woman swung her legs over the edge of the bed and sauntered to the door. Her cornsilk hair swayed at the curve of her hips and barely hid her breasts. She smiled at Ardis, and her lips bared serpent's fangs.

"Jesus Christ," Ardis said.

The vampire from Bulgaria. The one who had been so taken with Wendel.

"What's this?" the vampire said. "Dessert?"

She licked her lips, then sucked a drop of blood from her thumb. Her eyes flashed silver as they reflected the light.

"Back the hell away, bitch," Ardis said, her words a hoarse growl.

"I'm not a bitch," the vampire said. "I think you have us confused with werewolves."

Ardis swung her fist at her pretty little nose. The vampire caught her by the wrist and twisted her arm. Ardis gasped at the sharp pain and tumbled into a roll before the creature could pin her down.

Chun Yi lay in its scabbard on the dresser. Ardis lunged for her sword, but the woman hit her from behind. A fist yanked her hair and slammed her against the dresser. Winded, Ardis doubled over. The woman bent over her shoulder and sucked in a breath, sniffing her scent.

A tongue flicked out and licked her neck. "You taste marvelous."

Ardis struggled to inhale. Her sword's hilt hung balanced over the edge of the dresser.

"Women in your condition are a delicacy," the vampire said. "Something about the blood of an unborn child adds that zest."

Unborn child? A cocktail of fear and hope dizzied Ardis.

"Sorry," Ardis said, "but I'm not on the menu."

She lurched and grabbed the scabbard. The woman slapped Ardis's hand and pinned her wrist to the dresser. The vampire's weight pressed on her back. Ardis pretended to go limp.

"Take off your clothes," the vampire whispered, her breath cold against her neck.

"Not interested," Ardis said.

The vampire had a husky laugh. "He was."

Anger simmered inside Ardis, then boiled over. She ripped her hair from the vampire's grasp and elbowed her under the chin.

The vampire snarled, but it was too late. Ardis grabbed her sword.

Enchanted flames crackled down the length of the blade. The vampire sprang away, eyes narrowed.

Ardis slashed the vampire's neck to the spine. The woman collapsed like a marionette with its strings cut. To be safe, Ardis finished the job and beheaded her. Old blood oozed onto the carpet.

Ardis wiped her sword on a towel, sheathed it in its scabbard, and walked to the bed. Wendel still lay with his arm over his eyes.

"Wendel!" she said. "Wendel, wake up."

He murmured something she didn't understand. His eyelashes fluttered like black wings. Blood dripped from a bite on his neck.

"What time is it?" Wendel slurred his words.

"Time for you to tell me what the hell happened."

Wendel opened his eyes and stared at the ceiling. He blinked, then grimaced. "Room's spinning."

"How much blood did you lose?" Ardis said. "How much venom did you take?"

Wendel groaned and pressed his head against the pillow.

"Answer the question," she said.

"What venom?"

"The vampire venom. From the vampire who was naked in your bed."

Wendel sighed. "A mistake, Ardis. An accident."

"What do you mean?"

"Didn't meant to let it bite me like that. Had it under control."

"What"—Ardis took a steadying breath—"do you mean?"

"My necromancy wasn't strong enough."

"Did you let her bite you?"

Wendel closed his eyes.

Her heartbeat thundered in her ears. "Did you sleep with her?"

"I suppose I did." He twisted his mouth. "In the literal sense."

"Now isn't the time for jokes, Wendel. Was this what you wanted? Vampire venom? Opium wasn't enough?"

Wendel struggled to sit upright. He swayed and clutched the bedpost.

"No," he said. "That's not what happened."

"Then what's your version of events?"

His eyes cleared enough for him to glare at her. "I'm telling the truth."

She glared right back. "Really?"

Wendel rubbed his forehead. "Why would I lie to you?"

"When haven't you?"

He hauled himself to his feet. "The vampire hunted me here. It attacked me while I was asleep. By the time I woke, it had already bitten me, already drugged me with venom. I tried to fight it, but I wasn't strong enough."

Ardis stared at him. "Are you telling me the vampire forced herself on you?"

Wendel lowered his head. His cheeks reddened. "Perhaps."

"Don't lie about *that*." Tears stung her eyes. "Not to me."

Wendel met her gaze. "Why don't you believe me?"

He sounded hurt, but Ardis had seen the vampire in bed with him. Touching him.

"How can I?" she said.

"After all this, you still don't trust me? Damn it, Ardis, I don't know what else to say."

She shook her head. "I don't even know if I can do this."

"Do what?"

The vampire had mentioned her unborn baby. *Their* unborn baby.

"Should we even think about starting a family?" Ardis said.

Wendel's jaw clenched. "Are you saying you don't want the baby?"

He was still so certain of her pregnancy, when she wasn't certain of anything.

"I don't know," Ardis said. "You don't exactly have a stellar track record with family."

Wendel jerked back like she had slapped him. He sat on the bed and said nothing, though his eyes smoldered with emotion.

Ardis knew she had wounded him, and the sickness in her stomach intensified. She tossed aside her sword and strode toward the bathroom. Her footsteps quickened into a run, and she slammed the door. She dropped to her knees by the toilet. The stink of bleach stung her nose. She vomited into the porcelain.

Wendel rapped on the door. "Ardis?"

She coughed, shaking all over, and closed her eyes. She thought of the decapitated vampire bleeding on the carpet. "Go away."

The doorknob turned, but Ardis twisted the lock before he could open it.

"Are you all right?" Wendel said.

Ardis vomited again. Tears trickled down her face. She didn't want him to see her like this. She didn't want to see him at all.

"Go. Away."

Silence outside the door.

Ardis flushed the toilet and washed her hands, her face, her hair. She scrubbed herself dry with the towel. In the mirror, she couldn't meet her own eyes.

When she opened the door, Wendel was gone. And so was the vampire.

Ardis shuddered. She didn't think he could reanimate a headless corpse, so he must have dragged the body out. How were they going to explain the bloody carpet to the hotel? At this point, Ardis decided she didn't even care.

TWENTY-THREE

rdis waited in the lobby, tapping the hilt of Chun Yi. When the line at the desk cleared, she marched over to the concierge.

"Excuse me," Ardis said, "but I want another room."

"Any particular reason why?" said the concierge.

"I don't like it."

The concierge adjusted his spectacles. "Very well, ma'am. I can move you both to a room on the top floor tonight."

Both? Ardis didn't want to share a bed with Wendel tonight.

"Just me," she said. "I'm moving. He's staying."

The concierge coughed. "I will have to bill you double."

"Of course."

Ardis paid him for the second room, then walked to the restaurant for dinner.

"Just one?" said the waiter.

Ardis faltered on the threshold of the restaurant. She glanced around to see if Wendel was there, but he wasn't. Fortunately.

She needed to be alone. She needed to try cooling her burning thoughts.

Ardis sat at a table and unfolded her napkin in her lap. She rubbed her gritty eyes. The waiter slid a menu onto the table, and she stared blankly at the German. The words swam together.

"Should we even think about starting a family?"

"Are you saying you don't want the baby?"

"I don't know. You don't exactly have a stellar track record with family."

Her words echoed in her ears. God, she had been an idiot.

"Are you ready to order, ma'am?" said the waiter.

Ardis tried to smile. "I'll have the Westphalia ham."

The waiter speedily delivered her dinner, and Ardis ate in silence. The ham weighed down her stomach like stone.

After dinner, Ardis walked to her room alone.

Rain lashed against the window and rattled on the roof. A storm drowned out the stars. She cracked open the window to breathe in the icy air. Raindrops trickled down her face, and she closed the window again.

When Ardis climbed into bed, she shivered at the cold beneath the sheets. She wished she could sleep with Wendel at her side. She wished she could feel less alone, but wasn't sure she was allowed to feel at all.

Sand glimmered like gold dust along the beach. Mist drifted over the Pacific.

In her arms, Ardis felt something fidget. She looked down at the most beautiful baby in the world. The shape of the baby's eyes echoed her own, though the color was a pale green more like sea glass. Wendel's eyes.

Wind mussed the baby's wisp of dark hair. Ardis smoothed it back down.

The baby gurgled and gave her a toothless smile. It had quite a lot of drool. Ardis smiled and dabbed at its chin with her sleeve.

Her heart swelled until she wasn't sure it would fit inside her chest.

Seagulls shrieked and wheeled as a raven played in the sky. The silhouette of a man walked along the beach. Wendel. He bowed his head, his hair in his eyes, and he didn't see them. Ardis stood and waved at him.

"Wendel!" she said.

A knock on the door woke Ardis. She squinted in the sunlight. Another knock, hard enough that it shook the door.

"Just a minute!" Ardis said.

She kicked off the sheets, dragged on her clothes, and answered the door.

It wasn't Wendel. A telegram boy waited there, breathing hard, his hat askew.

"Urgent telegram, ma'am," he said.

She ripped open the telegram and read.

Return to pilot Colossus immediately

Ardis tipped the telegram boy, yanked on her boots, and hailed a taxi.

When she walked into the drydock, she dodged a swarm of engineers. The Colossus towered over the commotion.

"Ardis!" Konstantin waved her over to the Eisenkrieger.

She hurried to meet him. "What's the rush?"

The archmage gripped her shoulder. He looked skittish and pale. "It's time."

"Time for what?" she said, her hands already sweaty.

"The Russians are besieging Königsberg. They are marching through the farmland to the east. We can't let them capture the city. A Prussian division of the German army is advancing to fight, but they are outnumbered two to one."

Ardis whistled softly. "Will the Eisenkriegers even the odds?"

"Yes," Konstantin said, "but we only have three. And we need you to pilot the Colossus."

Ardis squared her shoulders and glanced at the metal giant. "My orders?"

"Find and kill the clockwork dragon. Before it does too much damage."

"Yes, sir."

Konstantin caught her hand and shook it briskly. His hesitant smile betrayed his fear.

"Have you seen Wendel?" Ardis said.

"No. Why?"

Ardis bit the inside of her cheek. "I don't know where he is."

"I'm sure the necromancer will turn up when we least expect him."

"I hope so."

"Good luck." Konstantin glanced into her eyes. "Stay alive, all right?"

"I'll try my best."

Ardis marched the Colossus from the drydock. She strode through the streets of Königsberg as soldiers directed traffic away from her earth-shaking footfalls. Townspeople leaned from their windows, and a little girl plucked a flower and held it out to her.

Ardis smiled and shook her head. The flower would only be crushed in her fist.

Trucks rumbled behind the Colossus, burdened with soldiers on their way to war. Children ran alongside them, laughing and shrieking as the tires sprayed slush from the road. It almost looked like a parade.

Ardis hoped most of them would live to see a victory parade.

They left the city proper and crossed muddy fields. The trucks flattened autumn's stubble, and the Colossus cratered the earth with its footprints. The soldiers joined a larger battalion of the Prussian division. Overhead, the USS *Jupiter* floated in the sky. Ardis wondered if it was on another observation mission, and if America would be able to stay out of this war forever.

No sign of the clockwork dragon, or the Russian army.

Ardis stood sentinel behind the Prussians. From this height, the men and horses looked like tin soldiers. Across the field, a ridge bristled with pines, their needles glittering with frost. An eagle soared over the trees.

It was a perfect day, one soon to be made grotesque by battle.

The Germans marched toward the ridge in regimented rows, armed with swords, pikes, crossbows, even a battleaxe or two. A handful of the blades glistened with the telltale iridescence of magic, but most looked like they hadn't been polished since the Middle Ages. Hopefully, each soldier knew how to wield them. Pines rustled on the ridge, and the eagle shrieked.

Russians marched from the forest. Konstantin was wrong—they were outnumbered three to one.

Ardis lumbered behind the Germans and halted when they did. Some soldiers grinned and whooped at the Colossus, like it was their big brother who the Russians wouldn't dare attack. Ardis wished she shared their optimism.

The Russian infantry stopped. Their cavalry rode to the forefront. Cossacks, or what was left of them after the Eisenkriegers.

Hooves drummed the dirt as the Cossacks galloped down the ridge, but the Germans held their ground. The horses charged nearer, mouths foam-flecked, riders brandishing sabers. A line of German soldiers advanced and, at the last moment, lowered their pikes. The Cossacks reined in their mounts, but for many, it was too late. They careened into the pikes and impaled themselves.

The remaining Cossacks wheeled and retreated.

Emboldened, the Prussian division advanced across the field. They halted halfway. Ardis flanked them, her muscles taut, and tried to ignore the screams of horses.

The USS *Jupiter* floated over the battlefield. On the ridge, the Russians lingered beneath the pines. The German infantry marched toward them, and a squadron of elite Prussian cavalry charged ahead, their lances lowered. But still, the Russians held their ground.

A glint of red caught her eye. The clockwork dragon sailed over the ridge.

The dragon's shadow darkened the battlefield. A Prussian officer shouted an order, and soldiers armed with crossbows fired a volley skyward. Bolts clattered uselessly off the dragon's armored belly. It soared overhead, out of reach, and looked down at Ardis with what she would have sworn was cunning in its eyes. Too intelligent for mere clockwork.

The cavalry charged across the field, their horses kicking up clods of earth, and the dragon dove into an attack. Flaring its wings, the beast swooped over the cavalry, plucked an officer from his mount, and crushed his spine in its claws.

The dragon landed with a thud, grinding the officer into the bloody dirt. Steam hissed between its fangs. It dropped the corpse and bit another man, jaws locking on his arm and tearing it off. The beast gutted, beheaded, and mutilated soldiers.

The Germans broke ranks, and Russians charged down the ridge and slaughtered them as they fled.

Ardis watched the chaos from her vantage in the Eisenkrieger. Adrenaline flooded her blood. This wasn't a battle. This was a massacre.

She could retreat. She could run away and could save herself—save her unborn baby. But if she ran, Königsberg was lost. And they were all dead.

Ardis clenched her jaw and shook her head, hard, to clear her thoughts.

She had her orders. Kill the dragon.

Ardis sprinted to meet her opponent and crushed a dead man underfoot, his bones crunching like a bug. She had less than a second to realize it, and no time at all to feel.

The dragon whirled to meet her.

Ardis focused on her ultimate goal. As she charged, the Prussians rallied. Her thundering footsteps punctuated their cheers and battle cries. The dragon reared into an attack, raking its claws down the Colossus's chest and gouging deep grooves. She rammed her metal hand under its neck and flipped it onto its back. The dragon writhed on crumpled wings.

She threw herself on top of it, driving her elbow against its throat. It struggled and snapped, its teeth inches from her face, but

Ardis bore down with all the weight of the Colossus. She punched the dragon in the jaw and knocked its head sprawling in the dirt. The blow rattled its fangs. She glanced at the steel plates armoring its chest.

Damn it, they looked impenetrable.

If she got out of this godforsaken mess alive, she was going to have a word with Konstantin about his impractical plans.

The dragon surged beneath her and bit the Colossus on the right arm, shaking it savagely, its fangs digging into the steel, wrenching wires and pneumatics. Her exoskeleton started to buckle. If she didn't act fast, the dragon would tear off the arm.

Ardis gritted her teeth and wedged the Colossus's hand into a crack in the dragon's chest armor. Her fingertips slipped, and she scrabbled for a better grip. Sweat poured down her face. Pain screamed through her muscles. She pried open the dragon's chest, tearing away the plate of armor.

The dragon's scream sounded almost human.

Deep within its ribcage, incredibly intricate clockwork ticked and whirred with oil for blood. A ruby crystal glowed at its heart.

Ardis reached between the dragon's ribs and closed her hand around the crystal. She sucked in a breath, then tore out the dragon's heart.

Magic surged up her arm and shivered over her skin. When the crystal darkened, the hum of Eisenkrieger stuttered to a halt. The dragon collapsed in the mud, its eyes flickering out, its jaws gaping like those of a dead fish on a beach.

Her ears rang in the silence. The Colossus dropped to its knees and swayed like a drunk. She strained against the Eisenkrieger, but had no control over its massive metal limbs. It balanced for a second before plummeting face down onto the field.

The crash deafened Ardis. Her scream sounded muffled.

Dirt splattered the outside of the cockpit. Sweat stung Ardis's eyes. She blinked and twisted in the cockpit, fumbling for the ignition. The engine failed to start, no matter how many times she twisted the key. Outside the Eisenkrieger, the sounds of the battle raged on. She strained to open the glass, but the latch didn't budge. Minutes passed.

Something metal banged the glass. Again and again, until it shattered. A man held out his hand.

"Thank God," Ardis said.

Soldiers pried her free. She staggered to her feet, knees shaking, ears ringing.

"Thank you," Ardis said, before she noticed their uniforms. "I—"

The soldiers around her were Russian. They stared at her with blatant hostility.

Slowly, Ardis raised her hands in surrender.

TWENTY-FOUR

O ne of the Russians shouted and waved his sword at her throat.

"I don't understand you," she said.

A soldier grabbed her arm and flung her onto the ground. She spat dirt and crawled to her knees. She wasn't the type to cower.

The Russians glanced between each other; she recognized that look.

Who would have the pleasure of killing her?

In that instant, Ardis wished she had seen Wendel one last time. She wished their last conversation could be something—anything—else.

But it was too late for that. She didn't see a way out of dying.

"*Grok!*" The wind carried a raven's croak.

Another Russian joined them, his uniform blood-soaked. He lifted his sword and stabbed his comrade through the back. The betrayed Russian stared at the blade in his chest, then crumpled in the dirt at Ardis's knees.

The other soldiers backed away from the turncoat. Ardis saw his dead eyes before she saw the necromancer who controlled him.

Wendel.

He arrived with his own army of the dead, an entourage of unbreathing soldiers, and a raven winging over his head.

"Kill the Russians," Wendel said.

The dead men did as the necromancer commanded. Wendel strode through the bodies and the blood and stopped by Ardis. He grabbed her arms and hauled her to her feet, then embraced her so tightly it left her breathless.

"Wendel," she said.

"Ardis." He looked her in the eye. "Are you hurt?"

"No."

She meant to add that she was more than a little bruised, but he kissed her with such sweet ferocity that she could think of nothing but kissing him harder. They shared an instant together where the world disappeared.

"Get me out of here," Ardis said.

"Gladly."

Without asking, he swept Ardis into his arms and carried her from the battlefield.

Wendel didn't put her down until they walked into Königsberg. Then he took her hand and brought her to the cathedral.

"Sanctuary," he said.

Ardis didn't tell him some men had no respect for all that was holy.

They sat together on the pew, their hands clasped between them. Stained glass windows transmuted sunlight into a faded rainbow.

"Where were you?" Ardis said.

"With Wolfram." Wendel looked at his hands. "After what you said, I thought I should be there for him."

She swallowed past the ache in her throat. "I should have never said that."

"It hurt," he said, "because you were right."

"No, I wasn't." She tightened her fingers around his hand. "Your family has treated you so badly. You deserve better."

Wendel's laugh was soft and broken. "Do I?"

"You deserve an apology from me. Forgive me?"

"If you have forgiven me for everything, it's the least I can do." He looked at her through his eyelashes. "Trust me?"

"If the vampire wasn't your fault, then yes, I trust you."

Wendel's face tightened, and Ardis poked him in the ribs to show him she was joking.

"I promised not to touch opium," he said, "and I promise not to touch vampires."

"Not even to try your necromancy?"

He hesitated, and she poked him again.

"Not unless absolutely necessary," he said.

All the bells of the cathedral began to ring. Their chimes echoed under the high ceiling.

Goosebumps rushed over Ardis. "Is it a warning?"

"Maybe we won," Wendel said.

She raised her voice over the clamor. "Maybe we lost."

"After you defeated the clockwork dragon?"

"They outnumbered us three to one."

Wendel arched an eyebrow. "That's rather bleak. I doubt we survived this long only to die at the hands of Russian soldiers."

"Why not?"

"I prefer to think I will have a grandiose obituary," he said airily.

They walked from Königsberg Cathedral and stepped into the daylight. Townspeople crowded on the streets. Their faces looked bright with excitement.

"Excuse me," Wendel said, "but what the hell is going on?"

A man grinned at him. "The Russians are retreating!"

Wendel tilted his head with a silver of a smile. "See?"

Ardis sighed. Wendel's smile widened, and he swept her into his arms again.

"I can walk, you know," she said.

"I know."

He carried her for a block or two, until she started laughing, and he set her on her feet.

"Are you sure you don't want me to carry you?" Wendel said.

Ardis swallowed another laugh. "No, thank you."

"But my reputation as a gentleman is at stake."

"You already saved me from the Russians." She touched her wrist to her forehead. "My knight in shining armor."

He snorted. "I'm not wearing any armor."

"I'd like to see you not wearing anything."

Wendel's eyes glinted, and he grabbed her hand. He led her to the doors of their hotel and almost hauled her upstairs.

"Slow down," Ardis said, breathless.

Wendel fished the key from his pocket and pantomimed unlocking the door very, very slowly. He kept a straight face.

Ardis laughed. "Don't be evil."

"I think you like it when I'm evil."

She rolled her eyes. "I think you're secretly too good for that. You're quite *nice*."

"Nice?" Wendel feigned a gasp. "Heaven forbid."

"You should work on your bastard skills. You're losing touch."

"Never."

Wendel swung open the door, hooked his hand behind her waist, and swept her into the room. She escaped and fell back on the bed. The day weighed down her bones. A long sigh shuddered from her lungs.

"We made it," she said.

He smirked. "It would have been quicker if you let me carry you."

"No," she said. "We're alive."

Wendel's smirk faltered, and he kicked off his boots.

"Alive, but filthy," he said. "Come bathe with me."

That sounded wonderful. While Wendel ran the bath, Ardis peeled away every layer of her clothes. The more naked she became, the more vulnerable she felt. They hadn't finished their conversation in the cathedral.

Ardis walked into the bathroom. Wendel knelt by the tub, his wrist under the tap. He glanced over his shoulder, and the heat in his eyes smoldered. He straightened, one eyebrow cocked, and unbuttoned his shirt. Blood flecked the white cotton; she wondered how many he had killed. She wondered if he felt proud for saving Königsberg. If he did, his face showed no indication.

"After you," Wendel said, with a lazy wave at the bathtub.

Ardis stepped into the water. She lowered herself to sit and tucked her knees to her chest. The heat of the bath soaked into her sore muscles and left her feeling delightfully drowsy.

"Where do we go from here?" Ardis said.

Wendel stripped off the last of his clothes and knelt by the tub. He dangled his arm over the edge of the porcelain and brushed his fingertips through the water, back and forth. His green eyes looked contemplative.

"Where would you like to go?" he said.

Ardis rubbed her knees. "I don't want to fight another battle like the last."

Wendel's hand drifted along her arm. He stopped on her shoulders his fingers working out the knots in her muscles. She closed her eyes and sighed blissfully at his touch.

"You're so good at this," Ardis said. "Yet another one of your talents."

Wendel laughed, though sadness betrayed his voice. "You frightened me today."

Somehow the soft way he said it clenched her chest all that much harder. She curled her hands, her fingernails biting into her palms.

"You aren't the only one."

"We should stop fighting." Wendel's hands slowed. "For the baby's sake."

Ardis stared at the ripples on the water. "I forgot to tell you."

Wendel stopped rubbing her shoulders. "Ardis. Did you—?" He let out a breath rather than finish that thought.

"The vampire knew."

Wendel leaned on the edge of the rub, grimacing at the mention of the vampire. "I don't understand."

"The vampire said I was pregnant."

The grimace vanished from Wendel's face, replaced by a blank look with a bit of joy leaking through the cracks. "We're having a baby?"

Ardis nodded.

Wendel kissed her on the mouth. His hand cradled her neck and his fingers tangled in her hair. She relaxed beneath him, her legs slipping to the bottom of the tub, her hands resting on her thighs.

Wendel smiled against her lips. "My tiny minion," he whispered.

Ardis scoffed and splashed water on him, but couldn't drown out his laughter. He shielded himself with his arm.

"You're supposed to be wet," Ardis deadpanned. "I'm helping."

Cautiously, Wendel lowered his arm and climbed into the tub. Ardis reached for the soap. Butterflies whirled in her chest.

They were having a baby.

They both washed in the bath, though they didn't linger. Wendel seemed rather intent on drying Ardis and dragging her to bed where they lay together under the soft, cool sheets. She listened to the rhythm of his heartbeat.

"I love you," Wendel said.

She didn't think she could ever hear him say it enough. He could say it a thousand times and she would still want to hear it again.

Ardis kissed him, the kind of slow kiss that melted your bones, and slid her fingertips down his chest. She found how hard he was, and stroked him.

"I'm all yours," Ardis said.

Wendel held himself over her and deepened the kiss. His skin scorched her own. She arched against him, and he kissed both her breasts. When he gave himself to her, she gasped at the intimacy of skin on skin. Nothing between them. She felt armor falling away from her heart.

They moved together, wordlessly, until their breathing became staccato. Wendel kissed her again, his lips insistent against her own. Trembling, she ached with unspoken emotion. The intensity overwhelmed her, and she closed her eyes. Tears escaped past her eyelashes, and Wendel kissed them from her cheeks.

"Why are you crying?" he whispered.

She opened her eyes. "I love you so much it doesn't fit inside."

"I could make a joke about fitting inside, but I won't." His mouth curled into a smile.

Ardis laughed and slapped him on the shoulder. "That's it. Moment ruined."

"Is it?" He grinned. "Or is it improved?"

He kissed her, his tongue sliding into her mouth, salty with the taste of her tears. He brought her to the brink of sweet oblivion, and held her when she fell. He moaned out a sigh and filled her with his seed.

They lay together, entwined. Wendel's magic shivered between the sweat on their skin, but she didn't even blink. His necromancy belonged to him, and this necromancer belonged to her.

Later that evening, someone knocked. Decent, though damp from another bath, Ardis answered the door.

Konstantin. He tugged at the collar of his dinner jacket and coughed. "Pardon the interruption, but we have been invited to the castle."

Wendel leaned against the doorway behind Ardis. "Who does *we* include, archmage?"

Konstantin waved an ivory invitation. "The heroes of Königsberg."

Wendel twisted his mouth, but before he could speak, Ardis beat him to it.

"Of course," she said. "We would be honored."

Konstantin nodded. "I'll give you a minute to change. I'll be in the lobby."

They dressed in eveningwear. As Ardis pinned her hair, Wendel fiddled with his cufflinks in the mirror.

"God," he said, "I hope don't get any blood on this shirt before the night is over."

She arched her eyebrows. "It would be nice to finish dinner unscathed."

"Otherwise I will be permanently indebted to tailors."

Properly attired, they descended to the lobby.

Konstantin waited for them, straightening the edelweiss pin on his lapel. "Shall we?"

They followed him into the street. Evening flowed overhead in a river of stars. Not a single cloud marred the sky.

The clockwork dragon never would again, a thought which immensely satisfied Ardis.

A scrap of black flew overhead. "*Grok!*"

Krampus flared his wings and landed on Wendel's shoulder. The raven's claws curled around the cloth of his jacket.

"There you are," Wendel said. "Abominable brat."

He stroked under the raven's chin. Krampus blinked and gurgled.

Konstantin sighed. "You can't bring that raven to dinner."

"Krampus?" Wendel said. "But he's a hero of Königsberg."

"Obviously," Ardis said, pokerfaced.

Konstantin shook his head with an exasperated smile.

Himmel fell in step alongside them at the next street corner. The zeppelin captain wore a dress uniform with a smart hat, replacing the one he had lost during the sinking of the *Wanderfalke*. Ardis thought the new captain's hat suited him.

"Theodore." Konstantin's eyes brightened. "Walk with us to the castle?"

"Himmel," said the captain, "and yes."

Konstantin blushed, though that may have had something to do with Himmel stealthily slapping him on the behind.

Krampus cocked his head and stared at Himmel's mechanical arm.

"Your arm is shiny," Wendel said.

"Thank you?" Himmel said.

"Krampus likes shiny things."

Himmel's mustache bristled. "And dead bodies." He held away his mechanical arm.

Wendel smirked and kept his gaze on the street.

Königsberg Castle looked rather ruined by night, the tallest tower crumbling, the conservatory smashed, but scaffolding propped up the stones. It would be rebuilt, after the war, maybe even before.

As they entered, winter wind flickered the candles in the entrance hall. Himmel closed the door behind them.

Juliana loitered by a carved column. A silver gown shimmered on her like rainfall.

"You're early," she said, in a bored drawl. "Dying to relive the last dinner?"

Wendel smirked. "It's good to see you, too, Juliana."

"*Good evening*," said a ghostly voice.

"Christ!" Wendel said.

Wolfram rolled from the shadows in a wicker wheelchair, pushed by a footman. A boyish grin split his face.

"Heavens, Wolfie," Juliana said. "Don't do that."

"Did I startle you?" Wolfram said.

Wendel snorted. "Hardly. I could hear that wheelchair squeaking."

"Liar," Wolfram said. "I don't need the wheelchair, though Mother insists on it. She's worried I might have another fit."

Wendel's eyebrows descended. "Is that what the doctors say?"

Wolfram shrugged. "Possibly."

"Please be careful, Wolfie," Juliana said. "You did hit your head fairly spectacularly."

Wolfram gripped the arms of his wheelchair and staggered upright. He winced. "Damn. My feet fell asleep."

"Are you sure you won't fall over?" Wendel said.

"Only one way to find out."

Wolfram stumbled against Wendel. The brothers hugged, then laughed over each other's shoulders.

Ardis grinned, and noticed Juliana hide a smile behind her hand.

A gust of wind announced the arrival of Nikola Tesla, who strode into the castle wearing an immaculate suit and an ivory cravat.

"Ardis," Tesla said. "You piloted the Colossus admirably."

She shook his gloved hand. "Thank you."

At the mention of Colossus, Konstantin stepped into their conversation. He clasped his hands behind his back. "The clockwork dragon was a formidable foe."

"That's an understatement," Ardis said.

"We have yet to understand its true power. Some experiments are in order."

Ardis suspected Konstantin might have his next endeavor after Project Lazarus.

Himmel cleared his throat. "Experiment all you want on the clockwork dragon, so long as you don't bring that thing back to life."

Konstantin looked at the ceiling and bit his lip. "Of course not."

The archmage sounded less than convincing. Himmel clucked his tongue.

"Where will you go now, Tesla?" Ardis said.

Tesla coughed. "I'm afraid we may have overstayed our welcome here. We acted in defense when the clockwork dragon attacked our airship, but that has certainly complicated diplomacy with Russia. We have orders to return to America."

Ardis touched her hand over her heart. "I haven't been home to America in three years."

"Oh?" Tesla said. "It takes only three days for the *Jupiter* to cross the Atlantic. You are more than welcome to travel with us."

Ardis twisted her fingers together. "Thank you, though I'm not sure I can."

"Nonsense, Ardis." Konstantin brushed away her comment. "I believe you are long overdue some leave. Perhaps a month?"

"I would love to," she said, "but there may be some legal issues."

"Oh?"

"I'm an outlaw in America."

"Oh, yes. That."

"I'd rather not be arrested the moment I arrive."

Konstantin had a sly smile. "The archmages can take care of all the paperwork. Diplomatic immunity and such."

Hope bubbled through her like champagne. "Thank you."

Konstantin shook her hand, and she tugged him into a hug. He patted her on the back, then tried to look professional. "I'll expect you to report back to the Archmages of Vienna."

"Yes, sir."

Konstantin laughed. "Please don't call me that. It makes me feel old."

"What," Ardis said, "have they found a younger archmage?"

He laughed again. "I doubt such a prodigy exists."

"Bragging, archmage?" Wendel said. "I approve."

Himmel grumbled in his throat. "Don't corrupt Konstantin."

"I'll leave that to you." Wendel smirked.

Their host and hostess made their entrance. Medals gleamed on Waldemar's uniform, and sequins glittered across Cecelia's seafoam gown. They surveyed their guests with as much pompous majesty as they could muster.

Wendel held his hand at his mouth. His eyes looked shadowed.

"It's my honor to invite you here tonight," Waldemar said. "Your heroics in the name of Königsberg will not be forgotten."

Cecelia pressed her hands together as if in prayer. "Thank you. Thank you all."

"You're welcome," Wendel muttered.

Wolfram elbowed his brother in the ribs.

"Please." Waldemar waved his arm imperiously. "Dinner is served."

Waldemar and Cecelia strode down the hall, with everyone following them to the dining room. Wendel lingered on the threshold.

Waldemar spread his napkin in his lap. He frowned at a candelabra for a moment. "Wendel."

Wendel glanced at him. "Yes?"

His father looked into his eyes, and an instant of understanding crossed between them.

"Sit," Waldemar said.

It looked like a weight lifted from Wendel's shoulders. He straightened and went to sit with his family, if only for a night.

TWENTY-FIVE

n the haze of dawn, the necromancer started singing. **Ardis** stood on the observation deck, wind blowing through the windows, and glanced sideways at him. Wendel leaned with his elbows on the railing.

"*So, so wie ich dich liebe*," he sang quietly, "*so, so liebe auch mich.*"

"What are you singing now?" Ardis said.

A smile stole over his face. "A folk song." He sang it again in English. "So, so, the way I love you, so, so love me too."

"Sounds like a love song to me."

"That, too."

She stood by him, and he held her close with an arm around his shoulders.

"It's New Year's Eve tonight," Wendel said. "I hope Tesla knows how to party."

Ardis laughed. "Don't get drunk on an airship. Again."

He wrinkled his nose. "I tried to black that from my memory."

Krampus hopped onto the railing. Wind ruffled the raven's glossy feathers as he peered down at the deep blue Baltic Sea.

"Careful, Krampus," Wendel said. "If you fly away, you might not make it to America."

Krampus blinked. "*Grok.*"

"Only a few days," Ardis said. "It's hard to believe."

Wendel narrowed his eyes against the sun. "I assume we will be traveling incognito. Since you *are* an outlaw in America."

"Konstantin promised diplomatic immunity. Besides, we're landing in New York."

"Will we travel to San Francisco from there?"

She shrugged. "Maybe."

"San Francisco is your home."

She smiled. "It's a long way. America is big, Wendel."

"I've never been." He frowned pensively. "Will we meet your mother?"

"Do you want to?"

He looked sideways at her. "Should I?"

She laughed. "She can be a bit intimidating."

"I'm game."

Ardis looked out over the clouds, and leaned against Wendel. With him beside her, she was game for anything beyond the horizon.

A TASTE OF...

KAREN KINCY

CLOCKWORK
MENAGERIE

ONE

Pity the clockwork dragon had been so violent.

Konstantin pushed his goggles over his head. Tugging off his leather gloves, he ran a hand over the clockwork beast's crimson scales, cold and smooth under his skin. Scars marked the enamel, raw steel glimmering in rough arabesques. If only he had a bigger laboratory. The bulk of the dragon's body rested on concrete, its head lying on a trolley, its tail looping among the wires powering the technomancy equipment.

"Falkenrath."

Konstantin jumped. Tonight, he had been alone in the laboratory; the other archmages and engineers had gone home long ago.

When he identified the interruption, his heartbeat skipped for an entirely different reason.

Captain Theodore Himmel smiled with a wicked glint in his honey-gold eyes. He smoothed his waxed mustache with steel fingers, still outfitted with the mechanical arm Konstantin had built for him.

"Are you alone?" Himmel said.

"Yes, which is why you shouldn't—"

Without any regard for who might walk in, Himmel marched over and kissed him. When Konstantin gasped against his mouth, Himmel growled out a groan as if savoring the taste of him. The captain tasted rather like peppermint himself, Konstantin noted absently, his mind not quite done cataloguing and analyzing.

His lips insistent, Himmel deepened the kiss, his tongue sliding into Konstantin's mouth, shamelessly bold. Heat scorched Konstantin's skin, his knees faltering as his muscles surrendered. Himmel supported him with his steel hand cradling his neck, the other gripping his hip. That was rather distracting.

Part of him wanted to seize Himmel, but the rest of him seized control.

He broke away, more than slightly breathless. "Theodore."

Himmel grinned. "You were saying?"

"You shouldn't startle me."

"It was worth it."

Konstantin licked his lips, tender from the kiss. "We can't be seen."

"Perhaps we should go somewhere more private." Himmel had eyes of molten gold.

Desire muddied Konstantin's thoughts. "I'm in the middle of an experiment." That sounded feeble even to his own ears.

Himmel glanced at the workbench, strewn with notes and papers stained by countless cups of coffee. "Don't you ever sleep?"

"Yes." Konstantin blushed. "I have a cot in the back of the laboratory."

Himmel's eyebrows shot heavenward. "You haven't been sleeping at the hotel?"

"The laboratory proved more convenient."

Himmel laughed, shook his head, and advanced with a determined glint in his eyes. Konstantin backed against the workbench. Trapped by Himmel's arms and the narrow press of his hips, he could feel the captain's—

"Theodore." He gasped. "Please."

Himmel swept everything off the workbench. Papers cascaded down and fluttered to the floor; pens rolled out of sight.

Konstantin's jaw dropped. "My research!"

"Your what?"

"All over the floor, out of order, and—God, Himmel!"

Konstantin dropped to his knees and started stacking papers into piles. Luckily, he had clipped the most important documents together, so it wasn't an utter disaster. He clenched his jaw and drew a calming breath.

Himmel's hand settled on his shoulder. "I'm sorry."

"Is that all?"

"I didn't know what you wanted."

Konstantin gritted his teeth. "It took me days to write down all this data. I can't afford to make any mistakes." The biggest mistake of all would be to let Himmel take him to bed. God, why he couldn't stop imagining him naked?

"Konstantin." His name brought him back to reality. "What are you thinking? You have that faraway look again."

"Do I?"

"Like your head is in the clouds."

Some of Konstantin's anger slipped away. "You should know, as an airship captain."

Himmel groaned at the pun, the sound reminiscent of how he had groaned during the kiss. Konstantin's trousers became rather tight, though he didn't dare correct that inconvenience here in the laboratory. How mortifying.

"Look at me." Though Himmel's command was gentle, Konstantin struggled to obey. His thoughts abandoned him and left him adrift. He hadn't the slightest idea of what to do. "Your eyes are beautiful. Blue like the sky."

No one had ever looked at him like this before. Remembering to breathe, he sucked in air. "You are the expert on atmospheric con—conditions." He stammered at the stroke of Himmel's knuckles over his cheek.

"Come to the hotel with me. I can think of a better use for your bed."

Konstantin retreated from his touch. "I shouldn't. I—"

"Stop working. For one night."

He blinked fast, mind scrambling for words. "I can't do this with you, Theodore."

Himmel's eyebrows descended. "Do what?"

"You—me—together." If only he could stop spluttering.

"Why?" Himmel said it evenly enough.

Konstantin dusted off his knees, his heartbeat thundering, and stared at the scattered papers. "I never have," he whispered.

"Pardon?"

"I've never been with a man. With anyone." Konstantin blurted out the confession. "Please don't laugh at me."

Himmel coughed. "I'm not laughing." Was that a hint of a smile? "Though I'm glad you aren't angry at me for your paperwork."

Konstantin scowled. "I didn't say that."

"Let me make it up to you."

"How?"

Himmel lowered his gaze. "I'll take things slow."

Stomach sour, Konstantin knew he must be cruel to a man who cared for him so much. "This is illegal," he murmured.

Himmel barked out a laugh. "You think I don't know that?"

The law in Prussia punished unnatural fornication with imprisonment. Austria-Hungary, Konstantin's homeland, was no more forgiving. God, once, he had been naïve enough to scour the legal texts for loopholes, but even royalty and the rich suffered the consequences. Just thinking about it made him sick.

Konstantin swallowed hard. "I can't risk my career."

"I would risk mine."

He stared at him. "Would you?"

"For a night with you." Himmel sounded husky.

Konstantin stepped away, distancing himself from a future he could never have. "I wouldn't."

Himmel jerked back, as if slapped, before lowering his gaze. "Understood."

Regret stung Konstantin. "Theodore."

"Good night."

Himmel turned on his heel and strode from the laboratory, leaving Konstantin alone again. Alone like he had asked.

The weight of silence bent his shoulders. Kneeling, he started sorting through his papers, but the formulas and numbers jumbled into nonsense. And no equation could solve the conundrum inside his heart.

Konstantin slept on his cot in the laboratory, like he did so many nights. It seemed strangely pitiful when he woke in the gray light of dawn. Dull pain squeezed his chest, no matter how many cups of coffee he drank.

He drifted outside and stared at the water with bloodshot eyes.

The Frisches Haff, a freshwater lagoon, rippled like silver silk along the coastline of Königsberg, a lace of ice edging the coast. The city still slept, only the seagulls already awake and squabbling over breakfast.

Where was Himmel now? Asleep in bed? Alone?

Maybe he had found another man. Surely an airship captain such as himself would have his pick of clandestine affairs. And in the Navy, before his promotion to zeppelin commander, who knew how many men there had been.

Konstantin held his cup in both hands and watched the waves. Damn it, he recognized the sick gnawing in the pit of his stomach—envy. He wanted Himmel to stay away from other men. He wanted him all to himself.

Even if he could never have him.

Sagging against a boulder, Konstantin pinched the bridge of his nose. He couldn't do this. He had a clockwork dragon to dissect. A war to win. Wearily, he straightened and poured his lukewarm coffee into the lagoon.

Back to work.

Konstantin laced his fingers and cracked his knuckles. His hands steady, he took up the blowtorch and burned the clockwork's dragon belly. The crimson scales blackened and melted away to reveal the metal guts within.

How fascinating! The smooth interlocking steel resembled the coils of a centipede.

He donned a pair of goggles with magnifying lenses and leaned so close, his nose almost touched the enamel. Sidestepping along the length of the dragon, he stopped at its gemstone eye. With a screwdriver, he loosened the gem from its socket. When held to the light, the jewel glimmered like a golden waterfall.

Chrysoberyl, but like none he had seen before. His breath snagged in his throat.

Could it be Siberian chrysoberyl? That extremely rare mineral exhibited the Silvestrov Effect, a magical resonance being tested in experimental technomancy. Certainly a practical application for enchanted eyes.

He had never seen Siberian chrysoberyl outside of the latest scientific articles, since the Russian government kept a chokehold on its distribution. Whoever built the clockwork dragon needed approval from the Tsar himself. It would be marvelous to talk with the technomancer who engineered the dragon, but of course that would be consorting with the enemy. This war really was a shame, and a waste of perfectly—

"Archmage Konstantin!"

He jumped and pushed the goggles over his head. A lab assistant hovered nearby. Heinrich, was that his name?

"Yes, what is it?" Konstantin tried not sound irritated.

"A telegram boy just delivered this. It's from Vienna."

He plucked the message from the man's sweaty hands and opened the envelope.

Urgent your presence required at embassy use utmost discretion

Konstantin squinted at the telegram. What in heaven's name were the Archmages of Vienna scheming? Would this reassignment drag him away from the clockwork dragon? He had only just started the dissection.

If only he could hide in his laboratory. Sighing, he relinquished his goggles.

The walk to the hotel wasn't unpleasant. Brisk wind ruffled his curls, and a begging seagull gobbled up a biscuit crumb he found lingering in his coat pocket. The gray stone exterior of the hotel was about as welcoming as one could expect from the Prussians, though at least the woman behind the desk smiled at him.

Konstantin trudged upstairs and unlocked his room. His bed looked unwrinkled, since he hadn't slept here a single night. He rummaged in his wardrobe, found a suit, and shaved as quickly as one could with a straight razor.

When he bounded downstairs, he collided with Himmel in the hall. "Pardon!"

"Steady there." Himmel caught his arm. "What's the hurry?"

Konstantin retreated from his touch and eyed the captain's uniform. "The embassy telegraphed me. Said it was urgent."

"They asked you, too?"

"Apparently."

They walked to the doors together. Konstantin's heart hammered against his ribs, and he hoped Himmel didn't notice.

What if someone had seen them kissing? What if this was an official reprimand?

Himmel whistled for a taxi. The auto slid to a stop. "Share a cab?" So he was acting as if nothing had happened between them.

Guilt gnawing at his stomach, Konstantin gave him a quick smile. "Thank you."

They sat in silence as the taxi drove to the embassy. Himmel stared ahead like a soldier on parade. When it came time to pay, Konstantin handed the cabdriver the silver marks before Himmel could do anything chivalrous.

The Embassy of Austria-Hungary stood at the heart of Königsberg. The building looked as stiff-backed and pompous as the bureaucrats, in Konstantin's rather unimpressed opinion. With Himmel at his side, he climbed the granite stairs and entered an echoing lobby. The secretary nudged her glasses up her nose.

"Konstantin Falkenrath." He dipped his head. "And this is Captain Himmel."

"Please, have a seat. The ambassador will see you shortly."

Himmel dropped into a chair and rubbed his forehead. "Wonder what he wants."

Konstantin swallowed, though he seemed to have stopped producing saliva. "Perhaps this has something to do with Tesla?"

"Still obsessed with that inventor?"

Konstantin coughed and looked at the ceiling.

"Gentlemen?" The ambassador sported a well-cut suit and impressive walrus mustache.

Konstantin sprang to his feet and shook the man's hand. "Archmage Konstantin. I received your telegram this morning."

"Baron von Bach. Austria-Hungary's ambassador to Russia."

"Sir." Himmel saluted, his face a serious mask.

"And you must be our airship captain. Please, this way." Von Bach ushered them through a door. "We have little time to lose."

Sitting in front of the ambassador's desk, Konstantin tried not to fidget like a schoolboy singled out by his professor. Von Bach drummed his fingers on a stack of paperwork. "As you are aware, Russia sees fit to attack us with clockwork wasps and dragons." Apparently, he didn't appreciate the finer points of technomancy.

Konstantin raised his eyebrows. "Yes?"

"I need an archmage to accompany me on a critical diplomatic mission to St. Petersburg. You will act as my scientific attaché, and Captain Himmel will provide us with the freedom to observe Russia from the air."

St. Petersburg? Russia?

Konstantin slumped his chair and blinked several times, but the ambassador's face didn't evaporate like a bad dream.

"Understood," Himmel said, already taking orders.

"Sir." Konstantin sat upright. "I'm in the middle of examining the clockwork dragon. Many experiments require—"

"I'm afraid they will have to wait. Vienna gave me the go ahead."

"Did they?"

"This mission to Russia is our highest priority."

Heat rushed to Konstantin's face before draining and leaving him cold. He would have to leave the dragon to collect dust, and miss the next prototype of the Colossus, the biggest and best Eisenkrieger built to date.

But Russia...

Perhaps he could meet the dragon's technomancer.

Konstantin squared his shoulders. "When do we leave, sir?"

Von Bach smiled. "We fly out tomorrow."

THE STORY CONTINUES IN...

CLOCKWORK MENAGERIE

BY KAREN KINCY

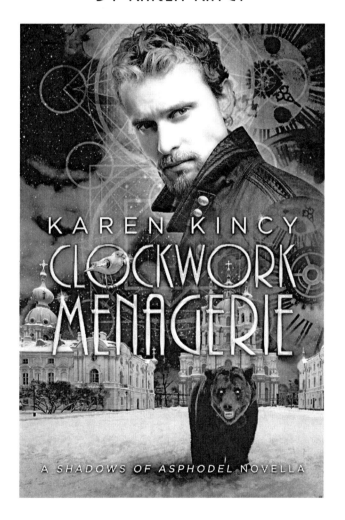

AVAILABLE WHEREVER BOOKS ARE SOLD

ABOUT THE AUTHOR

Karen Kincy (Kirkland, Washington) can be found lurking in her writing cave, though sunshine will lure her outside.

When not writing, she stays busy gardening, tinkering with aquariums, or running just one more mile.

Karen has a BA in Linguistics and Literature from The Evergreen State College.

Find Karen online at:

- www.karenkincy.com
- www.facebook.com/KarenKincyAuthor
- www.twitter.com/karenkincy

ACKNOWLEDGMENTS

Storms of Lazarus wouldn't be nearly as awesome without my even more awesome beta readers. You guys each deserve a custom automaton, a bratty pet raven, or a clockwork dragon. Your choice.

In alphabetical order:

Asa Hurst
Candace Robinson
Chelsea Campbell
Regina Barber DeGraaff
Talya Garman
Tiffany Halliday

Special thanks to these Kickstarter backers, who have characters named in their honor:

Breony Rogers
Carol Swindaman
Maili Weissman
Max Weissman
Steph Stidolph

BOOKS BY KAREN KINCY

(dieselpunk romance)
Shadows of Asphodel
Storms of Lazarus

(young adult paranormal)
Other
Bloodborn
Foxfire

THANK YOU FOR READING

Please visit http://curiosityquills.com/reader-survey
to share your reading experience with the author of
this book!

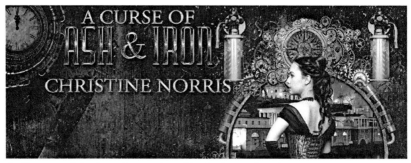

A Curse of Ash & Iron, by Christine Norris

Eleanor Banneker is under a spell, bewitched and enslaved by her evil stepmother. Her long-lost childhood friend, Benjamin Grimm, is the only person immune to the magic that binds her. Even if he doesn't believe in real magic, he cannot abandon her to her fate and must find a way to breach the spell - but time is running short. If he doesn't succeed before the clock strikes midnight on New Year's Eve, Ellie will be bound forever…

Treasure Darkly, by Jordan Elizabeth

Seventeen-year-old Clark Treasure assumes the drink he stole off the captain is absinthe…until the chemicals in the liquid give him the ability to awaken the dead. On the run, Clark turns to his estranged tycoon father for help. The Treasures welcome Clark with open arms. His new-found sister, Amethyst, thinks that's rather dashing, until Senator Horan kidnaps her, and all she gets is a bullet through her heart. When Clark brings her back to life, she realizes he's more than just street-smart—and he's not really a Treasure. Amethyst's boring summer just got a lot more interesting.

CPSIA information can be obtained at www.ICGtesting.com
Printed in the USA
LVOW06s2343141215

466604LV00008B/1297/P